Lock Down Publications and Ca$h
Presents

I0526624

LAND OF DA HOOLIGANZ

PART 1

Written By

IRA B

Lock Down Publications
P.O. Box 944
Stockbridge, GA 30281
www.lockdownpublications.com

Like our page on Facebook: Lock Down Publications
www.facebook.com/lockdownpublications.ldp

Stay Connected with Us!

Text **LOCKDOWN** to 22828 to stay up-to-date with new
releases, sneak peaks, contests and more...

Like our page on Facebook:
Lock Down Publications

Join Lock Down Publications/The New Era Reading Group

Visit our website:
www.lockdownpublications.com

Follow us on Instagram:
Lock Down Publications

Email Us: We want to hear from you!

ACKNOWLEDGMENTS

It is important for a writer to know he is in good hands, and I have always appreciated the hands in which I rest. First, to the big homie, CA$H, thank you for giving me this opportunity to do something great. Because of you, I can provide for my family now, and you'll always have my love & respect for that, my nigga. Hands down you the realest nigga in my corner right now.

My sincerest thanks goes to my mother "Mama BJ" and my other half, Krystal M. Schuster. You two women have been the rock in my life. And I'm sorry for all the hell I took you both through all these years. But never once did you turn your backs on me, and by God I will not put you through that shit again.

Endless gratitude to my haters and all you muthafuckaz who didn't believe in me. How can I even thank you enough for motivating me to be amongst the greatest of writers? Who's laughing now, bitches? Tonight, I'ma lay back and pen me another banger. My pen never sleeps!

To my brilliant & lovely daughter, Da'Jhana, I love you deeply, and never forget that. To my sons Delani & Olajuwon, you give me reason to wake up every morning. You are the best things to ever happen to me.

I owe a great debt to my aunt, Faye, for always being such a big positive influence in my life. You have no idea how far your encouragement went. I wish there were more people like you.

To my brothers, Rod, Marcus, Moby, Vic, Bear (R.I.P) Keylijah, I love you niggaz to death and I hope you are happy for me. My sister, Brittany, you are the sparkle in my eye and Lord knows I can't wait till we finally meet for the 1st time. Keep striving and being the best at what y'all do in life.

To producer Mann Robinson, @quavohuncho, Kwame "Dutch" Teague, Ghost, King Rio, K'wan Foye, Jamaica, Ernest Dukes over at Nottingham Agency, Tamika Mallory, EST Gee, Steven Ward, Rashia Wilson, I've never met any of you face-to-face, but I admire your hustle, and your unfailing drive to succeed has been my inspiration.

Last but not least, NBA Youngboy, your music has been the soundtracks to this book. And The Realest rapper in my book, MO3, I dedicate some of the murder scenes in the book to you. (R.I.P. MO3. You kept me in beast-mode while writing.)

Lastly, and perhaps, most importantly, thank you to all my readers and supporters. I'm honored to have you as fans, but even more honored to have you as my motivation to keep writing great stories. I promise to keep you all satisfied and give you something you can relate to. Not all that far-fetch bullshit, the real street gutter shit!

God Bless!

DEDICATION

I dedicate this book to Sandra Denise Murphy. My heart still longs for you and the lessons of life you taught me still guide me. It's been a long time, but you'll always have that special spot in my heart.

PROLOGUE

Once upon a time there were five young hooliganz who lived in a small town of Quincy, Florida. Two were identical twin brothers, one a girl, and the other two were statistics. Jamir, the runt of the litter, was just ten years old, the youngest and most audacious one of them all. Then you had Heaven, the cutest of the pack. She was twelve years old and suffered from a bad heart condition and epilepsy. And then there was Shamar, the only child of a well-known dope fiend, whose life only consisted of loneliness and fear outside of his circle of friends. He too was twelve and his life of poverty was a sobering experience. But it was the twins, Vermani and Delani, whom one always had to worry about, because they were two of the most bamboozling pair of hell raisers you could ever meet. Together they were all a team, a loyal crew, and a group of friends that loved one another like family.

To them there was nothing in the world that could come between them for any reason.

They were a solid gang of hooliganz.

Nothing could stop them.

Until one day when tragedy happened and it awakened something in them that changed for the worst, making them wreak havoc all across their small town.

The day Shamar snapped, the rest of the crew followed suit, bringing pure hell on earth amongst their community, one that eventually became the land of the hooliganz.

Chapter 1

For fifteen long years of heartache and misery, Dejah Cooper had been waiting patiently for this moment, the moment to finally breathe the fresh air of freedom. Having been incarcerated after all this time for a nigga who didn't keep it real with her, Dejah had learned to appreciate the smallest things in life. Prison makes you or breaks you. It broke her down to the lowest point. And in the process of keeping it real with her man by keeping her mouth shut, and protecting his honor by sacrificing her freedom, the nigga still did her dirty.

Dejah would never forgive Marlon for what he did to her. He literally left her for dead in prison.

So instead of finding him and killing Marlon dead, she knew his death wouldn't be desirable enough. Instead, she was going to fuck with his mind, destroy his pride, and attack his heart. What Marlon didn't know was that she was already up two on him. She had her freedom back and a decent stash put away. Dejah wasn't dumb by a long shot. She knew what type of nigga Marlon was, so she began skimming off the top of all the cash he would have her count for him. Dejah figured one day everything would go to shit and she needed a backup plan.

This was her backup plan, her money stash. Money that she still hoped was where she left it last, which was in her Aunt Sheryl's house, out in Pepper Hill. Her Aunt Sheryl was dead now. She died seven years ago from her battle with cancer. Last Dejah heard was her cousin MoMo had been living in the house with their aunt. That was the only place MoMo could go after burning the bridge with her own mother. Dejah's Aunt Wanda was a no nonsense having individual, and MoMo, being a mother herself, had to find out the hard way.

Motherhood was no simple feat.

Plus there was no wrath like a woman scorned.

Dejah's scorn.

When the Uber driver finally pulled up outside of her Aunt Sheryl's house, she had to do a double-take. Her mouth dropped into her lap with astonishment. She couldn't believe how much of a waste the house had become. One look at it and Dejah knew her aunt Sheryl was probably turning in her grave.

"Is this the address you were expectin'?" asked Roger, the driver.

Dejah swallowed. "This is it."

"Are you sure?"

"I'll only be a minute, Roger. I'm just going inside to grab something. Will you wait for me?" Dejah ignored the driver's mockery and turned her gaze on him.

"I'm on the clock right now."

"And I'll pay double the price," she said.

He nodded. "I need a cigarette break anyway," said roger.

Dejah tapped his seat and got out of the trashy car. He shrugged and reached for his pack of Kool's cigarettes.

As she made her way to the front door of the house, Dejah was almost scared to go farther.

What was once a beautiful yellow and white house, was now a sight of neglect. The body of the house was peeling of its tarnished paint, the landscape overgrown with pine needles and poor maintenance, the porch sagging, it was completely awful. It looked more like a haunted house than an actual home.

Dejah climbed the rickety steps up onto the porch. She approached the door and raised her hand to knock. But that was before she heard the slapping sounds and the unmistakable sound of a strangled cry from inside.

Without further reluctance, Dejah reached for the door knob, and surprisingly, the door was unlocked. But it's what she saw when she opened it and stepped inside that almost made her want to throw up.

She had definitely arrived at the wrong time.

It was MoMo, stretched out face down into the cushion of the worn sofa. On top of her was some homeless looking nigga. He was power driving his dick into her ass like it was nothing. The whole time while gripping the back of her neck as she cried out her pleasure beneath him.

And that's when Dejah couldn't take no more. Realization of what was happening in front of her made her snap.

Back in the federal pen, Dejah was considered a wallower, meaning she could fight and wasn't scared to get busy. She stayed getting in some shit with the other inmates and C.O.'s alike. Her fight game was proper, which is why she either had to get jumped or be put down by a shank. Yet she still prevailed against the odds and sustained her reputation to the bitter end.

Right at that moment was no different. Dejah walked right up to the man and punched him dead in the eye with a vicious right hook. Then she followed through with a two-piece combo of straight jabs that knocked him out cold.

"The fuck you got going on up in here, MoMo?" Dejah stared at her cousin as she struggled to get from under the weight of the unconscious man.

He looked penniless and just like a bum.

"Dej?" MoMo looked up at her with bloodshot eyes. There was a look of helplessness on her pathetic face.

With an exasperated breath, Dejah pulled the man off of MoMo's sickly thin form. He hit the floor with a heavy thump. Then Dejah slapped his dirty ass awake and kicked him out of the house. He was so high out of his mind that he didn't even realize that he'd left his pants behind.

"You should be ashamed of yourself, MoMo," said Dejah. She looked around the living room at its sparse furnishing, the sour musky stench of sex and body odor, the total loss of its former appeal. All she could do was shake her head. "Aunt Sheryl would have never settled for this. How could you even allow this shit to happen?"

"When she left us, I lost it," MoMo said.

"You lost your fuckin' mind, cuz. That's what the hell you lost." She was furious.

"When did you get out?" Suddenly, MoMo became attentive.

"Yesterday," said Dejah hesitantly.

Dejah watched with disgust as MoMo just continued to sit there, butt fuckin naked on the sofa as if she wasn't standing there.

A car horn honked outside, reminding Dejah that her driver was waiting on her.

The stash spot, she thought to herself.

Leaving her cousin sitting there, looking a hot mess, Dejah exited the room headed for the kitchen. Instinctively, she skidded to a halt at the sight of the mess before her eyes. When she switched on the light for illumination, nothing happened. There was no electricity in the house, no power whatsoever. It was no wonder the fridge was reeking of spoilage and sourness the way it did. There was nothing to refrigerate inside, at least anything worth looking inside for.

"This is so fucked up," said Dejah

But she didn't need any light to do what needed to be done. She'd done it so many times before that the performance would come naturally.

After locating a butter knife and coming into contact with a rat or a roach. Dejah knelt before the kitchen sink. Below it was a cabinet where Aunt Sheryl kept all her cleaning supplies. When she opened the cabinet, there was not one cleaning item present.

Please let it be here, she thought.

After removing everything that didn't belong inside, Dejah used the butter knife to pry open the floorboard of the cabinet. Below that floor board was a hollow space big enough to fit a briefcase. And sure enough, that's where it remained, fifteen years later, safe and sound.

MoMo had just entered the kitchen when Dejah was getting up from the floor.

"What in the hell?" said MoMo.

Dejah ignored her as she spun the dial to activate the code lock. She'd visualized this moment a million times over the years. The moment that was going to set her life straight for a while. This moment was worth every year waiting to collect.

And then the briefcase opened up to reveal the money inside. Three hundred thousand dollars she'd collected over the course of eight years dealing with Marlon.

"Is that all money?" MoMo snatched Dejah out of her thoughts.

Immediately, Dejah shut the briefcase and moved for the door. But before she could step foot out of the kitchen MoMo blocked her path.

"Move outta my way, MoMo," she replied.

"Gimme some of that money. I got bills to pay." MoMo told her, now dressed in a pair of jeans and a skimpy halter top. She even managed to put what little hair she had left in a ponytail.

"Don't make me tell you again, cuz. Move." Dejah tried to step around her but MoMo moved with her. Then she reached out for the briefcase and grabbed a hold of its handle along with Dejah's. "Bitch, you need to back the fuck up off me," she warned.

"No. Gimme some money." screamed MoMo.

"MoMo." Dejah made a move to remove MoMo's hand, only to get it slapped away roughly. She didn't want to beat her cousin's ass, but MoMo was pushing her to that limit. "Cuz, please let it go. Please."

"Fuck you." MoMo punched her in the face and tried to snatch the briefcase away. Instinct kicked in as Dejah released the briefcase and grabbed MoMo by her throat. Then she punched her so hard that it sent MoMo stumbling backwards into the kitchen counter. She fell and hit her head on the corner of the counter. That's when Dejah heard the sickening crunch of her skull cracking.

"MoMo?" she said

No response.

When she moved near MoMo's fallen body, she noticed the blood pouring from the back of her head. She knelt down to try to shake her awake, only to get no reply. MoMo didn't even stir.

"Oh shit," she muttered. "C'mon, cuz. Wake up."

Next, when Dejah reached for her arm to check her pulse, there wasn't any. She touched the side of her neck. Nothing.

"Oh no," Dejah panicked. "Oh no, cuz."

MoMo was dead.

Chapter 2

Shamar and Heaven had exited the school bus at the corner of their street. Their friendship was much like the closeness of siblings. Both were twelve, both shared the same homeroom class, and together, Shamar and Heaven had a mutual understanding of one another's way of life.

For as long as he could remember, Shamar had sought the love and guidance of all of his friends' parents. Since the terrible loss of his Aunt Sheryl, it was his friends and their parents that kept him sane, especially after having to put up with his mama's constant bullshit. Although he loved his mama with all his heart, Shamar stopped caring about what she did a long time ago. It was because of her foolishness that his life was so miserable and dark. Her lifestyle had caused him more pain and agony than the average kid would be able to withstand.

Hardship was the norm in his life.

His world was a very cold place to live.

If it wasn't for his friends, he would have frozen to death a long time ago.

As he and Heaven trekked along the sidewalk behind the other four kids, Shamar thought about the upcoming signups to join the school's football team. For a twelve year old, he was big for his age. He would make a decent cornerback or running back. But in order to earn those positions, he would have to knock Khalil Street and Donte Harris out of their spots, which meant he had to be vicious and just as dedicated to the game as them.

"I think you'll be great, Shamar. Plus, Khalil is into drugs now and Coach Richards will suspend his playing time and put in Brandon Jones, the second string."

"Brandon Jones?"

"He's a weakling, Shamar. He doesn't even have the athletic build, swiftness nor speed for even a second-string player."

"How do you know so much about football?" Shamar glanced ahead and spotted a white sedan parked in front of his house. He wondered who it was.

"Remember," Heaven gazed over at him with a knowing smirk on her pretty face, "I have four brothaz who made me play football with them. And you, out of all people, should know speed is your strength. You're faster than Khalil, brah. Once Coach Richards sees that, there's no doubt in my mind you'll make the cut," she said.

"You think so, huh?" He stopped.

"I know so, big head. Sign up to play. Stay focused. And I'll see you later, after I'm done with my homework." Heaven punched him in the shoulder and turned into the driveway of her house.

As he watched her leave for her house, Shamar's attention was stolen by movement coming from his own house, five houses down the street. It was a woman, dressed in Khaki pants and a white shirt. In her hand, she carried what looked like a briefcase. But her hurried pace and the way she was looking about cautiously made him suspicious.

Shamar headed in the direction of his house as he watched the woman get inside the white car.

"Oh yeah. Shamar?" Heaven called out after him as she stood in the doorway of her house. He glanced back over his shoulder at her. "Veronica does like you, too. She told me today," she said.

He smiled at the thought. "I knew that."

Veronica Jenkins. She lived out in the Joyland area, a beautiful clarinet player, eighth grader and funny. She wasn't Shamar's crush, but he did think she was cool. And to hear that she really does like him after confiding his feelings in Heaven, he wondered if she would want to be his girlfriend.

Why would one of the prettiest girls in school like a poor black kid like him? He had no clue. He was the son of a dope fiend, he wore hand-me-downs. He was walking in a pair of one of his best friend's shoes. He thought with silent discontent.

The approaching white car snapped him out of his reverie. Shamar looked in its direction just as it was passing by. In passing, he met the intense gaze of the woman he saw leaving his house. The moment he saw her, Shamar was hit with a brief instant of familiarity. For that momentary glimpse of her face, he stood there trying to recall where he knew it from.

When his mind went blank, Shamar proceeded on his journey to his house.

Upon reaching the front door Shamar noticed that it was slightly ajar. With a moment of hesitation, he pushed the door open and stepped inside the house. The instant he entered the house a sense of trepidation came over him.

Coming home to a broken house and its sullenness was something he could never get used to. Ever since his Aunt Sheryl, died everything had fallen to pieces for him and his mama. He was just five years old when she died. The past seven years of his life was spent ducking and dodging DCF and his mama's many boyfriends. Some of them wasn't right in the head, their intentions were cruel, but he never spoke on the things that haunted his dreams at night.

Shamar was forced to harden his heart.

He had no choice but to live through the hell he was confined in, or succumb to the darkness of fate.

"Ma?" Shamar called out to his mama. He spotted the lone pair of pants on the floor of the living room. He wondered which one of his mama's boyfriends they belonged to.

Tossing his backpack upon the sofa, Shamar went in search of his mama. She had to be home. Why else would someone leave their pants just laying around?

The closer he got to walking past the kitchen, the unmistakable scent of blood assaulted his senses. He stopped suddenly, looked into the kitchen, and saw his mama laid out on the floor. Shamar entered the kitchen and stood over his mama's still form.

"Ma?" He muttered. Shamar reached down to touch his mama on the arm, feeling the wetness of blood upon her flesh.

"Mama, what happened? Get up," Shamar replied, his heart thudding hard against his chest. "Ma?"

No answer. No movement.

His bottom lip trembled with fear of what he hoped was not true. But after several more attempts to wake her, to no avail, he got up and left the kitchen. His mama was dead. She was gone. And it was already too late to save her. There was never any time to save her.

Shamar was heartbroken.

He was crushed.

With each following step he took to distance himself from her, an explosion of tears threatened to burst from his eyes.

Then that same sofa, which he found the pants sitting in front of, he fell upon in a surge of sorrowful cries. He wailed like a wounded animal. The depths of his loss was drowning him in a river of anguish.

The pain was so intense that he couldn't breathe.

He couldn't even call for help.

He knew it was over now. The government was going to take him away. He didn't want to go. He wouldn't survive anywhere else.

And that's where he remained, right there on the sofa, crying his eyes out over his dead mama, until Heaven and

Jamir showed up at his front door. Shamar heard them knocking but he was too distraught to get up and let them in, not that he wanted to anyway, not with his dead mama in the kitchen. But Jamir let himself in anyway, followed by Heaven, both of whom had never witnessed him cry until that very moment.

To see Shamar crying the way he was made Heaven wonder what made him do so. Whatever it was had to be something close to his heart, which was all of his friends and his mama. And Heaven being the intelligent individual that she was, she knew it had to be his mama.

"Where is mama, Shamar?" asked Heaven

The mention of his mama only made him cry harder, which was evidence that her thoughts were right.

Minutes later, Heaven found her dead in the kitchen, and then she screamed, which brought Jamir entering the room next. When it was finally revealed what Shamar's sorrows were actually emitted from, everything suddenly changed. It all went completely downhill from there.

Chapter 3

Vermani and Delani were mad as hell because they couldn't go out and play. They had neglected to clean their rooms, do the dishes, and even their homework. So their parents made it obviously clear that if they didn't complete their chores, in that order, there was no outside for them. Nor was there any video game playing, for their father had taken both of their video games prior to their arrival.

Vermani sulked miserably as he went about his bedroom, cleaning and tidying it up. He was the humblest one of the two, the wiser one, unlike his twin, who was not doing a damn thing as such.

Instead, Delani was locked in his bedroom, flipping through a XXL Magazine he had stolen from the record store downtown the day before. While his mama was browsing the shelves for a new record (she was an old school traditional music freak), Delani was stealing. He couldn't wait to get back home to finish reading through the magazine, visualizing his life surrounded by the entertainment business. He had big dreams forming just from the pages of that one magazine alone.

Delani was the evil one of the two.

He was a nuisance.

And so was Vermani, but only by his brother's influence at times does he do the bidding. Together these two thirteen year olds were a force to be reckoned with. Vermani and Delani were worse than a pack of pit bulls.

They were two peas in a pod, two devilish creatures.

From where he was sitting on the bed, flipping through his magazine, the sound of sirens in the distance caught his attention. The alarm was growing closer by the second, indicating that there was trouble nearby. He climbed out of bed and moved over to his bedroom window to look outside. Then he opened the window as if hearing the sirens more clearly could pinpoint where it was going.

Right at that moment, Vermani came knocking on the door, asking to be let in.

Delani went over to the door to let him in. He noticed that his twin was no longer in his school clothes. Having not gotten the chance to change out of his own yet, Delani locked the door back and returned to the window in hopes of seeing something interesting.

"You heard those sirens?" asked Vermani. He picked up the magazine and started looking through it.

"I wonder where they were going."

"It sounded close."

A wicked thought crossed Delani's mind. "Wanna go see where it's at?"

Vermani stopped flipping through the magazine and looked up at his twin with a guarded expression.

"C'mon, Vee. It'll only be just to look and come back. Maybe somebody got shot or something."

"There was no gunshots."

"Or stabbed," he persisted. "C'mon, Vee. We're gonna be stuck in this house all afternoon anyway. We may as well go see what's going on. What if it's one of the others?" said Delani.

"Somebody woulda called and told us."

"Vee?"

"What?" Vermani answered.

"You're acting like a real bitch right now," said Delani as he moved the window curtains aside. When he moved forward to climb out of the window, he stuck one leg out and glanced over at his twin brother. "Cover for me 'til I get back," he replied.

"Hold up, Delani," said Vermani hesitantly. He then tossed the magazine onto the bed and stepped over to the window to assist his brother. "You know I can't let you go by yourself, right?"

Delani grinned mischievously.

Then the doorbell rang. Both of them froze suddenly, looking over towards the door.

"Wait a minute," Vermani said.

"Where are you going?" Delani was halfway out the window as he watched Vermani approach the bedroom door. Then he unlocked it, cracked it open, and peered up the hallway. Delani observed his brother quietly, feeling he was stalling on the mission to pull a fast one.

"It's Jamir," Vermani muttered.

"What?"

"Something's wrong, Delani."

When he saw his brother open the door wider and exit the room, Delani cussed under his breath and climbed back inside. Then he headed for the door to go see what was going on with Jamir.

Jamir was like their little brother, they loved him as though he were their own sibling.

As the two twins were entering the living room, they watched as their father, his big hand resting on Jamir's bony little shoulders, kneeled before him to speak. It was then that they, not only saw Jamir crying, but realized he was breathing hard, as though he'd run all the way there.

Something indeed was wrong, and from the looks of it, Jamir was extremely affected by it.

A sudden pull of fear tugged at Vermani's heart strings as he stood there watching his friend cry.

"Jamir, what's wrong?" asked Delani.

"What is it, son?" said Harold Taylor, a big powerful man, whose life consisted of working as a business contractor and running a firm household.

"She's dead," said Jamir, who only stood five feet even, but brave as any other ten year old.

"Who's dead?"

"Mama MoMo," he said.

"What?" both twins said in unison.

Jamir told them what him and Heaven saw when they visited Shamar's house. He was scared. Delani frowned and made his way to the front door.

"Delani?" Kiara called out to her son from the kitchen doorway. She had a chef's apron on, as she was in the process of fixing supper.

Delani didn't even acknowledge her. He walked through the front door without a backward glance. Then, when his feet finally touched the earth, he just took off running for Shamar's house, which was up the street and around the corner.

Vermani didn't hesitate and ran after his brother. Behind them, their parents bellowed in protest. But Vermani and Delani didn't stop. They were willing to accept the reprimand later if it meant reaching Shamar to be with him when he needed them most.

Their devotion to their brother was worth it.

Nothing came before that, nothing at all.

Chapter 4

Her name was Monica Lightfoot, and she was Heaven's mama. But the way she guarded her daughter's bedroom, you would think the president of the U.S. was inside. She already knew what was to come with MoMo's death, and nobody was going to take him away from her.

Anything that would bring her daughter any harm, she would go to the ends of the earth to prevent from happening.

Inside that same bedroom were both Shamar and Heaven. When her daughter came running and screaming about MoMo being dead, fear gripped her heart. She went down to the house to collect Shamar and had almost ran up out of there. The last time she entered that house was seven years ago, at Sheryl's repast. It was beautiful then, like a real home. But after she went in there today, she almost thought she'd walked into a fuckin' haunted house on Halloween night.

Monica got Shamar the hell away from that filthy place and brought him to her house.

The police and crime scene unit was there now, probably freaking the fuck out inside. The place looked like a death trap way before MoMo was found dead an hour ago.

It was no wonder why Shamar was always at her house, or the others, his own home was a nightmare. What Monica saw in there was enough to make her skin crawl.

Shamar didn't deserve to live like that.

He was just a child.

Little did she know, Shamar was not your ordinary kid. He'd seen and done things that an ordinary kid would be traumatized over. She could not understand what it was like to be so hungry that he contemplated eating his own vomit.

The hardships of Shamar's life were sad.

It was so surreal.

As she tired herself of standing guard outside her daughter's room, Monica made her way up front just as she heard pounding footsteps upon her front porch. Suddenly, the door exploded open and in rushed Delani followed by his brother. He didn't even knock, just barged in, breathing heavily.

"Where is he?" Delani asked breathlessly, then rushed past, her heading towards the back of the house.

Vermani hung back for a moment to catch his breath. This was the one Monica favored the most between the twins. His humbleness is what moved her, he was more respectable. He and she looked at one another, and just when she was about to speak, the front door opened. Jamir stormed in looking wild eyed and winded.

This was Monica's baby boy. If she had had a son, it would be one of Jamir's character. He was smart, inquisitive, brave, and cute as ever. His mama, LaShonda, and her were good friends. They lived just across the street.

But Monica loved all of her daughter's friends. They had become special to her, almost as though she had brought them into the world herself. They could always come and go like they please because, one thing she knew for certain, Heaven had four brothers who'd always protect her. And because of their love for her daughter, Monica was determined to see that they remained in their lives.

"Some police lady is coming," said Jamir.

Monica saw the astounded look on his face and said, "Is she coming here?"

He nodded.

At that very moment, there was a knock on the door. Monica shooed the boys away and told them to go in the back and keep quiet. They hurried towards the bedroom where the others were and went inside.

Keeping quiet would be the last thing they would do. She could hear Delani back there riled up already.

She made her way to the door and opened it. Standing on her doorstep was the last person she expected to see. Her name was Angie Galloway. She was a police detective and a friend of the family. Her son, Van, and she went to school together back when James A. Shanks High school was the high-light of its achievement of scholars.

"You got a minute?" asked Angie. She was a beautiful middle-age black woman with light brown eyes.

With a nod, Monica stepped forward instead of allowing the detective inside. She gestured toward one of the chairs occupying the wide spacious front porch. Angie shook her head and decided to lean against the porch railing.

Monica took her seat anyway.

"What's up?" she said and folded her arms.

"It's ugly down there, Monica," said Angie.

Monica glanced up the street, where a group of people stood across the street from the bloody scene of MoMo's house. They all wore sad faces. "So new developments have come up, back at the scene, that's very questionable. I'm told Monique's son was home when her body was found. Maybe he saw something that could be invaluable towards the investigation."

"Okay," said Monica very slowly.

"Will you let me talk to him, Monica?"

"What makes you believe he's here with me?" Monica had her game face on.

Angie gave Monica her dubious expression. "Look, Monica. Taking Shamar away from you is the last thing I want. He's been through enough already. But his mama was killed by someone and he may have seen who the killer was. I just wanna ask him a few questions."

"Hell no."

"Monica, please."

"I said no, Angie," she snapped.

"The killer could just be amongst that crowd of people standing outside MoMo's house. She was considered the biggest trick in the neighborhood. All types of niggaz have ran up in those guts, which was nearly typical for someone of her caliber. Word on the streets was MoMo had the best head game and ass in the hood," Monica explained. "At one point, I witnessed at least eight niggaz leaving MoMo's house one night, the same wannabe hustlaz who crawl about the hood and post up on street corners, slanging packs.

Det. Angie Galloway knew this for a fact herself, for she grew up in the same hood as them all.

"MoMo was murdered, Monica. There were bruises on her face prior to her fallin' back and busting her brain open. She was attacked by someone, and whoever that someone is, Shamar might have seen."

Down the street, a commotion erupted within the crowd of spectators on the sidewalk. A fist was thrown and someone hit the ground.

"Uh-oh. I guess Samantha just found out Jeremy's no-good ass been creepin' with MoMo late night, just like all the rest of 'em," said Angie.

"Shamar isn't here anyway," said Monica. "He's a smart kid, he isn't dumb. He knows now that his mama is dead, those DCF bitches are gonna take him away."

"Then where is he?" Angie saw the front window curtains move from inside the house. She knew it was one of the boys that she saw enter the house minutes ago, or maybe it was Shamar. "Do you trust me, Monica?"

"As far as I can throw you," she retorted with a wicked smirk on her face.

Samantha was beating Jeremy's ass all the way down the street as the neighbors looked on.

And that's when Harold pulled up and stopped in front of Monica's house. He and his wife, Kiara, got out of the big black '20 Camaro 2 SS and were making their way towards the front porch when Angie groaned in dismay. She knew once she laid eyes on her cousin, Kiara, her whole mission was doomed.

A smile appeared on Monica's face with the knowledge of Angie's sudden contempt.

She and Kiara never got along. There was a lot of tension between the two.

Bad blood, so bad that Angie lost her husband in the process, while her cousin lives happily-ever-after.

Chapter 5

Jamir had snuck back out of the room to go eavesdrop on the meeting between Monica and the detective. He had heard everything up until he peeped out of the window curtains at them. When he saw the woman detective look his way, he scurried back to the room.

Inside the bedroom, Shamar was sitting on the huge pink bean bag chair in the left hand corner of the room. Next to him, sitting on the floor, was Vermani. Both Delani and Heaven were sitting on the bed. No one was talking, the room was filled with despair.

When Jamir came bursting back into the room, Delani bolted to his feet instinctively. His instinctive reaction was to swing on anybody who threatened to disrupt their mourning process.

"What's wrong, Jay?" Heaven spoke up. She had been quietly picking at her chipped painted fingernails and watching Shamar for any reaction as to what he wanted to do next.

"She said somebody killed Mama MoMo."

"Who?"

Jamir said, "That police lady."

"What did she say exactly?" Delani asked. He was obviously the leader of their pack. A week from that day, he and his twin would be fourteen. Jamir's birthday was two days after that.

Parts of Jamir's recount were repetitive and verbose. He was very animated with what he was delivering.

Now all eyes were on Shamar. His tears were gone now, replaced by just constant heartache.

"Who was in that car earlier, Shamar?" Heaven was suddenly alarmed by the recollection. She bounced from the bed and went over to Shamar. "Remember the car?"

"What car?" Vermani stood up next. "What are you talkin' about, Hev?" He questioned. For a thirteen year old, he was tall, almost five feet seven inches tall. Basketball was his sport and he was damn good at it.

Delani was too violent for basketball.

"There was a white car parked outside my house. Some lady walked out with a briefcase in her hand. She looked familiar to me. I know I've seen her before. I think it's in one of the pictures Aunt Sheryl had in her picture book. I don't know. But I did remember her face, when I saw her," said Shamar.

"So, it's somebody you know," said Jamir.

Shamar shrugged his shoulders.

For more than an hour now, Shamar had been wrestling with his brain to remember where he knew the lady from. He kept going back to that picture book in his Aunt Sheryl's bedroom. He was sure that's where it was from.

"And this picture book is at your house right now?" Delani replied curiously.

"That's where I last saw it."

"Okay. We gotta get back in that house and find it. Once we find out who this lady is-"

"And what're we gonna do, Delani? Kill her?" Heaven replied in a sharp tone. One thing about having a girl in your circle, she would demand her two cents. Her voice of reason had to be heard, no matter what the situation was. "Whoever this lady is, I'm sure she has to be somebody important, right? I mean, you said she had a briefcase in her hand?"

"Yeah," Shamar nodded.

29

"Then who's to really say that she's the person responsible for what happened? Maybe she was a lawyer or something. Who else would carry around briefcases in the hood?"

"Except that she wasn't a lawyer, Heaven."

"How do you know?" Jamir beat her to the punch. He was just as eager to know as the rest of them.

When Shamar described the clothes the lady was wearing, he painted the picture of someone else, rather than a lawyer. Plus, the house was paid for, so it couldn't be anything in regards to foreclosure. But he did mention the strange occurrence of what he noticed in the kitchen earlier at his house.

"What did you see?" Delani asked.

He told them about the cabinet beneath the kitchen sink. Then about the base of its floor board being lifted up to reveal a hollow cove beneath.

"Could it be that's where the lady got the briefcase?"

"Really, Jamir?" Vermani said with a frown. "Why would a brief-case be hidden below a kitchen sink, stupid?"

"I think Jamir's on to something," said Delani. "But that's just something we need to find out. If this is true, then once we find her, we find the briefcase. Tonight we all are gonna go back to Shamar's house to look for that picture book. We find it, we get answers. Simple."

"Really?" Jamir responded excitedly. "Like a quest?"

"No. You're staying home, Jay. I don't care what Delani said. No exceptions." Vermani was always protective over the youngest member of their crew.

Jamir didn't even dare contest it.

He knew better.

Plus, his mama, LaShonda, and her boyfriend, Tony, were very strict about him being out after the streetlights came on. So the others would have to go at it alone and fill him in on what happened at the bus stop in the morning.

Once that was settled, they began to plot their next move and were looking forward to it.

Eventually Heaven's mama came knocking to check up on them. She was accompanied by the twin's mama, as both of them questioned Shamar on what he might have seen.

"I don't know nothing." Shamar lied.

By this time, Shamar was beyond tears, his sorrows locked inside, and his heart on ice. To know that his mama was murdered made him very bitter.

For the remainder of the evening, they all sat around the house amongst their families. Jamir's mama had come with her loud, flamboyant personality, always seeming to find humor in just about any situation. But her attempts were to no effect with the youngsters, no matter how hard she tried.

Before long, the twins left with their parents, then Jamir and his mama, which left Heaven and Shamar behind to eat a late dinner of fried chicken and mac-n-cheese, while anticipating their later mission.

Then Monica showed him to the guest room across the hall from hers.

"This is your home now, as long as you like," said Monica. She gave him a sad, forced smile that didn't work on him. Shamar just regarded her with silent understanding.

"Thank you," he replied softly.

Her restraint broken, Monica pulled him into her arms and held him for a long moment.

"Your mama is gone to a better place than this world, baby. You just have to be strong and fearless. It's not gonna be easy, but you have to understand something," she said as she released him. Monica met his humbled gaze and knew from the look in his eyes something very dark would become of him, if he wasn't careful. "If you allow this to tear you down, there ain't no gettin' back up from it. I don't mean to sound harsh about it, but that's the same shit your mama did," she replied.

"What did she do?" he asked.

Monica leaned against the door frame and folded her arms across her chest.

"Your mama lost herself after her mama kicked her out the house while she was pregnant with you. She had to live on the streets for a while. She was out there a long time before your great-aunt Sheryl took y'all in. By that time, MoMo was already knee deep in the streets, but when Sheryl died, that's what did it. That was the blow that sent your mama over the edge into the abyss," she said.

"What is the abyss?" Shamar wanted to know.

"A deep pit of whatever it is your mama found herself in and couldn't get out of, smoking dope and trickin' off."

He didn't want that for himself, he thought.

"But don't worry though, baby boy. We gotcha," said Monica, extending her arm towards him.

Reluctantly, he stepped forward and bumped fists with her. She nodded and stepped out into the hallway. The second she walked away, Heaven stepped through the door into the bedroom, carrying two flashlights.

"I'm ready," she said.

"Okay."

Now all they had to do was wait until Vermani and Delani arrived, as planned.

Chapter 6

An hour later, the four of them entered the house in which Shamar had lived his whole life.

Once they found the entrance of the house from the backdoor. Delani broke away from the group and said he wanted to go see the kitchen.

With the shake of his head, Shamar led the way to his Aunt Sheryl's bedroom. The trio entered the dark smelly room that appeared as though it was ransacked already by somebody. Maybe the cops came in and searched through the house looking for clues. Whatever it was they were looking for, Shamar hoped it wasn't the picture book.

"Where is it?" Vermani asked. He was both excited and freaked out at the same time.

"Check the dresser drawers, and under the bed, while I look in the closet," said Shamar.

"I'll check the dresser," Heaven was nervous as fuck in the creepy house where Shamar's mama had been murdered just hours earlier. With her flashlight in hand, she went over to the old dresser and began looking through the drawers that were already opened.

The closet had been once adorned with beautiful dresses and such, before his auntie died. Shamar then watched as those same precious dresses and jewels that she once had were taken by his mama to barter off for a high. His mama sold everything she thought was valuable. From the silverware to the old grandfather clock, and even the oil lamps were taken to be traded off.

MoMo had been a monster for that dope.

She didn't play.

Shamar entered the closet and searched through what was left of his Aunt Sheryl's belongings.

"Is this it?" Vermani asked minutes later, after getting up from checking beneath the bed. But it wasn't under the bed from which he had located the big brownish red photo album. It was on the bottom shelf of the nightstand that sat next to the bed. The photo album was amongst shopping magazines and coupons and a black bible with golden lettering.

It was a wonder MoMo didn't sell that too.

Both Shamar and Heaven turned the beams of their flashlights in the direction of Vermani.

"That's it, Vee," said Shamar. Then he hurried over to where Vermani stood and came to a sudden halt at the painful cry of someone other than them being inside the house.

"What the?" Vermani spun towards the door where the commotion was coming from.

POW.

A gunshot exploded, and this time, a loud terrifying howl came from what sounded like a grown ass man.

Intending on keeping Heaven safely behind him, Shamar said Delani's name and Vermani rushed for the door. Then the other two followed suit as they all exited the bedroom headed toward the tumultuous disturbance.

It was in the den area of the house where they found Delani. In his hand was a chrome baby .380 automatic pistol as he glared down at the man writhing in excruciating pain at his feet.

"He was hiding in the dark," said Delani with this strange look in his eyes. It was obvious that he was scared after what happened.

"Delani, is that daddy's gun?" Vermani spoke up with a look of surprise on his face.

"Larry?" Shamar stepped up and shone his flashlight down at the man. This was one of his mama's many boyfriends, Larry the base-head. He was holding his leg where he'd been shot just above his right knee. "What are you doing in my house, Larry?" he demanded.

"Mar? That's you?" asked Larry painfully, as he stared up at him, blinded by the light. "Don't y'all kill Larry. I only came back for my pants, just my pants."

"Your pants?" said Delani.

The instant those words left Larry's mouth, Shamar was reminded of what he saw earlier. He remembered seeing the lone pair of pants when he walked in the house, which meant that Larry might know something about his mama's murder.

"Looks like you got your pants on already Larry," Delani said with the gesture of the gun.

At that moment, Vermani was so scared he couldn't even speak.

After he and Delani found their father's gun in his nightstand drawer some time ago, he knew Delani would find the courage to get it. He had found that courage and now Delani's shot someone with their father's gun.

Heaven's fear made her immobilized. She was even afraid to blink her eyes.

"Had to get my good ones," Larry groaned in agony, panting in blatant fear of dying. I left something in my pants when I was here earlier."

"You was here? At this house?"

"With MoMo," he said.

"When was this?" Heaven found her voice. She glanced over at Shamar and stepped forward.

"Before that other bitch came and knocked Larry the hell out," he said. "That bitch."

"What other bitch, Larry?" Heaven replied.

35

That's when Larry told them about the unexpected surprise of MoMo's cousin, Dejah, catching them doing the nasty. Then she swung on him and knocked him out cold. Larry admitted that he was high as a giraffe's ass during the whole matter. He then told how Dejah woke him up and literally kicked him out of the house without his pants.

Larry had had a piece of dope and his pipe left inside the pocket of his pants.

"Dejah?" Shamar thought the name sounded familiar. He knew that name from somewhere. It was a name from long ago, one that was spoken throughout the family gatherings.

"Shamar? Where you going?" Vermani called out after him when Shamar suddenly dashed down the hall back toward his auntie's bedroom. It was then that he remembered tossing the photo album aside to get to his brother.

Heaven chased after him.

In the bedroom Shamar had found the photo album on the floor of the bedroom. He picked it up and laid it across the bed. Then he opened it to look inside.

"I know that name, Hev," said Shamar. He flipped through the pages of the photo album as Heaven entered the bedroom behind him, "I know Dejah."

"He said she was your mama's cousin."

"I know."

When Vermani came to the door, his shadowy figure made him look like a dark spirit. He wanted to know what they should do about Larry. When Heaven told him to kick him out of the house Vermani went to go do just that.

Moments later you heard Larry bellowing in pain and babbling and crying about them killing him. Under different circumstances, his actions would have been looked on as hilarious, but this wasn't no laughing matter at that point.

"Oh shit," yelled Delani in panic.

A second later, both twin brothers came trampling through the house yelling, "Police."

Without hesitation, Shamar snatched up the photo album and shoved Heaven towards the door. They all hit the backdoor the way they had come. From there, they ran through the backyards of the neighboring houses to get to Heaven's house. A minute later, they were in her bedroom, breathing hard and wide eyed with fear.

"We made it," said Heaven.

That's the moment when the bedroom door burst open and there stood Heaven's mama, glaring in at them all.

Everybody in the room gasped in surprise.

"Caught you little bastards," said Monica, barefoot in her pajama bottoms and tank top. When she stepped inside the room, she gave Heaven a dark look that could break steel.

Heaven sat her ass down on her bed.

"It's all my fault," said Delani.

"Shut the hell up, Dee." Monica approached him and snatched the gun out of his hand. "The hell you going with this? With my daughter out in the middle of the fuckin' night?"

Busted. Vermani dreaded the thrashing his father was going to do to him and his brother.

All Delani could do was shake his head. He had been so caught up in the moment. When he was literally kicking Larry's ass out the front door a police car was driving by. Then it had stopped and he panicked.

"We went to my house," Shamar insisted.

"What?" Monica shouted.

"I needed to find out what happened to my mama," Shamar replied before lifting up the photo album. "I think I know who killed her now," he said.

"What're you saying, Shamar?" Monica murmured.

Shamar then opened the photo album to the page he had stopped on when Delani rang the alarm. It was a picture of Dejah in her prison uniform. The perfect match of anything possible to identify the very same person that Shamar saw leaving his house.

Monica approached the little laptop desk where Shamar had the photo album spread open.

"Who is this?" He pointed at the picture. Monica glanced down at the picture and looked at it for a brief second.

Both Vermani and Delani held their breaths.

"That's your cousin, Dejah," said Monica with knowing.

Shamar nodded solemnly. "That's who killed my mama," he replied. "That's her right there."

Shaking her head, Monica said, "Dejah's in prison," she paused for a second. "This can't be right, Shamar."

"I know what I saw," he said.

She looked at him. "What did you see?" said Monica.

And he told her everything.

Chapter 7

The next morning Dejah exited the building of the federal halfway house facility that was assigned to her, per Judge Connelly's instructions. She had to live there for the next three to six months until the courts saw fit that she was ready to live in society. It was something like a primary probationary period she had to live through without getting in trouble.

Living in Tallahassee was way more suitable for her. Although it was only a few miles from Quincy, residing in its neighboring county just might be what she needed. Plus, her home-girl, Stacy, was living there now, too, having rid herself of the same old bullshit Quincy offered.

There was a point in time where Dejah was the queen of her small town, living the best life with one of the top money makers in the game on her side. Marlon had made her life feel like a dream, how beautiful it was.

But the good could only last for so long before something fucked up showed up and ruined everything, a dirty, disloyal, ungrateful nigga, to be exact.

Marlon was to blame for her downfall, and Dejah was going to enjoy watching him fall next.

His day was coming.

But until then, Dejah would enjoy her freedom the only way she knew how. After waiting at the curb outside the halfway house building, a blue corsa over cuoio Lexus LC

500 pulled up to a stop in front of her. Dejah stared at the car as its passenger window rolled down.

"Bitch, are you gonna stand your happy ass out there on the curb, or you gonna get in?" Stacy grinned up at her from behind the wheel of the car.

Dejah smiled and got inside the car.

The instant her ass hit the seat, she was pulled into her friend's arms for a long awaited hug. It felt good to be loved by someone who truly cared.

"Are you ready, Dejah?" asked Stacy.

"You know I am, bitch." *Fifteen long years waiting to claim this very moment*, thought Dejah.

"Good. Get your bag off the back seat." Stacy put the Lexus back in traffic. She too had served time in prison, about eight years ago, for fraud and drug trafficking.

With her hard earned money she hired a good lawyer that got her eighteen months in the pen. Shit, it was better than the twenty years she was facing.

Since her release Stacy had been on her hustle, trying to make up for time lost and money spent. Fast forward to today, she was living it up and enjoying life.

When Dejah looked in the back, she found a large white gift bag sitting on the backseat.

"No you didn't, Stacy." Dejah smiled when she pulled from the bag a bottle of champagne. Then her heart lit up when she also spotted the jewelry case inside the big bag. "Oh shit. Oh bitch. I love it." Inside was three thousand dollar Cartier red tulip wood frame glasses and the matching seven thousand dollar Cartier Ballon Bleu timepiece.

"And so that you know, Dej, that came outta my own pockets. So you better wear that shit proudly."

"Thank you so much for this, Stacy."

"Where to first?"

"You already know where I wanna go."

Stacy smiled at her private thoughts. "I thought you'd never ask," she said.

Fourteen minutes later, the Lexus eased into the entrance of Promise Lane Residential, which was a recently established gated community over on the eastside of town. It consisted of a wide spread residential area of lovely town houses. Stacy, herself, lived in the same location, but just not as close to where she wanted to be.

When they pulled up into the driveway of one of the townhouses, Dejah's eyes lit up in wonderment. Then Stacy handed her the keys to the house. She moved so fast tearing out of the car, Dejah damn near fell on her face. Once inside the house, she laughed out loud in obvious joyousness. She went about the house, going from one room to the other. Then she went upstairs to the second floor, where she found the other unexpected surprise. Dejah stepped through the door of the master bedroom and gasped in astonishment.

Lying in the big queen size bed were two beautiful bad bitches clad in the tastiest lingerie.

"Damn," was all Dejah could say.

One was a slim thick Latina with long dark silky hair. Dejah's mouth watered at the sight of her getting up from the bed. The other beauty was a petite redbone with adorable freckles and one of the biggest pussy prints Dejah had ever seen.

"I'm gonna leave you to it, bitch. Enjoy," Stacy said from the doorway with a mischievous grin. "You know how to reach me," she waved and left.

Right then, the Spanish beauty took Dejah by the hand and led her to the bed where she was helped out of her clothes. And that's where they got busy, exploring each other's bodies to its full effect. At one point, Dejah had one eating her ass while the other sucked on her clit like a pacifier. Then came the double-edge sword dildo that brought Dejah to the greatest pleasures. Although Dejah had indulged in the pleasures of other women during her life way before her incarceration, never had she had the pleasure of two women at the same time.

Kitten and Cherry. That was both of their names. And together they worshiped Dejah's body so good that she thought she was falling in love.

Two hours later, their sex games ended in the walk-in shower stall, where Dejah was pounded good from the back by Kitten and her large strap-on. By this time, it was the lunch hour as Cherry, the beautiful freckled redbone, hooked Dejah up with her favorite childhood food. Tuna fish sandwiches with pickles and extra mayo. Then both ladies said their goodbyes as they took their leave.

Left alone now in her new domain, eating tuna fish sandwiches and drinking champagne, Dejah allowed herself the simple pleasure of solitude.

Back in the federal pen, all it took was one cell phone, a few business books, and the game from other professional con artists to get to where she was at that very moment, which was occupying the comforts of her own house, earned from the telephone fraud licks she'd been hitting in prison. From the pen, she had secured the bag enough to send out to Stacy to put shit in position for her.

It all took just a year to do and here she was, taking it all in and loving the movement.

This would be her spot during the time away from the halfway house facility. But she had to look for a job and make it look good for her supervising official. Stacy had had it setup where she was working at her nail shop downtown. Stacy was a solid bitch, her game was on point, but now it was time for Dejah to make her own moves. Meaning, it was time to get her own wheels to get around.

The day she was released from prison, Dejah had to register in, get reclassified, and be present for all types of other bullshit management requirements she had to sit around the facility to deal with. Then, the next day, she had to go through her orientation attendance bullshit all that morning before she was allowed to go out for her primary noon job interview with Stacy. That's when she hailed an Uber driver and headed to Quincy for her stash.

And then her heart awoke with intense emotion at the thought of her cousin, MoMo. Without warning, her tears spilled from her eyes in thick splashes upon her half empty plate.

She cried because it hurt.

She was scared.

MoMo should have never forced her hand. She didn't mean for her to die.

"This shit is crazy." Dejah banged her fist upon the countertop of the chef island she was sitting at.

The front door resounded from the kitchen as someone knocked upon it. Dejah got up and left the kitchen to go answer the door. She peered through the peephole and saw Stacy and another one of her home-girls standing outside on her doorstep. With a broad grin on her face, Dejah snatched the door open immediately.

"Damn, bitch," Stacy said after Dejah pushed her aside to get to her friend.

"Fuck Stacy's black ass," said Dejah. "You're my real bitch. I love you. I love you. I missed you so much."

"What's up, sista?" said Sassy with a delighted smile. Unlike Stacy and her slim sexiness, Sassy was a plus size woman, but very shapely with it. She had a lot to hold on to and would put Lizzo to shame.

"Fuck both of y'all bitches," Stacy replied with attitude and strutted off to the kitchen with the two grocery bags she had in her hand.

Hand in hand, Dejah and Sassy entered the kitchen behind Stacy where a round of champagne was poured. They toasted and laughed. Then they talked and Sassy, whom Dejah had known since seventh grade, dropped the bomb that turned things around dramatically for Dejah.

"They locked up some crackhead last night for killin' MoMo yesterday," said Sassy.

"What crackhead?" Dejah asked.

"Larry Demps. You know Larry, sista. Peanut from High Bridge old man. Him. Yeah. Said they caught him leaving the house last night where he killed MoMo," Sassy answered.

"But he was shot too, wasn't he?" Stacy replied.

Sassy was an evening shift nurse at the Gadsden county hospital, over in Quincy. She was there when the paramedics brought Larry in to undergo immediate surgery.

Hearing this, Dejah thanked the gods for placing Larry in that position to become the scapegoat. She damn sure didn't want to become a suspect to her own cousin's death. She hadn't been out of prison a full 48 hours and already had blood on her hands.

The conversation then led to the subject of MoMo's son, whom Dejah had totally forgotten even existed. Sassy said the cops was looking all over for her son, Shamar, which meant that he was out there in the streets fending for himself alone, or somebody had him hidden away to prevent the government from taking him. Dejah knew all about that type of lifestyle, for it was where Marlon had come up from.

Dejah had to find Shamar.

He needed someone like her to hold him down.

It was the least that she could do now that there was no other relative in existence to claim him, or so she thought.

Little did she know the hell she was about to withstand. Dejah had no clue what was awaiting her.

Chapter 8

During that same moment, Shamar was in the process of utilizing his genius for information by taking advantage of Heaven's laptop computer. Since she had gotten the computer two years ago, they both had practically mastered its usefulness productively. Shamar's love for electronics and anything having to do with computers was the purpose for which his intelligence came. Information is key and Shamar understood the importance of how powerful information could be.

Again, Shamar wasn't your average twelve year old, his intelligence came from busying himself learning things as a distraction to keep from drowning in his own misery.

The rest of his crew were at school. Both Delani and Vermani had stopped by the house this morning to check up on him. Last night Monica gave Vermani back their father's gun to put back where it belonged. She knew Vermani was the responsible one to get it done without fucking up. Shamar learned this morning that Larry had been charged with his mama's murder. When he heard this from Heaven's mama, she was trying to convince him that Larry just might be the real murderer. Monica then told Shamar about how dangerous Larry Demps really was, despite his drug addiction. She had recounted some of the cruel things Larry had done to support his high, even catching a hustler lacking during the night and jacking them for all their products.

Some was said to have been killed by Larry, he had a reputation for doing dirty work.

Shamar was almost convinced of Larry's wickedness, but his heart just happened to be in the wrong place at the wrong time.

Having read about the murder investigation through the Gadsden County Times newspaper website, Shamar knew Larry had now been processed and booked. That very same morning, he would attend his first appearance where his case would go before the judge.

It was then that Shamar learned about all the serious crimes Larry Demps had been tried for over the course of thirty years. He'd gone to prison on two separate occasions for violent crimes and grand theft. He was even suspected of a list of attempted murders, battery, and even possession of weapons. Larry being the suspect of killing his mama made Shamar believe the cops and the judicial system was going to slam him just by his criminal history alone. Shamar felt sorry for Larry, only because he knew that he was innocent.

Somehow, some way, Shamar was going to help Larry. He knew that despite all his mama's bullshit, she favored Larry the most out of all her boyfriends. That's why Shamar wanted to do something about it, because his mama cared for Larry.

After he had completed his tasks on the computer, Shamar made his way up front. In the kitchen, he poured himself a glass of milk and thought about what else Monica shared with him the night before. When he demanded to know what she knew about Dejah, she gave him what he wanted. But that was after making it clear to her that he didn't want her to go to the cops about Dejah's involvement.

The last thing Monica expected a twelve year old to do was go after the person who was responsible for the murder of his mama. She thought he was too good of a kid to get his hands dirty. But Shamar had to remind her that he wasn't no ordinary kid. He had to re-familiarize her with the numerous incidents when he had to cause great bodily harm to those who hurt his mama and used him as a tool for bullying around.

Shamar was forced to strike back or else he would be considered a coward.

He'd once fought a grown ass man about his mama.

So once Monica got the point he intended to prove to her, Shamar told her that he would deal with Dejah on his own.

"You just need to be careful, baby boy," said Monica last night when he poured his heart out to her.

"I'm not the one you need to worry about." Shamar had responded. Monica read the pain in his eyes and then saw the hatred in its meaning.

That's when Shamar learned about Marlon. He and Monica had surprisingly stayed up late in the wee hours talking about Dejah and her life as a gangster's wifey. Marlon had taken Dejah the moment she graduated high school and paid her way into beauty school. In the process, he had spoiled her with the best that money could buy. From trips to Jamaica and London, to courtside seats at a Lakers game next to Ice Cube, and even shopping sprees on the whim. Marlon had taught her the game and gave Dejah what many other women only wished they had.

And then one evening during a traffic stop, Marlon bailed out on her, leaving Dejah to fend for herself. With four kilos of molly in the trunk, a pistol under the seat, and surprisingly, an unregistered Infiniti Q45 that was reported stolen from its lot two years prior out in Arizona. Dejah had embraced the hell the Feds had taken her through. She had refused to give Marlon up, who had went underground for fear of Dejah breaking under pressure. But he did manage to get her a high power defense attorney to represent her. That was the last Dejah had heard from Marlon, who apparently cut all ties with her, only because he couldn't face her after what he had done to fuck up her future.

Dejah had done fifteen years in prison for him.

Her loyalty was commendable.

Marlon today was a renewed kingpin with one of the strongest operations in the game. Shamar viewed the exclusive pictures of Marlon and his team on social media. They were really getting to the money. And Marlon had a new girlfriend now, Shamar had noticed. Her name was Anya Williams. She was from the Lake Skillet area, one of the most humbled, laid back hoods in town. And just like he did with Dejah, he caught Anya when she was young and tender. Now Anya was a college graduate and a dedicated school teacher at the local high school.

When Shamar learned this information after some careful research, he was struck with a devilish thought. He wanted to take this information to somehow use it against Dejah.

This is where his young intelligence came into play. Shamar was about to start some shit.

He knew Dejah must feel some type of way against Marlon for doing her the way he did. Let Monica tell it, he had really broken Dejah's spirit. So there was no telling what mischief Dejah already had in mind to show Marlon how she felt about him crossing her out.

And then, just when the plotting was getting good, there was a knock at the front door. Shamar exited the kitchen to look out towards the door. He eased toward the foyer, where the unwanted presence of a tall male figure peered inside at him from the stained glass window of the front door frame.

Shamar gasped and ducked back around the corner.

"I saw you in there, Shamar. You don't have to be afraid of me. I'm here to help you. Monica sent me here to check up on you," said the stranger.

Shamar didn't reply.

"C'mon little man. Open the door."

No answer.

Looking in the direction of the back door, Shamar felt he should make a run for it because Monica never mentioned that she would send someone to check in on him.

It was a trick to get him to open the door. Shamar may be young but he wasn't dumb by a long shot.

Without further hesitation he dashed down the hall for the backdoor. They would have to catch him because he wasn't going to allow them to get him that easy.

Heaven had always said that he would run so fast that the sole of his shoes would burn through. That's exactly what he was about to do at that moment. He was about to run until his feet started smoking.

Once Shamar made it to the backdoor and opened it, he hit the ground running. Right into the clutches of two big burly men, who caught him just as he turned his jets on.

"No." Shamar fought against them, but he was not powerful enough to defeat their combined strength.

Then, out of nowhere, stepped the big man that Shamar saw standing outside the door. He was dressed in nice casual linen and loafers. The look he had on his face was a look of trouble.

"Shamar Griffin. We can either do this the easy way or the hard way," he said.

"What do you want, man?" Shamar bellowed as both men held him by one arm each. "Lemme go," he yelled.

"My name is Emmanuel Thomas. I work for the Department of Children & Family. And I'm here to bring you in," he told Shamar.

"Fuck you." he spat angrily.

"Suit yourself," smirked Emmanuel and gave his two handlers the nod. "He chose the hard way," he said. Then he watched as they carried Shamar away kicking and screaming. But the triumphant expression he had on his face was about to get wiped off by the absolute unexpected, just as soon as they made it around the corner.

Chapter 9

Chuck had just turned his G550 G Class Benz truck onto Key Street when Dolo tapped him on the shoulder and pointed up ahead.

"I see it," said Chuck humbly.

"That's them bitch ass government people, huh?" Dred replied from the back seat, leaning forward, while placing the blunt of weed between his lips.

Up ahead the three gangsters watched as two big black men fought against the wild actions of a young black kid, who was attempting to fight himself loose from their grips. They were dragging him from alongside of a house, across the front lawn, towards the waiting minivan parked at the curb in front of the house.

"Hey, ain't that MoMo's boy?" Chuck said.

Dolo, who was the more dangerous one of the three, leaned forward to peer out of the windshield. "That's him, my nigga. Stop the truck. Stop the truck," he said, while pulling out his gun. "Got me fucked up."

Chuck didn't even question his homie's intentions because he was down for whatever he was down for. So he pulled the Benz over to the side of the road and parked it right behind the minivan.

"What's the move, y'all?" said Dred. He was the youngest of the three, twenty years old, but with a hell of a street reputation for putting in work.

These were a team of jack-boys that would rob and kill you without remorse. It was niggaz like them that gave hustlers nightmares. Their only rule was anybody from Quincy was off limits. They brought back to the hood instead of taking from their own.

Dolo hopped out of the truck, clutching his Glock .21 and closing the distance between himself and the two men who were handling Shamar. He didn't pay the lone guy no mind because he knew his niggaz had him.

"What the fuck y'all doing?" said Dolo. He stepped right in the path of the two sturdy handlers. "Let him go before I push your shit back like a bad haircut."

"Excuse me, but this is government business, so I suggest that you-" Emmanuel Thomas was punched in the mouth so hard by Dred that the blow made his head snap back. He stumbled backwards in a drunken manner, and then Chuck laid him flat out on his back with a vicious two-piece to follow up.

Both handlers were stunned by the sudden act of violence and didn't know what to do next.

"You think I'm playin' wit' you?" Dolo upped his gun and pressed it against the head of one of the handlers. He immediately released Shamar. "That's right, nigga. You ain't ready to die," he said.

Shamar then stamped down hard on the toes of the other handler's foot in an attempt to crush them. He let go and then Shamar whirled around and struck him across the nose with his fist. It started bleeding profusely almost instantly. Then Dred shoved him towards the truck and made him get in with him.

"Hold up," said Dolo, approaching the fallen man.

"What's up?" Chuck turned back to look at his right hand man and third cousin. "Fuck them niggaz, cuz."

"Naw, my nigga. I need some insurance," he replied.

"Cuz..." Chuck knew his cousin could be a real menace at times, but he sometimes also liked to go overboard with

51

his shit, too. And this was one of those times where he knew Dolo was about to do something crazy, in broad daylight.

But instead, he walked over to Emmanuel and dug his hand into his pockets. That's when he came up with a thick brown wallet. He opened it and examined the man's driver's license photo and information.

"Emmanuel Thomas. 2112 East Alabama Street. Oh, you're one of them Tallahassee muthafuckaz." Dolo sneered like a vicious pit bull at the man.

Emmanuel swallowed nervously.

"You make sure you people leave my lil nigga alone or I'm gonna come see you. Understand?" Dolo said.

"I understand," he nodded eagerly.

"A'ight. Cool. Now you pussy ass niggaz get outta my hood before I leave you dead out this muthafucka." Dolo made his way back to the truck and got in. Chuck did the same, and they peeled out. But before they got out of sight, Dolo made his hand into the form of a gun and pointed it at the three men.

It was wise to not take his threat lightly.

Dolo would kill you for real.

In the backseat, now riding next to Dred, was a silent Shamar. He was far from scared of being in the presence of the three killers. He knew them by reputation only, neither being involved with his mama, at least not in the way that made his stomach turn every time he thought about it.

"What's your name, lil homie?" Chuck said as he met the gaze of Shamar in the rearview mirror.

"Shamar," he replied, just above a whisper.

"Shamar. A'ight. Well you gon' roll with us today, or you got somewhere else to go where them government folks can't find you again?" said Chuck. "If you don't, then we gotcha, lil homie."

Beside him, Shamar watched as Dred relit the blunt he'd been smoking earlier. He inhaled a mouthful of weed smoke and looked over at Shamar to offer him the blunt.

"Hit that shit, lil nigga," Dolo said from the front seat. "That's your payment for us saving your ass back there."

"I don't smoke," said Shamar.

"Just one hit. Shamar. Like this," Dred put the blunt back to his lips and took a big pull from it. Shamar watched as he exhaled weed smoke from his lungs, while grinning over at him with a bottom row of gold diamond-encrusted teeth. "Just like that right there," he said.

"One hit," insisted Dolo.

As he contemplated the peer pressure of what these three killers were trying to get him to do, Shamar thought about Delani. He knew Delani would have done it without the pressure. Even Jamir's little brave ass would've took the blunt and hit it. And so that's where he got his motivation from, figuring if his little brother could do it, then he could as well.

Dred handed him the blunt.

When Shamar hit the blunt he pulled from it long and hard.

Then when he inhaled the smoke he gagged and begin choking, choking nonstop.

"That's that Moon Rock for your ass," Dred laughed as he patted Shamar on the back. He too was high as a kite and already knew what he was about to do with Shamar.

"Here," Dolo offered Shamar his red solo cup to drink, and Shamar downed its contents thirstily. But he just wanted, needed, anything to cool his burning throat. Little did he know, he had just drank a cup full of gin and juice.

Chuck exchanged a look with his cousin and shook his head with a facial expression of a man vexed.

Shamar was about to be fucked up.

A second later, Chuck's phone rang and he gestured for Dolo to answer it. Dolo reached for the phone in the arm console and answered it.

"Yo? Talk," said Dolo. From between the seats, Dred outstretched his arm, passing the blunt in rotation. He accepted the blunt and took a pull. "A'ight. I'll let him know. We about to get right on it, my nigga."

In the backseat, Shamar was slumped, eyes low and drooling from the side of his mouth.

"It's on, niggaz." Dolo disconnected with the caller and hit the blunt. "That was Amp. The play is up. We got a thirty minute window to hit this nigga," he said.

"It's on then," Chuck nodded.

Almost simultaneously, Dred and Dolo reach for their weapons and began checking their magazine and preparing for action. Behind the wheel, Chuck reached under his seat for the P89 Ruger he had there.

For about two weeks, they'd been laying on this nigga named Pimpin' Low. He was everything his name stood for and more.

Pimpin' Low was a big time club owner and pimp, whose hand in the adult entertainment business was bringing in loads of money.

The nigga was pimping hoes all across the south, from Quincy to Orlando. Word on the streets was that he'd just bought the old Platinum club building near PoleCat Alley and was planning on turning it into a strip club. It was located literally right across the road from the Gadsden County jail and a next door neighbor to a prison work camp facility.

And that's exactly where Dolo and his crew were about to lay his ass down.

The information that had just been handed to them was from a reliable source. Pimpin' Low was meeting with his investor with a big bag full of money. The money would go into the renovations of the club to spice it up a little more.

It only took them five minutes to reach the location. When they got to the club, there were only two vehicles parked out front. Pimpin' Low's candy painted red '67 Plymouth Belvedere and a black and silver 2019 Acura NSX. Chuck wasn't worried about the Benz truck he was driving. It came with the last lick they hit out in Madison, Florida several days ago. So when he parked the truck outside the entrance door of the club and left the engine running, Chuck didn't think twice abandoning it for the moment.

Shamar watched with a hazy vision as the three killers sprung from the truck. But not before Dolo looked back at him and told him to stay in the truck.

"Why do I gotta stay in the truck for?" Shamar responded in a slurred speech.

"Because I fuckin' said so, lil nigga." Dolo bolted from the truck immediately as he and his crew entered through the front door of the club.

Inside, Pimpin' Low was conversing with the investor and the architect contractor, whom he had brought along for the meeting.

They were standing near the bar when the killers rushed in bare faced and made them all lay down on the floor.

"Make this shit easy on yourself, Pimp. I came to collect that bag, nigga." Dolo stood over his man.

Pimpin' Low looked up at Dolo like he was crazy. "What bag? I don't know you-" Suddenly his words were cut short by the blast of Dred's gun. Next to him, the investor's head exploded from the hollow tip splattering his brains everywhere.

"I'm talkin' bout that bag," Dolo sneered.

Pressure busts pipes.

Another minute later, the killers exited the club with the money-bag, moments after two more shots rang out inside.

"What the fuck?" Dred skidded to a halt.

Shamar was out of the truck, stumbling towards the front door of the club. He was so high that he could barely keep his eyes open. The little nigga was fucked up.

"I told your stupid ass to stay inside the truck." Dolo jacked Shamar up by his shirt and shoved him back inside the truck. Then he hopped back in the front seat and they peeled away from the scene.

Chapter 10

When Vermani suggested that they skip class and go back to the hood to check on Shamar, Delani was all for it and thought that they should inform Heaven. Since it was lunchtime, they knew they would find Heaven in the school cafeteria.

Together the twins made their way to the cafeteria where they found Heaven standing in front of the vending machine amongst her friends, Veronica and Porchia. When she spotted them headed her way, a look of suspicion formed upon her face.

"Y'all look like you're up to no good," said Heaven, standing there in her fitted jeans and high top Air Jordans.

"We are," said Vermani

Delani said, "We're about to leave to go kick it with Shamar. You wanna come with us?" He reached for Porchia's bag of Hot Fries and helped himself to a few of them. On campus, many of the students considered him a bully, but Delani was far from it. He just did what he wanted to do without worrying about the consequences.

It only took Heaven a second to decide, and she nodded her head eagerly. "Let's go."

"I wanna go, too," said Veronica.

"No. We're not about to be responsible for you, Veronica," Vermani interjected. It was bad enough they had to watch their own asses, another ass was the last thing they needed.

"I know how to take care of myself, Vermani. Plus, Shamar's my boyfriend now and I wanna be there for him."

Delani laughed and mushed her playfully in the face. Veronica slapped his hand away and pushed him in the chest. He grinned and looked at his brother with that mischievous look of his. He liked Veronica, she was a feisty one.

"She'll only just slow us down," said Vermani. "No."

"I can keep up," Veronica stated firmly.

Vermani gave her a long hard look. She matched his expression and then he shrugged.

"You better keep up, too," said Heaven.

All it took was for Heaven to approve it. Then she looked at Porchia and knew that her scary ass wasn't down with it. So the two friends hugged, and then headed for the cafeteria's exit. Then they went to retrieve their backpacks.

Now the hard part was to get through the school's main entrance without getting caught. As they walked towards the front of the school, where the main office was, Veronica stopped them just before they reached its position.

"What?" said Vermani.

"I have a better plan," she said anxiously.

"What?" Vermani repeated.

"I can call my brotha, Thump, to come get us," she replied. "And he'll come, too." Veronica assured them. Before she could allow anyone of them to respond, she pulled out her smart phone and called her big brother.

Luckily, Thump was in the area, and pulled up on the scene in a greenish emerald colored Lincoln Aviator. When the truck swung into the parking lot out front, five minutes later, Veronica was the first to dash in its direction. The rest of them followed as Heaven and the twins hopped in the back of the big SUV.

Upon their entrance inside the truck, Delani extended his fist for some dap. "What's up, Thump?"

"What's going on?" asked Thump, a stocky built nigga, who was from the Lake Skillet area. Twenty-one years old and out there in the streets thuggin' hard, Thump didn't expect a crowd but that was just like Veronica, always unpredictable and using him to get her way.

"We need to get to Pepper Hill," said Veronica.

"For what?" her brother asked.

Heaven spoke up and told him the reason they were running off from school.

"I heard about that shit yesterday. I knew MoMo. She was good money," said Thump. He was dressed in the latest Purple Brand label and dripping in custom jewels. It was obvious he was getting to the bag. Veronica had always bragged about how her big brother bought her this and that.

"Turn that shit up, Thump," said Delani. He was bobbing his head to NBA Youngboy's "Outside Today" playing at a modest volume from the sound system.

Thump smirked and upped the volume.

Heaven, who was sitting in between the twin brothers, was rummaging through her backpack for her phone. She wanted to call her house phone to inform Shamar that they were on the way.

"You callin' Shamar?" said Vermani.

She nodded.

And that's when Heaven, with her phone to her ear, looked over and gasped. Suddenly, she lunged across Delani's lap to stare out his side window, causing him to look at her funny.

"What's the matter?"

"That's it right there," she bellowed.

"What?" Thump intervened.

"The car," said Heaven. "That's the white car I saw yesterday parked in front of Shamar's house." She was pointing in the direction of a white Dodge Challenger parked next to a gas pump at the 24 Kelly Jr. gas station across the street from Burger King and KFC. They were driving alongside of the 24 hour gas station on the side street toward

Pat Thomas Highway. "That's the car Dejah was in yesterday."

"Are you sure?" Delani asked

"Yes," she said excitedly.

Without further ado, Delani waited until the SUV stopped at the intersection before the main highway, then he jumped out and darted towards the car in question.

"Delani," Heaven shouted after him.

Vermani was out the truck next, hurrying around it to get to the other side. Then he chased after Delani to have his back on whatever he chose to do.

When Heaven moved to get out of the truck, Veronica grabbed her by the arm and told her not to go. Then Thump pulled out into traffic and Heaven screamed for him to pull the truck over.

"Where the fuck else you think I'm going, lil girl?" Thump snapped at her. After pulling out onto Pat Thomas and hitting the turn signal, Thump waited until another truck and car drove by before he swung his SUV into the central entrance of the Kelly Jr. gas station.

By this time, Vermani and Delani were already at the car, finding it empty.

"Where the hell she at?" said Vermani.

Delani headed for the store and went inside, searching for any sign of Dejah. But all he saw was five other customers occupying the store. Two at the front counter, while the others browsed around looking to purchase something. Then he was distracted by the alarm of an older white guy who suddenly bolted from the front counter through the door outside. Delani stepped over to the door and looked outside at the suspiciously enraged white man.

Vermani, who had been opening the door to the car at the pump, looked up and saw the white man headed in his direction. Stepping out the door, Delani watched as the guy approached his brother. A second later, Vermani drew back and punched him in the face. Instinctively, Delani was running straight for the white man and stole off on him from the blind side. Then together he and his brother pounced on him like ticks on a mangy dog.

And they were both wearing his ass out.

Heaven jumped in, and together, with the twins doing the most damage, they gave him a good thrashing.

"Where is Dejah?" Delani demanded, once the guy was down on the ground, having fell under the pressure.

"I don't know no De-jah. I'm just an Uber driver," the white guy cried out, his nose spewing blood and his split bottom lip also bleeding nonstop.

"Uber driver?" said Delani, kicking him in his head.

"I'm just a driver," he said. The man was now in a fetal position, curled up like a bitch. If it wasn't for the twins' different clothing, he would have sworn he was so fucked up that he was seeing double.

"It's true," Thump said from behind the wheel of his SUV, knowing better not to get out and be implicated in whatever it was that just happened. "That's Roger Rog. I know him.

He's tellin' the truth, y'all." he replied.

"I don't know nothing, guys. I swear," said Roger

"You don't know Dejah?" Vermani just had to make sure the guy was sticking to his word.

Before Roger could respond the blurb of a police siren alerted them all. A QPD cruiser was pulling into the entrance of the gas station. The twins looked at one another and took off running from the scene.

"Oh no," Heaven backed away from Roger, who looked like he was just as alarmed by the presence of the cop car. She looked and saw Vermani and Delani causing hell in traffic as they dodged getting run over, dashing across to the other side.

"We got a problem, Roger?" Thump replied in a serious tone.

Heaven got into the SUV behind Veronica and watched as the cop car approached their area.

"No problem, big guy. No problem at all." Roger picked himself up off the ground. By now all types of people were watching him and wondering what was about to happen next.

The cop car stopped behind Roger's car and the officer looked from Roger to Thump. Thump stayed back for a reason, he didn't want to seem too anxious to get away. The last thing he wanted was to give them reason to fuck with him.

"What's going on out here this afternoon?" said the black faced white officer exiting his cruiser.

"Nothing, officer. I'm just on my way." Roger opened the door to his car and got inside.

"A'ight, Roger. You be easy now." Thump saluted the Uber driver and went on his way. He got back into traffic and cruised on in the direction which he knew the twins would be. There was a back way behind KFC, which would take the twins to a side street behind the old Wal-Mart building and into Pepper Hill.

Minutes later, Thump found them walking alongside another backstreet behind the old pecan house where Big Tune grew up. Big Tune was yet another hood homie who used to run the streets real heavy before setting all that thug life shit aside and enjoying the family man lifestyle.

The SUV rolled up on the twins and stopped to let them inside. Heaven pulled the twins close to her.

"You know what, Vermani and Delani?" Thump said with a glance back behind him to look at them.

"What?" they said in unison.

"I love you two bad muthafuckaz," Thump laughed and sped up the street. "You niggaz are some real fools. But I respect y'all though," he said. "After that shit, y'all two bad muthafuckaz will always have my respect. For real."

Delani could only smile at the compliment.

Vermani's fists hurt still.

But they were good. It was time to go see Shamar. He would love to hear what they just did.

Chapter 11

When Marlon learned about Dejah's release, it was through his little brother Chad's wifey. Her name was Eboni and she was the manager over the beauty parlor that Chad owned. She heard it through the grapevine that Dejah was home and decided to inform Marlon of the news, since it was mainly his fault she was even coming home from prison.

But of course, she didn't tell him that for fear of Marlon and Chad beefing over her and her slick mouth.

Marlon hadn't thought about nothing much, except for Dejah and what life for her was about now that she was out. He knew Dejah reaching out to him was not going to happen. He knew she would rather lie in a pit full of rattlesnakes than pick the phone up and call him.

Marlon couldn't believe he had forgotten her release date. He had been so busy ripping and running the streets, trying to maintain his reign over the game that he didn't think to remember. Now that he knew she was home, Marlon decided to take it upon himself to find out where she was located and what she was up to, because he knew that he couldn't sleep on a bitch like that.

He had cut her deeply, Marlon had to admit that. Her getting all that time behind him scared Marlon. He figured if he remained connected to her that a case would be built against him. He didn't trust Dejah to keep solid under pressure, but she had proved him wrong.

She kept it all the way real.

She stuck to the G-code and didn't say a thing.

Back then, Marlon did what he had to do to survive. He had just gotten where he needed to be in the game to become who he was today. Marlon never feared anyone as much as he feared Dejah all those years ago, when the Feds snatched her. It was just a bullshit traffic stop, but when they found what was in the car, the Feds took the case. And that's when Marlon took his chances and skipped town.

One peep and he was dead.

Marlon had to disappear.

He was scared as a snitch in a room full of gangsters. But he eventually made it through and was now one of the biggest niggaz in the game.

Marlon was just leaving from seeing his grandma Betty at the local senior citizen community center she was attending when he got the call from Eboni. He climbed into his shiny burgundy Mercedes Benz S65 and contemplated his next move. There was only a few people he could think of who would know where Dejah would be. His first candidate would be Sassy, who was Dejah's closest friend, next to Stacy. So he decided to call Sassy first.

Getting back in traffic, Marlon hoped his grandma at least won one game in bingo this time. She used to be the lucky one before her eyes started getting worse, but Betty was still sharp as a razor.

Marlon called his boy Nate, whom he knew was messing around with Sassy every now and then. He didn't have neither one of Dejah's friends' numbers in his contacts. After what went down with Dejah all those years ago, they pretty much cut all ties with him.

Then Marlon ended the call. Even if he had a way to contact Dejah, he didn't think he would actually follow through with calling her.

That would be like waking a sleeping lion.

His pride wouldn't let him do it.

But what Marlon did do was put a call in to his business attorney, Jacob Lynch, to get all the information he could get on Dejah. He needed to know where the blow would come from if there ever would be one.

After connecting with Jacob, he still called Nate back to see what he could find out.

"Are you sure that's what you want, dawg?" Nate was another go-getter that Marlon practically grew up with over the Sub Division area. But he wasn't into the drug trade, he got his bag slanging that iron robbing niggaz, before going legit. All he needed was the start-up money to fund his business plans, and he made it happen.

Now Nate was just as successful as Marlon.

Life was good.

"I'm sure, Nate," he said.

"Because you know there's talk about her having somethin' to do with MoMo gettin' killed yesterday." When Nate said those words, Marlon almost lost control of his car. "Don't ask me how I know, dawg. I just heard about it myself. It's crazy," he replied.

"From who? I mean," Marlon didn't know what the hell he meant. He paused and said, "Where is this shit coming from, Nate?" This was shocking to Marlon, for he hadn't heard such talk as this.

"Holla at your girl Tia, she knows."

"Tia?"

"Yeah. When she told me this morning, I had to put the muzzle on the bitch. She talk too fuckin' much. Shit like that can get a bitch fucked up in the game," Nate spoke from his own knowledgeable perspective.

What a coincidence that Marlon chose to call Nate to do some investigating for him, only to be told by him something that could definitely get a bitch killed?

Marlon told Nate to call Tia and tell her to meet him at her house, if she wasn't there already. If this shit about Dejah was truc, then somebody had to be dealt with accordingly.

Before he made his own conclusions on the matter, Marlon needed to know the full truth.

Dope-head Larry had gone down for the death of MoMo which was a shock to many people. If one knew of their relationship, they would know that Larry would never hurt MoMo. That was his woman, his partner-in-crime, his road dawg for life. It was even said that Larry killed crackhead RonRon about MoMo, and left him slumped on the train tracks behind the New Projects. So all that shit about Larry killing MoMo was some other shit that wasn't adding up, which was what planted the seed in Marlon's brain about Dejah's involvement. And if so, why would Dejah kill her own cousin the day after she was released from doing a fifteen year prison bid? A bid that Marlon left her to rot on, while he climbed the charts of being the next top dawg.

It didn't take Marlon long to reach Tia's house. She lived two houses down from MoMo's but across the street, next to his homeboy Roe's house. When Marlon pulled up, he was surprised to see Nate's BMW parked at the curb in front of the house. A knowing smirk came over his face at the thought of Nate being there at the house the whole damn time.

Both Nate and Tia were hanging out on the front porch, enjoying the company of one another. Also present was Tia's young bad ass nephew, Donte, and some teenage cutie with long turquoise weave and bow-legs.

Marlon parked behind the BMW and made his way toward the front porch.

"What it do, Marlon? I'm still waitin' for you to put me in the game. A nigga tired of ridin' the bench, pitchin' pennies and shit," said Donte in passing.

"Your day coming real soon, big shot," Marlon responded without breaking stride. He made it up to the porch and embraced his homie Nate.

"I laced her up on everything already, bruh." Nate replied, receiving a head nod from Marlon.

Sitting down on the padded bench in the corner of the front porch was Tia Reynolds. She was a jet black chick with green eyes and slim sexy. The mother of two young girls and a hell of a crack rock chef when you needed one, which was how she and Nate met, after Nate kicked in her door one night, looking for pressure. He had gotten a call from a source saying the nigga he was looking for was up in Tia's spot cooking up dope. By the time he got there, the nigga was already gone.

Nate caught him two days later though.

He always got his man.

"I'm listenin', Tia," said Marlon, taking a seat on the bench beside her.

Tia sat her bottle of Mountain Dew aside and crossed her long firm legs. She wasn't all that in the face department, but her looks made up in sex appeal.

Then she recounted the moment she saw Dejah pull up in an Uber, driven by white boy Roger. She had just let her girls in from school yesterday afternoon. After what seemed like a second after she entered the house, Larry came running out the house in his underwear.

"What?" Marlon looked at her incredulously.

"Yep. His dirty ass was in his dirty drawers," Tia gave a disgusted shiver to emphasize her meaning. "A few minutes after that Dejah left the house carrying a black briefcase. She got in the car and left. Then MoMo's boy, Shamar, came home and found her dead in the house. Poor thang. It's bad enough he had to deal with all his mama's constant bullshit. But to find her in there dead," she said, and shook her head sadly. "That's the worst thang a child should ever want to see."

A briefcase? Thought Marlon perceptively.

"She had a briefcase, not a bag?" he replied, holding Tia's gaze intensely. He needed her to reassure him that what she said she saw was accurate.

"These beautiful green eyes do have 20-20 vision, Marlon. I don't miss much when I'm focused," Tia said in regards to her known coke and liquor habit.

A briefcase. The briefcase. Marlon was taken back all those years ago when he somehow misplaced his custom black leather briefcase. He used it at times during business meetings with his elite and eloquent associates to look the part. The very same briefcase that contained most of his earlier wealth. Back then Marlon had been so busy doing so much shit that it was difficult to keep up with everything at once.

"She came back for her stash," muttered Marlon.

"Huh?" Tia answered.

Marlon shook his head in disbelief.

Dejah had had money in that briefcase hidden somewhere in her auntie's house. She had been waiting, dreaming, hoping for the opportunity to come home and collect her stash, which meant that she had already expected trouble would eventually come and put money up safely to bounce back with.

How much money though? Marlon wondered. Then another thought invaded his consciousness that made Marlon suspicious as to what he hoped Dejah hadn't been doing all along.

Was Dejah stealing from him, too? Did the money she came to collect come from her skimming off the top of his richness?

That was something he could not tolerate, a thief. And of all people, the woman he had given whatever her heart desired. To think that Dejah stole from him really hurt.

It fucked with his pride.

He had to find out the truth.

He felt crossed.

And that's when he looked up and saw Thump's green SUV pull up on the scene across the street. And then the twins got out, along with two other girls, one of them that steals his breath away every time he looked at her.

Chapter 12

Dejah sat amongst the other five people in the reception area of the car dealership. She waited patiently for the manager to finish with her paperwork. Today she would be driving straight off the lot in a brand new black Mustang Dark Horse. The very same car that stole her heart the moment she saw it advertised in the USA Today newspaper back in the pen. She committed it in her mind that one day she was going to be rolling clean in one of her own.

Today was that day, and Dejah couldn't wait to leave the lot, driving in style. With Stacy backing her, she was able to drop a nice fifty thousand dollars easy on the car. The rest she would handle later, after her investments started progressing. She had a masterplan and today she would get that plan in motion, by any means necessary.

Dejah was focused, she was on her game.

On her way to the car dealership, she stopped by the Sprint store and bought herself a smartphone. And that's what she was tinkering with while she waited, programming the phone to fit to her liking.

After about thirty minutes of waiting, the manager approached Dejah with her car key and paperwork. They shook hands and she skipped out to her brand new Mustang parked out front. Before taking off, she selected what she wanted to listen to from the sound system, then sped out of the lot, booming Moneybagg Yo in the wind.

"That's what the fuck I'm talking 'bout," Dejah yelled in excitement as she floored the engine, making the Mustang roar one good time. Good thing Stacy let her get re-familiarized with driving her car. Now Dejah was back in her groove, like she never left.

This time she was on her own shit.

No nigga to tie her down.

The next stoplight she came to, she plugged her phone into the connecting circuit and called Sassy. She had had taken an early lunch break from her job at the local Credit Union to reunite with her childhood bestie for the moment. But she did say she could call her at any time, whether she was at work or otherwise.

"Miss me already?" came Sassy's voice through the speakers of the sound system moments later.

"Bitch, I don' bought me a horse," Dejah laughed.

"A horse?" Sassy stated puzzled.

Dejah put the car in neutral just as another car eased up to a stop next to hers. Then she applied pressure to the gas pedal to let the engine growl for a second. Then she pumped the pedal a few more times just to feel it rumble.

"You hear that, bitch?" she said.

"I heard it, so you got your new car now?" Sassy sounded amused about the matter.

"Naw, bitch, I got a big monster ass vibrator. And this muthafucka got my pussy like whoa." Dejah and Sassy laughed together. "I love you, bitch."

"Love your crazy ass more," Sassy said, chuckling.

Back moving again, Dejah checked the time on her watch and saw that it was nearing 3:00, which meant that school was about to be out soon, and she wanted to check into the situation regarding Shamar. From what Stacy told her earlier, he was MIA and nobody seemed to know where he was at. But it was hinted that Shamar was still somewhere in the hood, she just had to find out where exactly.

Dejah got onto Tennessee Street and headed for Quincy to find her little cousin. Once she found him, she would see to the funeral arrangements for MoMo. She felt guilty about what had happened the day before. Shamar had to be devastated right now, feeling as though he had no one else to turn to.

From what she'd witnessed of her auntie's house yesterday, Dejah knew her little cousin must had been miserable. No child deserved to live like that, ever, nobody at all, for that matter.

A prison cell seemed like a luxury hotel suite compared to the rodent infested, sour, and filthy pit of a home that she walked into only just the day before.

Taking Shamar back to her place, where he could live like a king was the least she could do.

He would be the only man of the house.

Then she thought about her two home-girls, LaShonda and KeKe, both of whom Dejah still considered all right with her. At least they were supportive enough to write when they could. Dejah cherished those brief letters throughout the years. She was grateful for both of them for keeping it real with her.

By the time Dejah made it to Quincy, she headed straight to her old stomping grounds of the Pepper Hill community. She was so amazed at how much of her town had changed and how it yet still remained the same.

As she cruised through the neighborhood, Dejah felt a tightening in her chest. It was just two blocks away from where she was when it all happened all those years ago. The worst moment of her whole entire life, one fuckin' bogus ass traffic stop had taken fifteen years of her life. Years that cut her deeply, but still strengthened her and preserved her in major ways.

At 38 years old, she was still a bad bitch and could run it with the best of them.

Dejah was far from just a pretty face now.

She was a warrior.

In passing, Dejah watched as school buses dropped off school kids, niggaz roaming the streets and posted up on street corners. The brand new Mustang was definitely making a good impression as she cruised through the hood.

Her gas light started blinking on and off, indicating that her new beast needed some fuel in its system. Dejah was surprised by this, figuring the new car should have come with a full tank. But she didn't sweat it at all, because she was coming up to a Kelly Jr. gas station anyway. It sat just at the corner of Key Street, which was where she was already headed. She parked the car next to the gas pump and got out to go inside to purchase her gas.

Upon entering the small store, Dejah was instantly shocked to see who was standing behind the cash register.

"Goddamn, Mike. You're still running this fuckin' place?" Dejah asked, acknowledging the aging Arab store owner, whom she remembered running the place since she was a little girl herself. "You don't remember me?" she asked.

Arab Mike regarded her with a look of perplexity, trying to wrack his brain to remember her. The man was about seventy years old now, degenerating, and probably couldn't see the way he used to see.

"I know what'll spark your memory." Dejah smirked devilishly, then moved toward the back of the store toward the Little Debbie cake section. "I got his ass, watch this."

The door to the store opened and a young girl and a boy entered. Arab Mike gave them a fleeting glance as he kept his eyes on Dejah. And that's when he saw it, her pocketing two Star Crunch pies, and he yelled in alarm.

And then he remembered. The young girl he caught stealing in his store one time and made her work for the two pies. That afternoon, Dejah had to sweep the floor of the store to earn her keep.

"Remember now?" Dejah looked up at him expectantly.

He nodded with a smile. "You all grown up now."

"Yep," Dejah made her way back up front with the two pies in her hand.

"Where you been? It's been very long time."

"I've been in prison, Mike. It's a long story. But I'm back home now." She sat her items onto the counter.

"Good. No more trouble?"

"No more," she replied. "Just business and living life."

"Good," said Arab Mike. "Business is good."

She paid for her purchases, pumped her gas, and got back on the road. She didn't have much longer before she was to return back to the halfway house facility. Dejah just wanted to get Shamar and be on her way.

When she finally brought her car to a stop outside of LaShonda's house, Dejah got out and approached the front door. In the process, she glanced in the direction of her Aunt Sheryl's house across the street, and a deep emotion burned in her chest. The house looked scary, it even looked depressed. She still couldn't believe how MoMo just let the house go the way she did.

Now it would become just another bando that the dope-heads and the trappers would make their new spot.

Suddenly Dejah came to a halt upon LaShonda's front porch as a thought crossed her mind. What if she could fix the house back up and bring it back to life? Make it look like a home again? Aunt Sheryl would love that, and besides, the house still had potential.

The front door opened, snatching Dejah away from her current thoughts. When she turned to see a little boy standing before her, she automatically knew whose child he was by his little bunny ears.

"Is LaShonda home?" she asked.

"Why do you wanna know?" he frowned at her.

Dejah gave him a sideways glance. "Because I wanna see her, you little shit. Where your mama?" she retorted, fighting the thought to kick his little ass.

What happened next really put Dejah in her feelings, the door was slammed in her face. Then she heard the boy scream for his mama through the other side of the door. Dejah let out an annoyed breath and reached for the doorknob to let herself in.

"LaShonda? Where you at, woman!?" said Dejah, stepping through the front door.

"She's in our house, mama," said the boy at the mouth of the foyer doorway leading into the living room. Then he charged up the foyer toward Dejah, she braced herself for the collision, but the boy did a shake and bake move to get past her for the front door and out of it.

A moment later, LaShonda appeared in the living room doorway in a pair of boy-shorts and low top Air Max sneakers. When she saw Dejah, her manicured hands flew to her mouth in surprise, then she screamed in glee and rushed her with open arms.

"Bout time you made it home," LaShonda hugged her.

Dejah smiled. "And the first ass I'm kicking is that little hooligan of yours, too," she said.

"That's Jamir," LaShonda said laughing.

"Then Jamir's ass is on my shit list already," said Dejah. From there, LaShonda welcomed her back into her home and they went inside to celebrate over a glass of wine, while they talked. But it was what was about to happen next that was going to really shake things up.

If only Dejah knew the hell she was about to experience at that very moment.

Trouble was headed in her direction because Jamir went to go get it, and they were coming.

Chapter 13

When Shamar opened his eyes from his slumber, he found himself laid out on a living room sofa. He sat upright in his seat and was overtaken by a sudden wave of highness. The effects from the Moon Rock weed he'd smoked earlier was still kicking. He looked around the room and didn't know where he was at, or how he even got there, and where he needed to go to get answers.

Shamar stood up and swayed on his feet a little, then he looked around the spacious living room again. On the low coffee table in front of him sat stacks of cash money, a glass ashtray full of blunt roaches, a half bottle of Gatorade, two PS5 game controllers, and other miscellaneous shit that gave him no clue where he was.

One thing for sure, was that whoever house he was in, it was laid out nicely. From the plush sofas to the large Sony flat screen TV taking up majority of the wall, Shamar was in the presence of some of the best things money could buy.

That was when it all slowly came back to him. Dolo, Chuck, and Dred. They had rescued him from Emmanuel, the DCF agent and his two Bullmastiffs. Then he let Dred talk him into smoking weed with him, which was pretty much the last thing he remembered. All Shamar knew was that it felt good and even now, the buzzing feeling he was having at that moment made him feel as though he was floating. He was still high. Now he knew why people smoked weed, because it made you feel terrific.

With a shitfaced grin, Shamar went exploring through the house to see what else he could find.

That's when he heard the sounds coming from a bedroom down the hall. Shamar knew those sounds very well, for he'd lived with it many nights. They were sounds of sex being made and it made him curious as to who it was doing it.

As he made his way down the hall, Shamar heard Dolo's voice as he talked shit. Dolo was very vocal about how he was putting his fuck game down while whoever was on the receiving end only grunted and moaned audibly.

Then came the voice of Chuck, whom Shamar reeled back in dismay as he listened, wondering what in the hell was really going on. Shamar refused to believe what he hoped wasn't true, and stepped up to the ajar bedroom door to peer inside.

"That's right, bitch. That big black dick good, ain't it?" Chuck replied, standing behind a naked white chick with a big booty as he pounded her hard from the back.

Lying across the bed on his back while the white chick hovered over him with his dick in her mouth was Dolo. He was gripping both sides of her head as he fucked her mouth. He was trying to cave in the back of her throat how hard he was fucking her face.

"Suck that dick, you white slut. Swallow my shit," Dolo was saying as he got busy.

Chuck was having fun behind her.

Next thing later Dolo glanced over at the door and saw Shamar standing there looking in.

"Come get some of this shit, lil nigga," he said.

Shamar gasped and shook his head no, then he hurried back down the hall. In passing, he grabbed some of the bills from the money pile on the coffee table. Then straight out the front door he went, hearing Dolo laughing at him in the background. He had to get the hell away from there.

Outside, Shamar scanned his surroundings and already knew where he was. He was in the Shaw Quarters area, which is where his grandma Wanda used to live before she passed away. He still had friends in the neighborhood, but not as important enough to seek their help.

Looking down at the money in his hand, Shamar counted out four fifty dollar bills. He peeled one from the stack and put it in his left pocket. Then, after disposing the other bills in his right pocket, he stepped off the doorstep, moving up the street. Up ahead was the neighborhood corner store, where he hoped to catch a ride back home.

Ten minutes later, Shamar exited the corner store, drinking from a bottle of Peach Faygo soda, while clutching a bag of Sour Cream & Onion chips. He stood outside the store for a minute before he recognized someone he knew from around his area. She had driven up in her car and parked it next to the gas pump. Shamar walked right up to her with a twenty dollar bill and asked her to take him to Pepper Hill. She didn't even ask questions, just took the money and told him to get in the car.

Her name was Dominique, and Shamar knew her from kicking it with his big homie, Rico, from the hood. She was a down ass bitch and Shamar wouldn't have chosen a better helper.

When Shamar noticed it was 4:01 p.m. from the time on the screen of her digital sound system, he panicked. He had been gone from the house for four hours. He knew everybody was probably worried sick about him.

After dropping him off outside of Heaven's house minutes later, Dominique handed him back the money he had given her. Shamar gave her a strange look and told her that she was a real bitch.

Dominique smiled and tossed up the deuces.

Watching her drive away, Shamar was interrupted by the front door of Heaven's house opening. That's when he saw Jamir bolt from the house with the rest of the crew in tow. When they spotted him, they all rushed towards him with a look of earnestness in their eyes. Shamar was almost intimidated by their approach.

"Where you been, bruh?" Vermani asked.

"She's in my house, Shamar. That lady Dejah's in my house with my mama." Jamir couldn't help it, he needed to get it out of his system. He made it sound as though he had just discovered Big Foot or something.

Shamar turned his gaze on Vermani, then Delani, and then Heaven, all of whose expressions read the same exact thing. They wanted a confrontation and it was written in all of their eyes. They were waiting on him to give the call.

"She's over there right now?" Shamar replied.

"Jamir just told us," said Heaven.

Turning his gaze on the shiny black car parked in front of Jamir's house, Shamar felt his heart quicken at the prospect of finally confronting his mama's killer. He couldn't believe she had the audacity to show her face after what she did the day before.

The bitch was one valiant muthafucker, way more bold than Delani.

As if he couldn't take waiting any longer, Delani made his way across the street. On the way there, he scooped up a brick laying alongside of the road and leapt over the curb into the front yard of Jamir's house.

The rest followed as Jamir hurried along to take the lead. They then entered the house to the sound of Jamir's mama and Dejah talking. They were in the living room talking and laughing, like everything was all good. But all that came to a cease when the five young hooliganz entered on the scene.

Instinctively, Dejah looked at them all and rose up to her feet. She sat her glass of wine down on the table and faced off with the crew. There was a challenging look in her pretty but cold brown eyes.

"What's wrong with y'all?" LaShonda asked. She sensed trouble was amiss and stood up next.

"Why did you do it?" Shamar approached Dejah, then Delani eased over near her as well. Dejah glanced in Delani's direction and sized the brick in his hand, then back at her cousin with obvious bewilderment by his actions.

"Why did I do what?" Dejah said.

Shamar said, "Don't play dumb wit' me, Dejah. You killed my mama." He clenched his fists tightly, glaring Dejah dead in her eyes and ready to strike.

The instant Dejah opened her mouth to respond, Delani hit her in the face with the brick. Dejah stumbled back against LaShonda, almost knocking her over. Then Shamar went in for the attack. In the process, Heaven pulled the arm of Jamir's mama to remove her from the possibility of being harmed in the process.

But to all of their surprise, Dejah did not cower under the attack of Shamar, Vermani, and Delani. She fought back and was hitting their asses like a grown man.

"Stop. Stop this mess right now," LaShonda screamed to the top of her voice.

"You killed my mama." Shamar was rocked by the vicious blow to his right ear that sent him tumbling sideways onto the couch. He climbed back to his feet and charged after Dejah like a madman.

While both twins were also standing up against Dejah's calculated punches and swift movements, Jamir located the brick off the floor and was about to bash Dejah in the face with it. But his mama grabbed him by the arm and slapped the taste out his mouth.

"Sit your muthafuckin' ass down," LaShonda told her son with a second slap upside his head.

Suddenly, Vermani let out a deadly cry when Dejah put him in an arm bar and mercilessly snapped his arm out of its socket. She had blood pouring from her cheek, where Delani had hit her with the brick.

"What you did to my brotha?" Delani paused when he saw his brother hit the floor howling in tremendous pain as he held his wounded arm. This scared the hell out of Delani.

Dejah then stole on Delani and knocked his ass out with a wicked left hook to the face. "I'll kill you little bitches. C'mon. What's up, nigga," she glared at Shamar.

Shamar, who was bleeding from his nose and mouth, his right eye swelling up gradually, was far from done. "You killed my mama," he growled.

"No I didn't, Shamar." Dejah braced herself.

"You did. Bitch." Shamar charged in again, but this time with Heaven with that same brick in her hand. He and she had gotten a few hits in with the brick and their fists, before the unexpected happened. All it took was one blow to Heaven's chest to send her falling to the floor convulsing and seizing while foaming from the mouth.

"Oh no. No. No. No." LaShonda rushed in and dropped to her knees to render aid to Heaven's situation.

Shamar looked at Heaven and feared the worst.

That was Dejah's cue to get the fuck up out of there. She pushed past Shamar and headed for the door. Shamar didn't even bother to chase after her. His concerns were for Heaven at that moment, kneeling down to lay a gentle hand upon her shoulder as she lay seizing on her side.

"She'll be all right, Shamar. Go help you brothas," said LaShonda, now understanding where his fears arose from.

Shamar didn't even budge, not even for Vermani crying out to him, not until Heaven stopped shaking.

Delani was still knocked out cold on the floor, and Jamir was too shocked to move.

They had all lost against the enemy.

Dejah had won.

Again.

Chapter 14

When Marlon got the call from Tia saying that Dejah had just shown back up in the hood, he bust a U-turn and headed back to Pepper Hill.

Marlon was told that Dred and his crew had saved Shamar from the DCF officials and took him with them. After calling Chuck several times to reach him, and getting no answer, he hit Dred up. Dred informed him of everything. Then Dolo was contacted, that's when Marlon was summoned out to Shaw Quarters.

Then, just as soon as he arrived at the location, Tia called with the new information on Dejah's existence.

Without thinking twice, Marlon deviated from his mission to take Shamar off them niggaz hands to go back to Pepper Hill to catch Dejah.

Dejah was top priority.

The drive there was spent with Mo3 pumping from the speakers and thoughts of murder on his mind. He knew Dejah had been stealing from him and Marlon refused to allow her to get away with that.

His phone rang and Marlon answered it when he saw it was Anya calling.

"Is it true, Marlon?" she asked. By now Anya should either be home already or attending some after school function or another, which had become regular as of late.

Marlon already knew what Anya was referring to.

"It's true," he replied.

"And has she contacted you?"

"Not yet."

A pause. "Not yet?" Marlon could just imagine the look of curiosity she had on her face at that moment.

"She'll find a way to contact me sooner or later. But I'm not gonna hold my breath on it," he said.

Marlon turned onto High Bridge Road to cut through the backway around the Old Projects on Stewart Street.

Anya sighed. "Okay. Whatever," she muttered.

"How was your day, my love?"

"Progressive." she said. "I punched your little mannish-ass homeboy again today after class. He pushed up on me talkin' 'bout when he graduates in a few months, am I gonna let him smash one time."

"Just one time?" Marlon chuckled.

"Oh. You think that shit is so funny, huh?"

He said, "One time, bae? If he knows like I know, that pussy is like crack. One time ain't enough."

"Then again I just might let him smash," said Anya.

Marlon's grin was wiped away fast.

"I heard them young boys got stamina," she rubbed it in thick and Marlon began to fume. Anya was laughing because she knew her teasing was getting to him. It was okay for him to tease her, but he couldn't take it himself. "A good graduation fuck just might be what I need."

"Oh yeah, bae?"

"Yeeepp," she sang.

Marlon disconnected the call, not because of her teasing, but because he was turning onto Key Street just as a black Mustang shot past him like a bullet. He looked in the direction of the shiny black car, wondering what the hell their problem was, driving along a residential street so recklessly like that. Didn't they know there were children in the area? He mused.

After pulling up outside LaShonda's house, Marlon got out and went to the door. From the other side of the door, he heard somebody screaming in pain. Marlon paused briefly, then he opened the door and went inside.

"Marlon." LaShonda looked up at his entrance and beckoned him to help her.

Marlon felt his heart squeeze with panic when he saw Heaven laid out on the floor. Then there was one of the twins, who also was laid out on the floor unconscious. The other one was a few feet away hollering madly and cussing his ass off.

"Quiet him down. Please," LaShonda gasped in frustration, lifting Heaven up into her arms, cradling her head and stroking her face.

Shamar glanced up at Marlon and stood up to face him directly. "Dejah did this," he said.

"Where is she now?" Marlon approached Vermani.

"She just left," Jamir interjected.

"Somebody fuckin' help me," Vermani bellowed and kicked the leg of the coffee table. He howled in pain when the blow of the impact journeyed up to his injured arm.

Kneeling down next to Vermani to examine his arm, Marlon noticed that it wasn't broken but dislocated. He helped the twin up to a sitting position and told him to stop crying like a little bitch. When Vermani opened his mouth to say something slick, Marlon reset his arm. Vermani roared in agony and shoved him away from him.

"Shit." Delani came to and sat up on the floor, looking around the room dreamily.

Moments later, LaShonda helped Heaven up to her feet and helped her into the kitchen. Heaven was still a bit unsteady but she managed the journey.

"Okay," Marlon stood before the four hooliganz. "Somebody tell me what the hell is going on?"

"And who the fuck is you to be talkin' to us like that, nigga?" Delani rose up to his feet at once, his left eye swelling and his temper flaring.

"Lil nigga …" Marlon moved toward Delani and the other three hooliganz advanced on him to stand guard around Delani and shot him a cocky smirk.

In response, Marlon smirked back and nodded his head in respect. He had heard all about these four youngsters causing hell everywhere they go, including Heaven, whom Marlon was surprised to hear such a lovely girl as her could be so fitting amongst likes of these four. Even at the young tender age that they were, their reputation was solid and their courage was admirable.

"What are you doing here anyway?" Jamir asked. Marlon looked at the youngest of the crew and thought he had to be at least sixty or seventy pounds. He was a little scrawny badass muthafucker.

"He's here for Dejah." Shamar replied.

"And how do you know that?" Marlon perched on the arm of the couch. That's when Jamir stepped over and pushed him off of it.

"If I can't do that, you can't either," Jamir said.

Marlon had to respect his mind. Why did he feel like he was being pushed around by a pack of hooliganz? He was the king of this town, yet here he was being challenged by ten, twelve, and thirteen-year-olds. "Okay. Y'all win. I'm in your shit so I gotta respect the game. But yeah, I'm here for Dejah. She did all this to y'all?"

"You should see her, too," said Shamar.

Marlon looked around the room and it looked like a tornado went through the place.

"Why though? Why all this shit?" said Marlon.

"Because she killed my mama," Shamar spoke up.

"She killed your mama?" Marlon looked at Shamar and recognized the dark hate in his eyes.

"So we beat her ass," Delani said, as he located the bloody brick Marlon had spotted moments ago.

"Any idea where she might've gone? I need to get down to the bottom of this shit right now."

"But you didn't ask me how I know, Marlon. Ask me how I know she killed my mama, and not Larry," Shamar replied with a straight face.

"That's enough of this mess, Shamar." LaShonda entered the room next with a cold pack of frozen corn and green peas to offer Delani and Shamar to put on their faces. "I don't wanna hear any more of that mess, okay?"

"It's the truth," he blurted out.

"It isn't," she argued. "Dejah wouldn't dare do that."

"You're only saying that because she's your friend, but I know that bitch killed my mama yesterday."

"Don't tempt me, Shamar," she warned.

"Or what? You're gonna slap me around like you do my little brotha? I wish the fuck you would. But you don't know what happened to my mama, probably only what Dejah wanted you to hear. You never know stuff, always assuming thangz you think you know." Shamar slung the pack of green peas across the room and it burst open against the wall, scaring Jamir.

"Where you going, Shamar?" she called out.

"Fuck you," he shot back. Shamar was moving towards the front door and snatched it open to leave. Then he came to a sudden halt when he came face to face with the last person he expected to see.

"You thought this shit was sweet, huh?" said Dejah, pressing the tip of the pistol against his forehead. She glazed into Shamar's eyes and dared him to test her gangster.

Dejah held his intense gaze and saw the hate he had for her in his eyes.

Marlon sensed the danger amiss and moved over to see what was happening in the foyer. When he saw Dejah and what she was doing, he was tempted to intervene. But the look she shot back in his direction was so cold he even felt the chill coming off of her.

"Back the fuck up, lil nigga." Dejah shoved Shamar backwards as she stepped through the door.

"You gonna kill me, too, Dejah?" Shamar looked like he was really about to test her.

"Try me," she said fiercely and threateningly.

Not even Marlon was stupid enough to test her. He knew Dejah was capable of killing him first, before anyone else in the house. He gave her reason to want him dead and Dejah would not hesitate doing it, if he provoked her.

When Dejah entered the living room, her presence brought absolute shock to all their faces. She asked where Heaven was and ordered her to come out.

"Don't do this, Dejah," said LaShonda.

"Shut up, Shonda. Damn. I'm in control now. I want everybody together." Dejah said once Heaven eased from out of the kitchen and Marlon reached to pull the girl close to him. There was something about that gentleness and affection she saw in his handling of Heaven that made her want to question his actions.

As he held Heaven protectively in his arms, Marlon's heart thudded rapidly in his chest. He was scared and it had nothing to do with him dying.

Once everybody was huddled up together on the couches facing her, Dejah took the pistol and tucked it into her waistline in front of her.

Dejah was a bloody mess. Her face was scarred and swollen. She walked with a limp, her body ached and it showed every time she moved. But overall she was still standing tall and firm throughout her troubles.

"Shamar," she directed her focus on her little cousin. "I loved your mama, whether you believe it or not, but right about now, I don't give a fuck what you think," she said.

Shamar sneered up at her.

"But I'm sorry about what happened to MoMo. The same way you found her is how I left her. But it wasn't intentionally, little cuz. I swear it wasn't." Dejah watched as Shamar's eyes glazed over from pure hate to something else that she couldn't put her finger to.

Then Dejah went into detail about what she did the moment she entered the house until she left. She admitted being terribly sorry for what happened to MoMo. Her confession was heartfelt and to Marlon's surprise, Shamar separated himself from the group to approach Dejah.

"If you wanna hate me for the rest of your life, then hate me, Shamar." Dejah then drew the pistol and extended it towards him. "Or you can kill me now, and don't have to hate me no more. I'm not gonna stop you, cuz. I'm sorry. And I promise to make it up to you for every wrong that ever happened in our life."

Without a word, Shamar took the pistol away from her and Dejah let him do it.

She was far from afraid to die. Dejah lifted her head high and embraced her fate.

"Shamar…" LaShonda called out when she saw Shamar lift the pistol up to aim it at Dejah's face. "Baby, put the gun down. Don't do this, Shamar."

"I promise to love you and support you, like any motha would do her child," said Dejah.

"My mama never loved me." Shamar had tears welling up in his eyes.

"But I can prove it to you, Shamar."

"No she won't," said Delani

Dejah didn't pay him no mind. "Give me a chance to prove my love, little cuz. Or you can kill me. Your choice. I'm ready for either one you choose." Shamar cried silently as he stared Dejah in her eyes, the pistol never wavering. Even with his finger on the trigger, he could not bring himself to pull it.

After what seemed like an eternity, Shamar lowered the weapon, then he stepped forward to wrap his arms around Dejah. She sighed deeply and wrapped her arms around him next, loving him already.

And all Marlon could do was shake his head at the performance. He saw that Dejah still had the gift for gab, for she could talk a cat off a fish truck. She still could be just as persuasive as she had been all those years ago. A sense of pride came over him as he watched the one person he should have never allowed to slip away by his own selfishness.

Seeing Dejah now reminded him of just how much of a damn fool he had been.

She was back, back like she never left.

And now he didn't know what to do with her.

Chapter 15

MoMo's funeral turned out to be more entertaining than it should have been, far as funerals go. All the dope-heads and hustlers and players in the game showed up to pay their respects. It turned out to be just another hood get-together, which was what MoMo would have wanted.

Even Detective Angie Galloway and a few other police officials showed up in honor of MoMo's last ride. Despite her difficult and conflicting past, MoMo had been a good woman, just young and troubled by her circumstances.

But one thing that made MoMo so respected was the fact that, despite her lifestyle, she still found a way to make people feel good about themselves.

There was a point in time where Shamar had caught a glimpse of the woman his mama was before the drugs. She hadn't always been a dope-head, she had plans and goals, too. She just went by accomplishing them the wrong way.

Shamar got high as fuck that day, listening to stories of MoMo and her cherished moments in life. How ironic it was that Shamar learned more about his mama in death than he had when she was alive. MoMo was well loved and respected, but Shamar never received such regard from her as a mother. All she'd ever been to him was a lying, deceiving junkie. Monica, Kiara, and LaShonda, and even his great-aunt Sheryl was more a mother to him than his very own.

But Shamar still celebrated her death because, at the end of the day, MoMo was still his mama. She could have just swallowed him or had an abortion, but she chose to give him a life, although it didn't much account for anything. So for that he would love his mama on her final journey to a better place.

Meanwhile, all his cronies were there to support him, and their families, including Dejah, who was keeping her word to give him what love, respect and honor she could give. Even some of his additional neighborhood friends showed up to be with him on this emotional day. But it was the presence of Larry's son Peanut, who showed up at the repast block party that made things more interesting. Here it was this twenty-eight year old man, one of the most respected figures in the game, trying to pick a fight with a twelve year old. He was mad about Larry being locked up, plus about him being shot by one of the hooliganz, so he took it to Shamar instead.

"You need to back off, Peanut," said Veronica, who had shown up to the block party with her brother, Thump. She was talking to Peanut after he swaggered over in his Gucci linen and Balenciaga shoes to confront Shamar.

"Naw," said Peanut, never taking his eyes off Shamar, as he stood there smirking up at him. "I think this lil nigga know who really killed MoMo and just too much of a bitch to say it."

"Just leave him alone, punk, before we kick your ass," said Jamir, with an air of bravado, stepping up to face Peanut, like he wanted some action.

The crew had all been sitting down at the big picnic table in front of Shamar's house in the front yard, eating BBQ ribs, chicken, and smoked sausages and baked beans. They were surrounded by hood family and this nigga just walked up with the bullshit, like shit was sweet.

He had no clue what was in store for him, if he didn't turn around and leave.

"Get the fuck outta my face, lil busta." Peanut mushed Jamir in the face, knocking him down.

Moments later, Delani snuck up behind him and went across the back of his head with a beer bottle he found lying around on the ground. When he saw Peanut coming, he had gotten up from the table to find a position behind him. He had already peeped the bullshit in Peanut's eyes.

The bottle didn't break, but Peanut still stumbled from the impact, and righted himself quickly.

"You bitch ass lil muthafucka," he said and made a move to go after Delani. But Jamir lunged for his right ankle, throwing him off balance, holding on and biting into the back of his calf really hard.

Peanut screamed bloody murder.

That's when Delani swung the beer bottle again and it shattered across his face this time.

Immediately, Shamar, Vermani, and Heaven jumped in and began punching and stomping Peanut's head into the ground. Then, out of nowhere, another young warrior jumped in and Shamar swung and socked him hard in the mouth, before realizing who he was.

"Kahlil?" said Shamar

Kahlil spat out a slob of blood and rubbed his jaw. "Who else?"

"Oh shit, my bad. You're home?" Shamar said excitedly.

"I am," Kahlil rubbed his face some more.

Shamar was then shoved aside as four of the older hood homies rushed in and separated the hooliganz from Peanut. He had been catching pure hell before the big homies came and dragged him away.

Dejah had approached them, along with Sassy and Jamir's stepdaddy, Tony, who looked down at Jamir proudly. It always made him proud to see his stepson stand up for himself.

"You good, lil cuz?" asked Dejah in concern.

With a shrug, Shamar nodded and went over to go inside his house. The rest of the crew followed, including Kahlil, whom the rest of them were also happy to see, especially Delani, who was a relative of Kahlil. Their mamas were sisters, and very close, like any siblings should be.

Inside the house, it looked nothing like the home Shamar had shared with MoMo after Aunt Sheryl died. It was clean, bright, and lively now, with new furniture and wallpaper and everything that makes a house feel like home. Dejah had done well for herself and brought amazing color to Shamar's world.

It was an awesome start at making things right in the world for him.

Finally, he could breathe with ease now.

He wished his mama was still alive so she could see the changes that were being made in their lives.

"When did you get home, Kahlil?" Shamar asked, once they all were occupying the living room.

"This morning," said Kahlil, who was sixteen and had been gone for the past ten months at boot camp. He had been facing prison time, but somehow the judge found it in his favor to allow him to slide with just a juvenile sentence.

Vermani punched his cousin in the chest, complimenting him on how big he had gotten. Boot camp had Kahlil looking brawny and fit, like he'd been pumping iron.

Kahlil had gone in for violent crimes committed against his mama's boyfriend and his family. It was really him who had initiated the crew to a life of crime at a young age. From stealing video games out of Super Wal-Mart to extorting all the other kids in the hood, they did it all. And by Kahlil's influence, they had continued their torrential rascal behavior while he was gone to do time at boot camp.

For the remainder of that day, the hooliganz hung out inside the house, while the adults partied outside. It was then that Shamar showed Kahlil that he was into smoking weed now, and together, they all got high, except for Heaven and Vermani.

When Dejah eventually walked through the door to find Jamir laid out on the floor, laughing at nothing in particular, and both Kahlil and Delani looking like Chinese hooliganz and grinning crazy, she snapped.

"You," Dejah pointed a firm finger in Shamar's direction and said, "In the den. Now." Then she stomped down the hall just as the twins' mama and Tony entered the house.

Heaven shot Shamar a troubled glance as he smiled highly and got up to go follow Dejah. By this time, the block party was winding down outside and everybody was going on about their lives as usual.

MoMo's celebration had turned out well, despite the little bullshit that happens at any typical black get-together.

Little did they know, Peanut was still on one.

He just better beware.

When Shamar found his cousin in the den area of the house, she was pacing back and forth, like she was mad. This was the behavior of a concerned individual, who was fed up.

"What's up, Dejah?" he said slowly.

"What happened to you playin' football, Shamar? Huh? How in the fuck you gonna keep up in the game with no wind? All that smokin' you doing is gonna break your ass down." Dejah was really upset with him.

"I'm still gonna play football."

"And smoke, too, huh?"

"I haven't smoked in like... three days," he said.

Dejah wanted to slap him upside his damn head. "The only way for you to be the best you can be out there on the field, Shamar, is by being in good shape and health."

"I know," said Shamar.

"Then act like you fuckin' know, cuz. I wanna see you win, but you won't win like this." Dejah gestured towards him, as if Shamar could see the reflection of himself.

Heaven entered the den next and sat down on the sofa chair next to Shamar.

"I told him the same thang, Dejah." Heaven and Dejah weren't the best of friends since their altercation seven days ago, but only through their devotion to Shamar would they eventually find it worthwhile to share one another's space.

And that's how it went for Shamar, being attacked by both of them in regards to his well-being and future.

When Shamar was left with nothing else to believe in except for his circle of friends and Dejah's promises, Dejah stepped up to the plate and was doing her part. Within the week, she had had restored the house, fought to earn guardianship over him, signed the paperwork to approve of his playing football, took him shopping to get his wardrobe up to par, and even became the confidante that his mama never could be. Within the week, Dejah had done everything in her power to represent him.

She was standing firm for him.

Her heart was involved.

So when Shamar made it to his first football practice for the school's team, he had really made his mark. And Dejah was right there on the scene to cheer him on. And Coach Richards, who was impressed with Shamar's speed and aggressiveness, still didn't let him start in its first two games because he had Kahlil Street running the show.

But the twins knew just what to do to put an end to Shamar's let down.

Somebody had to get hurt.

It was only right.

And Dejah was down for the cause, always had been, especially when it came down to someone she cared about.

Chapter 16

Since the day he had finally come face to face with Dejah again, after fifteen years, Marlon had not been the same. She was constantly dominating his thought process. That day back in LaShonda's house had shown him another side of her that he'd never seen.

She had murder on her mind and in her eyes, eyes that he never thought possible to show anything other than the kindness and the realness that he remembered. Her whole demeanor had become hardened and a cold. That could not be denied.

Prison had toughened her up.

His betrayal had made a warrior out of her, a beautiful beast.

On that very same day, Marlon had noticed that the pistol Dejah had in her possession had come from the hidden compartment installed in the floor beneath the steering wheel of his car.

Dejah was present that day, all those years ago, when Marlon had that same set up installed in his Jaguar XK. She must have seen him in passing that day, in Pepper Hill, to round back and search his car to retrieve the pistol. She knew what to expect when faced with him, and if Shamar hadn't accepted her that day, Marlon just might be dead. Killed by his own pistol, which he never got back.

The only reason why Dejah didn't shoot him that day was because she had obligations to fulfill. Shamar was holding her to her word to be there for him.

Marlon didn't press her, he knew what was going on. He knew if crossed Dejah, she would not have hesitated to put him down.

He felt really chumped by her and her little clan of badass hooliganz. So Marlon left her there without exchanging words with Dejah. But the lingering look he gave her was more than enough to assure her that it wasn't over that easy.

Dejah just shrugged in nonchalance, like she already expected to see him later and would not bow down to him.

Since then, Marlon had learned everything he needed to know about Dejah. He knew she was spending her nights in Tallahassee in a halfway house facility. During the daytime, she juggled her time between her Promise Lane townhouse and building a life around Shamar. Then in the afternoons, she was in Quincy, loving on her youngins and reconciling with old friends and associates. Dejah was doing well for herself, and Marlon found himself being proud of her.

Even Anya violated protocol and visited the beauty shop one Saturday, where she knew Dejah would be. She had established a beauty class for the youths to show and teach them the importance of being beautiful and creative.

Anya had met and enjoyed Dejah's performance dealing with all the young girls, until Dejah got wind of who she actually was and gave her the cold shoulder.

Marlon even found himself attending Shamar's football games in hopes of seeing Dejah. Was he obsessed with her now? Was he still hoarding feelings for her, after all these years? Could he forgive her for stealing from him? Money that now made her present existence worth admiring.

Marlon needed closure with her, or he was never going to be rid of her haunting existence.

He was driving himself crazy over Dejah.

She had come and disrupted his life to the point that she had begun to damage his relationship with Anya, without even being physically involved.

Something had to shake or he would lose his mind.

The passenger door to his BMW M8 convertible opened and PJ slid into the seat next to him. This was Marlon's right-hand man, who was brought up in the Lake Skillet area. He had been out of town, down in Miami, when Dejah had come home and fucked up the flow of things.

"What did she say?" said Marlon, starting the engine of the only BMW M8 in town and all the other surrounding areas.

PJ was a tall brown skin nigga, who thought he was God's gift to women. The muthafucka had game that many niggaz couldn't match, but he could never keep a bitch. There had been numerous occasions where either Marlon, or a chosen few of their other team players, had to bail him out, getting caught up with all the bitches he couldn't seem to keep tamed.

"Dalphnie said she agrees to the terms," he said.

"How much is she talkin' though?"

PJ fired up a Black & Mild cigar to blow in the wind. "She wants twenty thousand up front."

"That's all?" Marlon said in disbelief.

PJ looked like he wanted to add more.

"What else, nigga?"

With the shake of his head, PJ said, "And she wants to have dinner with me tonight, at her place, to go over the plans she got in mind."

"Oh. I see," Marlon replied with a grin. "That old cougar bitch wants some dick," he laughed. "I knew it was the best move to send you in there alone."

"I'ma fuck the shit outta that old, fine white bitch," said PJ, laughing. "Real shit though, I prolly can get her to lower the price on that muthafucka."

"You do that."

The person they were referring to was Dalphnie Santa Cruz, a lovely sixty-two year old Brazilian woman, who owned a bunch of land out in the country area of Midway, way back off in the cut. It was once a cow pasture, a wide span of open field of green, and with a lake nearby, which is the area of land Marlon wanted to buy.

He was planning on building his mama's house on that land, a countryside view that she said once that she would love to have. She wanted space to build her own greenhouse and grow a big garden. That's what Marlon wanted, for his mama to be happy with her dream house, other than the big Stucco-style five bedroom home he had purchased for her out in Perry, Florida.

Mama wanted to come back home and spend the rest of her days on familiar territory.

Marlon promised to honor that.

"Let's do it," PJ said as they headed back to Quincy, where their presence was needed.

An hour later, Marlon, PJ, and their chief of enforcers, Lyonell, were all occupying the bar downtown up on The Block. The news Lyonell had for them wasn't good, especially when he couldn't handle the situation himself.

"So you're tellin' me somebody hit three of my trap houses, on the same fuckin' day, and nobody knows who the fuck is behind it?" Marlon wanted to splash his drink in Lyonell's face, but that would've been on some hoe shit.

"I did my part, Marlon," said Lyonell.

"Where's Hot Boi, Blacc, and Rallo now?"

Lyonell said, "Gettin' fitted for their muthafuckin' graves, but only after I interrogated their asses and didn't get the answers I knew you'd want to hear."

"You killed…" PJ lowered his voice and leaned in closer to Lyonell. "You're tellin' me you killed my muthafuckin' cousin, nigga? Huh? Is that what you're tellin' me?"

"PJ." Marlon touched him on the arm.

"Get the fuck off me, nigga." PJ snatched away from him and drew his Glock .21. He then stood up at the table and glared down at Lyonell, like he wanted to blow his fuckin' brains out right there. "You don't even bother to tell me first, muthafucka?"

Lyonell shrugged. "I did my job accordingly, PJ. And that was to never contact y'all unless I have no other choice. I honor every muthafuckin thang I do, and you know that."

"And I honor everything I do, too," PJ sneered.

"What're you saying then, PJ?" Lyonell wasn't positioned as chief of enforcers for nothing. He didn't take no shit from nobody, and his street rep was immaculate.

When Marlon saw that murderous glint in his man's eyes, he calmly spoke up.

"PJ, I suggest you put that gun up, sit your ass down, and handle this shit like bosses do. Or you can get the fuck out because you're causing too much unwanted attention right now," said Marlon.

A deeper shade of darkness clouded PJ's eyes as he stared from one gangster to the other.

"Fuck all this bullshit," he growled and marched toward the exit door of the bar.

In his wake, people steered a clear path of him for fear of being one of his next victims.

"They made an oath, Marlon. They knew the consequences behind not being able to uphold their position."

Marlon nodded. "You did what you had to do. Now you gotta find out who took my money and product."

"Can't do that if I have to watch my back around PJ. We both know that nigga is a fool. I am, too, Marlon, and I will not hesitate killin' his ass, as well."

"I'll deal with PJ, my nigga. Don't worry about him."

"Somebody better deal with him."

"I got it," Marlon reassured his homeboy.

Lyonell nodded solemnly.

"And Ly?"

"Yeah?"

"Look into Chuck and 'nem," he stood up.

"But they don't work in town, Marlon, you know that," said Lyonell, with a look of certainty.

"Niggaz change every day, Ly. There's no honor amongst thieves, so leave no stone unturned. Understood?"

"For sho'."

Chapter 17

"Damn, everybody came out tonight, huh?" said Kahlil, led by his crew of young hooliganz.

They were walking through the entrance gate of the football field to watch Shamar do his thing. They were playing some other school out of West Gadsden, over near Marianna. The bleachers were packed on both sides, with droves of people still coming in for a night of action.

Also amongst the crew were the twins, Jamir, Heaven, and two more hooliganz from the hood, Antwan and Jeremy, both who were closer to Kahlil. Delani only dealt with them off the strength of his cousin, but until either one of them fuck up, he was down by law and honor.

"Look at this chump," said Vermani, nodding in the direction of the home side bench, where the players were sitting and standing alongside the field.

"Shut up, Vermani." Heaven pushed him in the back. "I still can't believe you two idiots did that to that boy."

Delani said, "Only for Shamar. The nigga lucky we didn't break his fuckin' arms, too." He chuckled as he stepped out in his purple label attire and fresh Air Forces.

The person they were referring to was Kahlil Street, the team's starting running back, whose leg was now encased in a white cast all the way up to his knee. When they realized the coach wasn't going to let Shamar start in the games because he was a third string, the twins thought otherwise.

It was all Vermani's idea to lure Kahlil behind the school's gym one day, during their period, to smoke some weed. Kahlil was one of the biggest weed heads at the school, so he didn't hesitate taking him up on his offer. Delani was waiting on him. The moment he made it around the back of the gym, they beat his ass and used a cinder block found nearby to smash his leg up.

That same day, Vermani and Delani cornered Brandon Jones in the boys' restroom and put the fear of God in him. They lumped him up good. Brandon, the team's second string running back, no longer wanted to play. That bumped Shamar up to the top spot. Now here he was, his second time starting in a game.

The crew walked past Kahlil, who glanced back at them and looked petrified. He hurriedly turned back around and dropped his head. He was obviously ashamed to even be present, despite his useless condition.

Even Kahlil, who was now the leader of the crew, laughed at the other Kahlil. "Good for his bitch ass," he said. "I'm the only Kahlil that a muthafucker better recognize."

"That's right," said Vermani.

"Hey y'all," Dejah yelled from the bleachers.

The crew climbed up to the top of the bleachers next to the school's marching band, across the underway gangway. Dejah was in the company of her girl, Sassy, both looking jazzy and excited to see Shamar do his thing.

"What y'all up to?" said Dejah, when Kahlil came to sit down beside her.

"You know we had to come out and watch lil brah run all over these clowns," said Kahlil.

"I see you lookin' fly too, lil nigga." She nudged him.

Kahlil looked down at his thirteen hundred-dollar Palm Angels tracksuit and nine hundred-dollar Lanvin Curb snake-embossed, leather, low-top shoes. The day before was his seventeenth birthday and he went all in, shopping and getting his gear up to par.

"Thanks to you, I can afford to look like this on the regular," said Kahlil.

Dejah nodded her head.

"And since we're here, I got that money for you, back in the truck. I gotcha after the game," said Kahlil, who was also dripping in customized jewels.

"You done with that pack already, Kahlil?"

He shrugged. "What can I say? You chose wisely when you put me on, Dee."

Kahlil had shown Dejah a hungry, fearless side of him that she automatically knew could be of great use to her game plan. So she put him up on what Marlon had going on, and Kahlil hit him where it hurt, his pockets. Instead of hitting the trap houses on separate occasions, Kahlil did all three on the same day. Him, Delani, Jeremy, and Antwan had hit for twenty bricks of heroin, five bricks of coke, and a total of ninety-seven thousand dollars in cash. Dejah took half of the money and Kahlil divided the rest between his team. Then she set Kahlil up in his own trap house out in Tallahassee, where he was making a name for himself.

Dejah knew one day that she would get Marlon back for what he did to her. But what Kahlil did was the least of his worries, because what Dejah had planned for him next would no doubt crush his spirits.

The starting of the game kicked off and the visiting team got the ball first. Then they turned the ball over on a fumble, during the second down, on the 45th yard line. When the home team offense headed out to the field, the hooliganz rose up and cheered as they watched Shamar get into position.

"What the fuck are they doing?" said Delani when the ball shopped and the quarterback, Quavon Mitchell, threw a short pass to one of the wide receivers. A big boy defensive tackle dropped him with a hard take down.

"Give Shamar the ball, nigga," shouted Jeremy.

And sure enough, Shamar got the ball during third down, after a gain of five yards. Shamar came out the back, like a raging bull, trucking other players over and dodging tackles left and right.

He made it all the way up the field and was stopped short, inches from the goal line.

"Watch this," said Dejah expectantly.

"I already know what's about to happen," Delani glanced back at her and said.

The offense took their positions, Shamar got into his stance. He was ready for the ball. The anticipation was intense. Then Quavon hiked the ball, passed it back to Shamar, and Shamar drove it hard down the middle for a touchdown.

"Oh shit." Heaven bolted out of her seat, when she saw Shamar run through the defensive line, like it wasn't nothing. Then he did a two-step dance move that sent the stands in a thunderous cheer for the victory.

Two and a half hours later, the James A. Shanks, Tigers won by 20 points. Three of those touchdowns Shamar earned for himself, putting him at 5 touchdowns total in two games. Tonight proved just how much of a great asset he was to the team. Coach Richards was a proud man. However, he suspected foul play to put Shamar where he was, but he didn't say anything because he knew the seriousness of the situation.

After the game, Delani, who was 14 years old now, treated the crew out to the Waffle House to celebrate.

It was there that Kahlil noticed Antwan, who was sixteen years old, trying to touch up on Heaven. She was 13 now, too, as her birthday was just a week ago. Antwan was sitting next to her, grinning and laughing with the others, but at the same time sneaking feels on Heaven, under the table. Kahlil had also noticed Vermani watching them and mean mugging Antwan, like he wanted to punch him in his shit.

"Aye, Twan?" Kahlil got his comrades attention, and said, "Lemme holla at you real quick, brah."

Antwan pulled his hand back from Heaven's leg, underneath the table, and got up to see what Kahlil wanted.

Kahlil beckoned him in the men's restroom, and Vermani got up and followed. Delani was too busy entertaining the rest of the crew to notice anything out of sorts.

Kahlil saw the look on his cousin's face as he entered the restroom behind them. Antwan glanced back at Vermani, then back over to Kahlil, with a look of question on his face.

Without saying a word, Kahlil watched as Vermani stepped forward and got up in Antwan's grill. Antwan took a cautious step back and Vermani then wrapped his hand around his neck in a vice grip.

"Don't ever let me catch you touchin' on my sista like that again, or I swear on everythang I love I'ma break your fuckin' hands," Vermani announced menacingly.

Antwan frowned as he grabbed Vermani by the arm and tried to break free of his grip.

"Get the fuck off me, Vee." he shoved him.

Vermani was bigger than him by thirty pounds and four inches. He liked throwing his weight around, when the situation called for it. So when Antwan shoved him back, Vermani just smirked wickedly and counter-attacked, with the sole purpose to test his fight game.

For about a minute, Kahlil watched as the two battled it out. Vermani, for the sake of Heaven's honor, and Antwan, out of sheer fearlessness to protect himself.

"A'ight. Y'all break that shit up." Kahlil stepped in to intervene and separate the two.

Right then, Delani entered the room, drew his .9mm, and was about to go across Antwan's head with it before Kahlil stopped him.

"Naw, lil cuz. Don't do it," he said. Kahlil stepped before Delani and stared him dead in the eyes. "Fall back and let Vee handle this shit himself."

"What's going on?" Delani asked him curiously.

Vermani snatched the gun from his twin and pressed it against Antwan's temple. "Please don't make me kill you about my sista, nigga. Heaven is off-limits. One more time and I'ma show you," he hissed.

"I'm good," said Antwan.

"No more, Twan."

"I gotcha."

After a long moment, Vermani lowered the gun and stepped away from Antwan. He gave Delani back his gun, who was now glaring at Antwan. The mention of him doing something to Heaven made him want to do something very bad to Antwan himself.

"He got the picture," said Kahlil. Because he knew, with Delani present, the situation could turn a little dark for Antwan, and he didn't want that for his homeboy. "Just keep your hands to yourself, brah, because I'm not gonna always be there to save you."

Chapter 18

It had been two months since Kahlil and his crew robbed the trap houses in Quincy. Since then, Kahlil had become the thoroughbred hustler that he was destined to be. Now he was trapping over on Magnolia Drive at Rhonda's house, who was the aunt of Sassy, and an occasional dope head, who worked as a professional chef. She had traffic coming in and out of the crib, and Kahlil and Delani were making all the money. They were running through at least 10 ounces of crack and heroin a week.

"We got work to do," said Kahlil, when Delani showed up one morning, ready to get back to the paper. He had been skipping school lately to focus solely on his hustle game. Today, Kahlil promised to school him on how to cook crack.

Delani rubbed his hands together anxiously. "Let's do it, cuz," he said.

"Well, c'mon then, nigga." Kahlil led him into the kitchen, where he retrieved the freshly shrink wrapped kilo of coke from the deep freezer, beneath a box of fish sticks.

Next, Kahlil grabbed a plate, an old Pyrex container, and a box of baking soda, along with the digital scale. Then he showed Delani how to weigh the first ounce and put it in the container. He then took 6 grams of baking soda and used the coke mixer to mix the two together. Then, he put enough water in the container to cover the powder, and then put it in the microwave for a couple of minutes. Delani watched as the heat from the microwave broke the coke down into an oily substance.

Kahlil then removed the container from the microwave and hit it with just enough cold water for the remix, until the coke begin to harden up into crack.

"That's cool shit right there, cuz," said Delani, as he helped his cousin spread newspaper down across the kitchen counter, where the crack was dumped from the Pyrex to dry.

Then Kahlil, with the assistance of his little cousin, repeated the same process until they had cooked and weighed the whole entire kilo. The process took them three hours total to complete, but it was all good because the money they were about to make was worth every minute.

"I can move some of this shit back home in the hood," Delani replied. He was already considering setting up shop at crackhead Ashy Pete's house, over by the Steven School Park.

"You think you can work this shit back home?"

"C'mon, Kah, look where we from, nigga. We live in Pepper Hill, that's Crackhead Central," said Delani.

Kahlil nodded. "A'ight then. We'll bust this shit down the middle and push from there. If you think you can handle it, then I'ma give you the benefit of a doubt, Dee."

"I can handle it, cuz."

"We'll see."

Late that afternoon, when Delani made it back to Pepper Hill, he didn't waste any time. He gave Ashy Pete the proposition that he couldn't refuse, and made his home his trap house.

After giving the crackhead five fat twenty-dollar pieces to smoke for himself, Delani then promised him an additional twenty-dollar piece for every hundred dollars he brought to him. Ashy Pete got on his job, and before Delani even knew it, he was pulling in at least seven thousand dollars a week. At fourteen years old, he was doing better than the majority of the hustlers who'd been in the game longer than he was alive.

The only problem was the Billy Blood Gang members, who lived in the area. They were a ruthless crew that was known for putting in work. But Ashy Pete's daughter, Toby, was a member of the Blood set, and Delani was cool with her. So he brought her aboard to assist him, locking the hood down now that he had the best dope in the area.

Another week flew by with Toby as his sidekick. The money bag nearly doubled its original weekly gross. Toby was twenty years old and had a knack for hustling. She knew how to handle her customers. But she was dead serious, too. Toby would bust your head without thinking twice, especially when some of her gang members had come to confront Delani about him hustling on their turf. Toby, who had stepped up for Delani by using her influence, didn't need to because Delani had done so himself.

"No disrespect to your set, but y'all niggaz just became Bloods here in the hood. Quincy never even seen a Blood set 'til one of our homeboys came home from prison, reppin' the set. So don't come around here like that shit been going on since day one. We all know whose area this is." Delani knew the history of the county's gang activity, since it became essential way back in the early 90's. Back then, if you wasn't a Crip or a Gangster Disciple, no other gang was allowed to rep in their town. But times had changed, and this was a new era. However, one still couldn't act like that blue and black flag didn't exist.

"How old you is, lil nigga?" asked Billy Blue, one of the older gang members, who confronted Delani.

"Does it matter, nigga?" Delani shot back.

"You talk real gangsta for a lil nigga," he replied.

"And I can back it up, too, Blood. Matter of fact." Delani stepped back, pulled over his shirt, and handed over his gun to Toby. "Let's get this shit outta the way right now, so I can get back to my money."

Billy Blue looked amused by Delani's performance.

"Look at this fool, Blood." Billy Blue laughed, along with his other three homies. He was nineteen years old and had a reputation for causing hell in the streets.

Without further ado, Delani punched him in his face and then, just because he knew what would happen next, he punched one of the other three members before they jumped him. But he was a young lion and didn't back down from nobody.

That day, Delani earned his respect with the Billy Blood Gang, and was left alone after that.

Toby was happy to have him as her right hand man. She knew, one day, Delani would own this town, and when he did, she wanted to be there to witness him claim it.

By the third month, Dejah had connected with another cocaine plug. She brought Delani and Kahlil along, as her loyal shooters, when they met for the first time. His name was Oscar Rafael, the brother of Dejah's former Mexican roommate back in the pen, Amelia. Oscar was residing in San Antonio, Texas, and that's where Dejah, along with her two vicious hooliganz, had flown out to meet in person. Upon seeing the two young hooliganz, Oscar regarded Dejah with a look of skepticism. He was initially skeptical about their abilities, but almost immediately changed his mind when Delani and Kahlil conducted themselves accordingly.

After arriving back in town, two days later, Dejah had fifty bricks of the purest cocaine in the game waiting on her.

From there, she let her faithful hooliganz do what they did best, while she busied herself collecting money and washing it thoroughly. There was no looking back for her, it was to infinity and beyond from there.

"This is my destiny, Vee," said Delani, when he picked his twin brother up from school in a shiny black BMW M5 sedan. It had been six months since he was in the kitchen with Kahlil, cooking up crack for the first time.

"Define destiny, Delani?" Vermani accepted the blunt his twin was smoking and took a pull from it. He had never deviated from going to school, because he still had dreams of one day becoming a professional graphic designer.

"Destiny: What will happen or has happened to somebody or something." said Delani. "That sounds like fate to me.

"So being a big dope boy is your fate?" Vermani replied.

Delani shrugged his shoulders as he drove.

"What happened to just graduating high school and becoming your own businessman first, Delani?" said Vermani, with a hint of vex. "People can try to reinvent themselves. I don't really think you can change who you are, though, because who you are is pretty much where you came from and what you've done up to now," he added as the weed smoke took effect on him.

"And what I've done up to now is make sure you don't have to need for nothing. We are good, brah."

"There's only two outcomes with being a dope boy, Delani. That's death or prison,"

Again, Delani shrugged his shoulders. "You sound like our parents right now, Vee. I'm not tryna hear that shit."

"I had a dream last night that somebody robbed and killed you, twin. That's why I'm on that level right now. I don't want nothing to happen to you," he said with earnest.

That's when Delani pulled his Beretta .9mm from beneath his seat and sat it on his lap. "You don't ever have to worry about that shit happening."

"Promise me you won't let no one take you away from me, my nigga," Vermani looked over at him and said.

"I promise," Delani said. But he still couldn't shake the unsettling feeling that his brother had just planted in his brain.

He was going hard out there in them streets and Delani hadn't even reached his full potential in the game yet. To let his twin down was the last thing he wanted, so Delani knew that he had to tighten up his game. Shit was real in the field.

Chapter 19

One afternoon, while out grocery shopping with his aunt LaVetra, on his dime, Marlon was contemplating how he was going to make his next move.

Just an hour ago, he learned that PJ was locked up on a bullshit possession of weapon and DUI charge. His source informed him that PJ was stopped and pulled over in his Benz truck, after he was caught swerving in traffic.

They found an open container and pistol in the car, and PJ was a convicted felon already. That was last night out in Tallahassee, and just this morning, the judge denied PJ bond, so now he had to sit in jail.

Since the trap house robberies and Rallo getting killed in the process, PJ had really been on some reckless shit. He and Marlon hadn't been talking all that much lately. Rallo's murder put them at odds. He felt Marlon was siding with Lyonell, and PJ wanted some smoke about that.

After continuously avoiding his calls and pretty much giving Marlon his ass to kiss, PJ stayed out of sight and was doing his own thing.

He needed some time to get himself together and get back in the game.

At least that's what Marlon thought, until Lyonell called and told him that PJ tried to take his head off one night after leaving Club Top Flight. This was two nights after Chuck and his crew were murdered. PJ caught Lyonell just as he was leaving the club with two of his loyal goons at his side.

From the passenger window of a dark sedan PJ protruded with a Mac-11 submachine gun and sprayed that bitch, like a can of Raid. He sent everybody scattering, like roaches, hitting one of Lyonell's men and killing him on the spot.

Since then, Marlon had been desperately trying to reach his right hand man, but to no avail. Lyonell was crossed, and he wanted blood for the attempt on his life. But out of respect for Marlon, he didn't go after those whom PJ loved to draw him out. Because those same people Marlon loved, as well, and going against him would not turn out how he might want it to.

PJ had become a serious problem of late.

He had become a renegade.

Now here he was having been caught slipping on a bullshit traffic stop. It was a wonder that PJ had even stopped the car in the first place.

Marlon surmised that Lyonell would find a way to touch PJ, while he was on lock, which was why Marlon had called his chief enforcer to try and prevent him from making that move.

But Lyonell wasn't picking up his phone, so Marlon thought it best to go find him personally.

"What's ailing you so, boy?" said LaVetra, snapping Marlon out of his busy thoughts. "I'm talkin' to you and you ain't even payin' attention to me. You a'ight, boy?"

Marlon had been pushing the grocery cart on autopilot, as he thought about his situation.

"Just got a lot on my mind, auntie. PJ got locked up last night and I gotta figure out a way to get him out of there." Prior to retrieving his aunt to take her grocery shopping, Marlon contacted his lawyer to go see what he could do about PJ and his situation.

Marching right alongside of the cart and gesturing toward the left of the produce section, LaVetra said, "What he got locked up for?"

"A DUI," Marlon left out the gun part.

"He should be okay, if it's just a DUI, unless somebody got hurt, too?"

"Nobody got hurt."

"Then don't worry yourself sick about it, boy." LaVetra stopped in front of a freezer of pork chops and chicken breasts, scanning her choices. "Besides, PJ need a little sit down to get his head back on straight," she said. She exchanged a look with him.

"What make you say that, auntie?" he asked.

"Just know that I know he's been not the same lately. PJ came and sat with me the other day, and he had a lot on his heart about y'all two. Don't ask me what, just know that boy loves you like a brotha. So do whatever you gotta do to look after your brotha. Because, at the end of the day, y'all all you got. Okay?"

He nodded. "Okay."

"Now," stopping before a rack of lamb chops, LaVetra grabbed a pack and said, "How is Anya? And why haven't you fulfilled her dreams yet, Marlon?"

"Her dreams? What're you talkin' about, auntie? I give her everything a woman could ever hope for."

"Except for her own family."

Marlon paused.

"Yeah. That woman wants to be a motha, boy. It's about time you start thinkin' about settling down and enjoying what life you got left. But I don't wanna talk about it, it's not up for discussion. Just do your part and be happy at the same time," said LaVetra.

The crazy thing was, Marlon and Anya had been talking about raising a family of their own. His only problem was the game, and he was where he needed to be, having finally accomplished his mission.

Anya was becoming consistent about her feelings of becoming a mother and raising her own family. She had shown him countless times just how dedicated she was. Anya loved children, which was why she decided to become a school teacher. And Marlon desired nothing more than her being the mother of his children one day. But she wanted him to leave the streets alone before she could bring his child into this cold world. She wanted a devoted father and loyal husband, and not the gangster that he was today. Anya didn't want to raise her child, while he clung to the streets. Her own father had done that and look where it got him, an early grave and a daughter who desperately needed him.

Anya didn't want that for her child, and Marlon was seriously contemplating her wants and wishes for him to leave the game alone.

But all those thoughts were put aside when Monica suddenly appeared before him. In her hand, she carried a shopping basket filled with purchases. She was dressed casually in her usual real estate agent attire. Monica stepped around him and hugged LaVetra, glancing over at him with an earnest look in her eye.

It was then that Marlon decided to finally confront Monica, after so long of dodging one another. They had some long overdue unfinished business to tend to.

"Can I talk to you for a minute?" he asked. Marlon didn't wait for her to respond, he just stepped away from her and his aunt for some personal space.

With a deep sigh, Monica spoke her piece to LaVetra and approached Marlon. He had moved down the aisle and was standing in front of the frozen pizzas section.

"What is it, Marlon?"

"I think it's about that time she knew the truth," Marlon replied.

"Who?" she said.

"Who else, Monica? My daughter," he said. "I can't take this shit no more. I want a relationship with Heaven. I deserve to have a life with my daughter."

"Now you wanna play daddy? You shoulda thought about that thirteen years ago, Marlon."

"Thirteen years ago, you threatened to take her away and never come back if I so much as looked your way."

"That's the decision you chose," said Monica. "The life you lead is too dangerous and I would never subject Heaven to get hurt from it. You chose the streets over your own child. And from what I see, you're still in the streets, Marlon, more so than you'll ever be, and that's why Heaven won't be sharing a life with you."

"She deserves to know that I'm her father, Monica."

"She deserves a father who truly cares."

"Then I'll tell her myself," Marlon shrugged.

She glared up at him. "You so much as go near Heaven and I'll murder your ass myself. I've worked too damn hard keepin' my daughter safe and I'll be damned if I allow you to jeopardize that."

"I'll never hurt Heaven," he professed.

"But the streets will, Marlon. Just as soon as the streets find out that she's your daughter, that alone places her in grave danger," she sneered.

"They know better than to hurt my child."

"Just like they knew better than to kill your brotha, too, huh? How that worked out for ya?" Monica sat her shopping basket down on the floor between them. "I'll take my chances raising my daughter alone."

Before Marlon could stop her, Monica turned away from him and hurried away. When he moved to go after her, he was stopped by a hand taking ahold of his arm. When he looked behind him, there stood his Aunt LaVetra, gazing up at him intently.

"This isn't the time or place for that," she said.

"But," he protested

"Not buts. That woman is right about her child. Either you gonna man up or stay doing what you been doing. But that child doesn't need to be hurt behind this. I love you like my own son, but you have to live and learn, boy. The world doesn't revolve around you just because you got money and power. You better get it together before it's too late to repair the damage you're causing."

Marlon knew she was right, like always. And if his mama was standing in front of him right now, she would have said the same exact thing.

He needed to really get his own shit straight.

For the sake of his daughter.

His family.

His future.

Chapter 20

Speaking of Heaven, she was in the company of Porchia and Veronica at the Rec Center that afternoon. Across the street, Sonny Boy and Shamar were attending football practice for their upcoming Friday game. Sonny Boy was Porchia's new boyfriend, the second string wide receiver, one whom Shamar himself didn't think too kindly of.

The girls had decided to step over across the street at the Rec Center to see what was going on. But really it was Heaven's suggestion after spotting Antwan's green Chevy Impala pulling up on the scene.

Heaven knew it was dangerous dealing with Antwan. She knew her brothers would fuck him up, if they found out they were seeing each other behind their backs, especially Vermani, whom she knew had already warned him once about her. Her brothers had confronted Antwan that night a while ago in the restroom of the Waffle House restaurant. But there was something about Antwan that made him irresistible to her. Maybe it was the fact that, despite her brothers threatening him, he still found a way to pursue her. From sneaking her special gifts of jewelry and money to late night phone calls. Antwan did what he felt would make her happy, despite their situation.

He was a young bold muthafucker, and arrogant, too.

And Heaven wanted nothing more than to bask in the glow of puppy love that Antwan had planted in her heart. He was one of the young bosses in their small town and he wanted to make her his girl.

Outside the Rec Center, the spot was jumping off with youth activities. They were hanging out in the parking lot, some were coupled together, hugging and sneaking feels upon one another, the typical actions of teenagers. Then Veronica led the way inside the building's entrance, where they were instantly hit with a blast of sweat, musk, and cheap perfume. A four on four game was going on the basketball court. Other guys stood courtside, waiting their turn to play ball. Some were older, high school drop-outs, as well, who had nothing better to do than hang out with the younger crowd.

The trio entered the main area of the indoor rec center.

Heaven looked around for Antwan and spotted him amongst the group standing at their left. But what Heaven saw at that moment didn't sit well with her.

"Dog ass nigga," said Veronica

Heaven watched as Antwan, flanked by two of his homeboys, stood leaning against the wall near the restroom area. Shayla Moore, from Hill Side, was all up in his grill and fondling his gold Cuban Link chain. Antwan just stood there, smirking at her, like he found Shayla's advances quite amusing to him.

"All you gotta do is say the word, gurl," Porchia said, removing her earrings in preparation for battle. "Either his ass or her stank ass, I'm ready."

Veronica said, "Give his ass a beat down!"

"No." Both of them said in unison.

"I got this," Heaven said, and began walking toward the group with her girls following. When Antwan looked up and saw her coming, he pushed himself away from the wall, and then away from Shayla.

"What's up, Heaven?" he asked.

Heaven looked from Shayla's salty expression back to Antwan. "What's up with you, nigga?"

He shrugged in his hundred-dollar CPG t-shirt. "Just chillin' and gettin' to the bag," said Antwan.

"Looks like you was gettin' to more than the bag, Antwan," she checked him firmly.

"What? Shayla? That ain't bout nothin'," he said and reached for her hand. "The bitch just thirsty like the rest of 'em. You the only girl that I'm focused on."

"That's straight up bullshit, gurl, and you know it," replied Porchia, feeling vexed.

Heaven glanced at her friend and said, "What I just saw ain't a good look, Antwan."

"I'm scheming on the bitch, baby," Antwan said in a whisper, as he brought himself inches from her face. "Her big brotha, Pound, is a person of interest, and to get to him, I must go through Shayla. It's all game, Heaven. Nothin' more than that," he told her.

"You promise?" Heaven held his gaze.

Antwan leaned in and kissed her on the forehead. "I promise it's nothin' else but that."

"Okay, Antwan. I trust you. Do what you gotta do." Heaven stepped back from him and shot a hard look in Shayla's direction. Shayla tooted her nose up at her and Veronica caught it. Then Veronica moved in to smack the shit out of her.

"No. No. Chill out, baby girl." Antwan's homeboy Junior intervened and snatched her back, just as she swung in Shayla's direction, barely missing her face by mere inches. "It's not going down like that." he said.

Shayla said, "The fuck is her fuckin' problem? If you woulda hit me, bitch, we woulda tore this bitch-"

Porchia didn't even give her the opportunity to finish her statement before punching her in her mouth.

"Oh shit," Antwan muttered.

At once, Heaven and Veronica snapped into action. Heaven went after Shayla's home-girl and hit her with a mean overhand. Her name was Mona and she was the pretty girl type, not a fighter. So she tried to get away from Heaven, like the coward she was.

"Junior, Lil John." Antwan turned a gaze to his two homies. "Stop them from stompin' her into the floor. I got Heaven," he yelled, and they nodded.

Both Veronica and Porchia were double-teaming Shayla, and she could not stand under the pressure she was getting. She fought back, but it only made her attackers go harder. She had forced herself into a corner, where she couldn't run, like her home-girl had, and Shayla went for what she knew.

Antwan pulled Heaven away from Mona and dragged her all the way towards the exit door.

By this time, some of the others occupying the gym had their cellphones out and were recording the incident. Nowadays, you couldn't do anything without being the next viral sensation. Technology had fucked up the whole game.

Outside, Antwan tossed his arm over Heaven's shoulders and escorted her over to his car.

"I just told you what the fuck I'm tryna do," Antwan replied angrily. "Now this bullshit done fucked up my whole game plan."

"It's not my fault. I fell back, Antwan."

"I know." He stroked Heaven's face and helped her inside his car. Antwan glanced behind him at his two homies exiting the Rec Center with Veronica and Porchia. Porchia was bleeding from her nose and she looked deranged. "Take them with y'all."

"I'ma take her home."

"I'm not going nowhere without Shamar," Heaven said.

"Where's he at?"

Heaven pointed across the street at the football field. "He's over there at football practice."

Antwan looked out towards the field.

"Plus, my mama will be here to pick us up anyway," Heaven told him. "I'm good," she said.

"You sure? Because now I gotta go deal wit' this nigga, Pound, before he find out what happen. I can't miss out on this opportunity." Antwan had money and murder on his mind, and what just went down inside the Rec Center would, no doubt, put Pound on some dumb shit.

"Go do what you gotta do, Antwan."

"You're gonna be a'ight?"

She nodded.

"I love you."

Heaven paused and looked up at him. "I love you, too. I'm sorry I messed up your plans.

"It's not your fault, remember?" he grinned.

"Right." she grinned. "My friends are crazy."

"But I admire your girls' loyalty, though. I like that," Antwan said.

Right then, Monica's car pulled up on the scene across the street and parked outside the gate circling the football field.

"Looks like it's that time," he said.

Heaven got out of the car, and together, her and her girls made their way back over across the street.

"That bitch busted my damn nose," Porchia said. She had been given a t-shirt by Junior and was now holding it up against her face.

Veronica said, "That's my bad, Hev. I don't like that grimy bitch. I didn't mean to mess up what you and Antwan had going on." She brushed a hand against Heaven's as they walked next to one another.

"It's all good, y'all," was all Heaven said.

Across the street, Monica had gotten out of her car and was watching as they approached. Heaven looked at her mama and saw that she had a worried look on her face.

Behind them, Antwan and his crew screeched into the street in their two cars and roared away from the scene.

"What happen?" Monica asked the moment the trio made their way over to her.

It was Veronica who owned up to the incident, then Heaven and Porchia added their two cents on the matter.

Monica looked between her daughter and Veronica and nodded, then she stepped toward Porchia and reached for the bloody t-shirt in her hand. She examined her face and told Porchia that she was still flawless and beautiful.

"We need to talk, Heaven," Monica said to her daughter, and Heaven nodded. "In the car. Now."

"We'll be over there." Porchia gestured towards the football field, where others were occupying the bleachers.

Heaven said, "Okay."

The two girls left and both Heaven and her mama got inside the car.

Inside the car, Monica just sat there for a long moment, contemplating her thoughts. When Heaven turned a gaze at her mama, she saw that worried expression again.

"What's wrong, mama?" she asked.

"I've been misleading you all along, and I knew I shouldn't have done that. But just know that I only did it to protect you, baby. I love you more than anythang in this world, and lying to you is the worst thang I've ever done."

"Lying to me about what?"

"Your daddy." A lone tear escaped Monica's left eye, where Heaven couldn't see it fall from her chin onto her lap. "Your daddy isn't dead, Heaven. He didn't die in no car wreck." Monica hated herself for ever coming to this point.

Now Heaven was looking at her with a curious expression. "Then who is my daddy, mama?"

Monica swallowed nervously. "Marlon," she replied. "Marlon Jones is your father, baby."

After a brief moment, Heaven turned to look at her mama and said, "I knew that already, mama. I was just waitin' to see how long you was gonna wait to tell me."

The stunned look on Monica's face was priceless.

"You knew already? How? Has he spoken to you? How do you know this, Hev?" There was anger in her voice now, and it was evident that Monica was feeling played.

"One thang you always taught me to be was observant, mama. I only knew it for about two years now."

"Two years?"

Heaven nodded her head.

"And you didn't say nothin'?"

"MoMo slipped up and told me during one of her high spells," said Heaven. "That's when I began lookin' at him closely, mama. I mean, I look just like him. We share the same nose, eyes, chin and all. I didn't say nothin' because I knew you had your reasons for not tellin' me. I understand now. My daddy is a gangsta and a drug dealer, and you didn't want me to be a part of that life."

"I'm sorry, Hev. Really. I was only protectin' you from possibly gettin' hurt behind what he had going on."

"My pain has come and gone now, mama."

"So what do you wanna do?"

Heaven let out a deep sigh. "I wanna go finally meet my daddy and share my life with him," she said.

Monica feared she would say that.

"And while I do that, you need to go and make amends with Dejah. She was your friend and you slept with her man. Go do what's right, mama. I got me." Then Heaven kissed her cheek and got out of the car. Her tears threatened to burst, but she held them in.

Chapter 21

Two days later.

Dejah and her girl Sassy was in the house chillin' with Shamar and Jamir, while they battled one another on the PlayStation 5 game. It was one of those rainy days of mid-September, where everything seemed so boring and dull. But not for this group, for they found themselves making the best out of their situation.

While Dejah sat between Sassy's legs, on the floor, getting her dreads re-twisted, they conversed over the latest news about PJ's situation.

That very moment, the streets of Quincy were mourning another fallen soldier. Late yesterday evening, PJ was stabbed to death in his jail cell by two inmates. Word on the streets was that PJ's death was a hit, authorized by another well-known goon by the name of Shawdy. Shawdy was from the St. Hebron area, who too had a stronghold in the streets as well. Come to find out, it was Shawdy's niece who had been hit in the leg by one of the bullets PJ sent at Lyonell outside the club that night.

"Ain't Shawdy about to come home soon?" said Sassy. "Didn't he get like ten years or somethin' for runnin' that girl over with his truck?" she asked.

"He comes home in a few months."

"Now all this shit is going on," Sassy replied.

Dejah said, "It wouldn't surprise me if Marlon have him killed the second he walk outta them prison gates. PJ was like a brotha to him, and you know he won't let that slide."

The day before yesterday, her and Monica had had a heart to heart about her dealing with Marlon, after the bullshit that he took her through.

Dejah pretty much told the woman to go fuck herself and to never look her way again, or there would be pressure.

It was out of her love for Heaven that she didn't spank Monica's ass, right then and there. Lord knows she wanted to punish her badly for pulling a move like that.

Her betrayal hurt Dejah.

"Real talk, though, sis. I don't think Marlon's gonna respond to that mess," said Sassy.

"Why do you say that?"

Sassy thumped her in the back of the head. "You know why I say that," she said.

"Heaven?"

"Yep."

At the mention of Heaven's name, Shamar glanced back over his shoulder at them.

Dejah met his gaze and tapped a finger over her heart to signal that she loved him.

"Despite his foolishness, I don't think he'll jeopardize his relationship with that little girl. If there's anybody who'll get his shit together, it'll be Heaven. Watch and see. I'll bet lil mama gets his mind right," Sassy added, as she finished twisting up the last dread. Then she pushed Dejah away from her and stood up to stretch her thick legs. She then hurried down the hall for the bathroom.

Right then, there came a knock at the front door, and Dejah went over to answer it.

Shamar paused the game and looked up towards the front door as Dejah approached it. He stood up and moved towards the door, along with her. Lately, Shamar's cautiousness had been on alert, ever since Heaven decided to commit to Marlon.

He understood the dangers of that commitment, and was ready to respond, if ever Heaven found herself in a situation. Her safety was what mattered to him.

When Dejah made her way to the door, she was shocked to find Anya standing on the doorstep. She was soaked to the bone and looked very sad.

"I need your help, Dejah," she said.

After a long glaring moment, Dejah stepped aside to allow the other woman to enter. Then she told Shamar to go get some dry towels for Anya.

She then led her through the house into the bathroom.

It was pouring down outside and Anya was caught in the downpour without an umbrella. Whatever her reason for showing up in the middle of a rainstorm, it had to be of importance. When Sassy exited the bathroom, she looked at Dejah like she'd stepped in a pile of shit.

"What the hell?"

"She needs help, Sassy."

Sassy just shook her head in dismay, then said something about Marlon and his bullshit.

"Change outta those wet clothes so I can put them in the dryer." Dejah handed her the two towels from Shamar and hurried across the hall to her old room, which she had refurnished to her liking.

"Why the hell she came here for some damn help?" replied Sassy, a second later, as she appeared in the bedroom doorway.

"I don't even know," said Dejah.

"And you just accepted the bitch, just like that?" Sassy didn't even know Anya except for her relationship with Marlon, the very same person she had grown to hate over the years, after what he did to Dejah. So anybody he was associated with, she wanted no parts in dealing with them.

She even kicked Nate to the curb, after finding out that he and Marlon were associated.

Dejah gathered up some dry clothes for Anya to put on. She didn't share the same sentiments for Anya, like her friend did. She couldn't fix herself to dislike the woman, just because of her involvement with Marlon. To be real, Dejah felt sorry for her.

Minutes later, Dejah returned to the bathroom door and knocked before entering. And that's where she found Anya, still fully dressed, sitting on the lid of the toilet, sobbing into her hands.

"What's happened, Anya?" This wasn't the first time Dejah ever spoke to Marlon's new woman. There had been quite a few times they'd spoken in passing throughout the months of her release from prison.

Dejah stepped into the room and shut the door behind her, tossing the dry clothes on top of the closed hamper in the corner.

"What did he do?" Dejah asked.

"They made me do it, Dejah. I didn't wanna do it, but they made me," cried Anya miserably. "They said they'd kill me and my baby, if I didn't do it."

"Do what?" Dejah replied as she stared down at the other woman. "What did you do, Anya?"

"I killed him," Anya sobbed harder. "I killed Marlon."

At hearing those words, Dejah felt her heart squeeze with sudden dread.

"You killed Marlon?" she questioned. Dejah's disbelief was written all over her face, as she watched the woman before her bawl her poor heart out.

After trying to get through to Anya, to no avail, Dejah left the bathroom for the living room, where she left her cell phone. Sassy said something to her, but Dejah's thoughts were stuck in a dark place at that point. She retrieved her phone and searched her contacts for Marlon's number, which she had attained for some curious reason. She figured there might come a time where she needed to reach him, and so she installed his number.

That time had come, and now Dejah was wrestling with the thought of going through with actually calling the man's phone, who had been the cause of her heartache.

"Fuck it." Dejah called the phone and waited for Marlon to answer, still not believing what Anya claimed she'd done.

After about the sixth ring, the phone was answered, but it wasn't Marlon at all on the other end of the line.

"Who is this?" she demanded.

"This is Homicide Detective Patrick Renkoski, may I ask who is speaking?" said the male voice.

Dejah disconnected the call and dropped her head. Her heart was pounding hard in her chest now.

"What's going on, sis?" Sassy inquired from the sofa.

"He's dead," murmured Dejah.

"Who's dead?" Shamar interjected. He had paused the game again, and Jamir groaned in protest.

Without a reply, Dejah marched back down the hall and into the bathroom, where Anya still sat in her grief. Dejah slapped the hell out of her and demanded that she tell her what she had done.

"You need to start talkin'," she sneered.

Sassy appeared in the bathroom doorway.

"They made me do it," Anya cried.

"Say that shit one more damn time, and I'ma beat your ass to death in here," said Dejah. Her heart was pounding hard in her chest. Her blood pressure was rising quickly.

And so Anya told them everything.

She had just made it home after a hard day teaching at the local high school. A FedEx delivery man rang her doorbell, and forced himself inside the house, the second she opened the door.

Then two more entered next, and demanded that she call Marlon and make him come to the house.

"They even threatened to kill my Nana Rosa, and me and my child," Anya touched her stomach as tears continued to spill from her eyes. "I couldn't let them harm my baby."

"So you just gave Marlon up, just like that?" Dejah clenched her fists, fighting the urge to strike her.

That's when Anya added that they had beaten Marlon within an inch of his life before they made her shoot him in the head. When Sassy heard this, she watched as her friend cringe with the mental image of Anya killing Marlon.

"And they just let you go after that?"

Anya nodded sadly.

"I wonder why," Sassy replied.

"Because one of them was my cousin," said Anya in a tone just above a whisper.

"Your cousin?" Dejah replied.

"Donte and his crew," Anya told them.

"Donte Brown? From Lake Skillet?" Dejah shared a knowing glance with Sassy, and knew without a shadow of doubt what this might mean. Donte Brown was the man in her life before Marlon, the very same man she once loved dearly, but then cast him away after she got her taste of the dope boy lifestyle.

Dejah excused herself from the bathroom and went into her own bedroom, where she shut the door behind her. She couldn't believe what had just been revealed to her. Just a couple weeks ago, she had bumped into Donte out in Tallahassee, at the mall. It was then that Dejah realized that he wasn't that sweet, smart kid she remembered. He was all man now, and with a flavor of gangster.

Sassy and Stacy were with her that day, and it was evident that Donte was gettin' to the money. He had "hustler" written all over him.

"Dej," said Sassy, moments later, after letting herself inside the room. "I bet you're wondering why Donte let her kill him instead of doing it himself, huh?"

Dejah looked up at her.

Sassy said, "To get back at her for lettin' his mama die on her watch, nine years ago. She just told me."

"What a strange fuckin' coincidence that Anya is the cousin of the man I once loved and the wife of the second man I once loved and became my enemy." Dejah could only shake her head sadly, as she dwelled on the matter.

"So what're you gonna do about it?"

"What can I do?"

The look Sassy gave her was filled with earnest.

Dejah said, "I gotta see Donte."

"And," Sassy said. "You need to be there for Anya, too. She obviously trusts you with her truth. She needs you. Work it out the best way you can. Okay?"

"And this coming from the bitch who doesn't even like Anya," replied Dejah.

"It's not that I don't like her," said Sassy. "I feel sorry for her. And my loyalty is to you, honey bun."

Chapter 22

When the rainstorm subsided, four days later, Delani finally left the trap house and made his way to his home, on the other side of the hood. When he pulled his car up outside, on that Friday afternoon, he noticed his parents' cars parked in the driveway. Delani took one last pull from the blunt he was burning and stubbed it out in the ashtray.

The moment he opened the door and got out, a black on black Dodge Charger pulled up to a halt behind his car. He turned towards the car and instinctively reached for the pistol tucked at his waistline.

"Well, look who it is," smirked Detective Angie Galloway, as she exited the car.

Delani just gave her a straight face look.

"Just the person I need to see," she said. Det. Galloway, who was his mama's first cousin and archenemy, eyed Delani, like a wolf to its prey.

"What's up?" Delani gave her his look of contempt.

"Nice car," she stepped around the shiny BMW, while running her claws along its side as she came to a rest in front of him.

Delani sneered at her.

"Heard you've been quite the young hustla lately. Word in the hood is Dee-Money 'got' em packs, he got them thangz fat," she said. "And that's why I'm here, Delani. I want a piece of the pie. You pay me and I'll keep my people off your trail."

"I ain't payin' you shit. Get the fuck outta my face wit' that bullshit," he said and turned away from her.

"Or how about I arrest you now? I'm pretty sure you're carrying a concealed weapon on your person right now, and drugs in this nice car of yours." She leaned against the hood of his car and folded her arms. "Then arrest your brotha and parents for conspiracy and manufacturing a drug house. I know you don't want that, huh?"

Immediately, Delani came to a halt, then he glared over his shoulder at her.

"All you gotta do is pay your dues. Dee-Money," said the detective, with a serious look on her face.

"How about I blow your fuckin' brains out right now, and pay your grave a visit afterwards and piss on it?" Delani had turned fully around and made his way over to where she was still leaning against his car.

Behind him, the front door opened and there stood Kiara in the doorway, looking out at them.

Detective Galloway peered around him at her cousin and waved sweetly at Kiara. In response, Kiara shot her a look that was so cold it could freeze Jamaica.

"Today is Friday. You got twenty-four hours to pay me ten thousand, or else I'ma make you suffer, ya hear?" Detective Galloway slapped him on the shoulder and made her way back to her car.

Delani then drew his pistol, and she stopped, sensing what he had on his mind to do.

"Delani," Kiara called out after him. "Come in the house, baby. Come to mama, baby," she said.

"Yeah, Delani, go to your coward mama," chuckled the detective, without looking back at him. Then she got into her car and drove away, honking the horn in the process.

Right then, a school bus turned onto the street and stopped at the corner, next to his mama's house. Suddenly, young elementary school kids descended the bus and Delani tucked his pistol back under his shirt, at his waist.

Three of the children hurried down the sidewalk in Delani's direction. Two of them begged him for money to go to the candy lady's house. Delani reached in his pocket and pulled out a huge wad of money. He peeled off three twenty-dollar bills and handed them each one. One of the little girls, whose name was Royaltee, hugged him and told him that she would buy him something from the candy lady. Then the trio ran for the candy lady's house in a race to get there first.

With a grin on his face, Delani turned away from the memory of being that same little kid, once upon a time.

"No guns in my house, Delani," said his mama.

"Huh?" Delani paused mid-step on the front porch.

She said, "You heard me."

Without argument, Delani returned to his car and put the pistol away.

A minute later, he was standing in the kitchen, where he found his mama standing over the stove. She was in the process of cooking one of his favorites, chicken casserole and buttermilk biscuits.

"I see you've found your way back home, after being gone for days, without hearin' from you," said Kiara.

"That's why I'm here, to check up on y'all." A week or so ago, Delani and his father had gotten into a big fight about his street dealings. Before they could get into a physical altercation, his daddy decided he wasn't welcome in his house anymore.

"I miss you, baby," she kissed his cheek.

"I miss you, too, mama."

"What are we gonna do, Dee? You must make thangz right wit' your daddy," said his mama.

At the mention of his father, Delani reached inside the jacket pocket he was wearing and pulled out another thick roll of bills. He then handed it to his mama. He knew she would put it up for safe keeping. She understood him more than Harold, and would always be there for her sons, no matter what, which was really why Delani was so adamant about staying away from home. He didn't want to hurt her by killing her husband, if he ever tried him again like he did last time.

MoMo's death, and the situations that came after it, were what changed Delani so dramatically. It was like he'd lost all sense of control of self, once he put that pistol in his hand and shot crackhead Larry. That had awakened that inner demon in him, and now Delani was lost on the old him. He did everything now for the love of power and money.

Delani's legend was growing by the day.

"I like it just the way it is already, mama. All I care about is takin' care of you and Vee. As long as I'm breathin', y'all will never have to worry about a thang," he vowed.

"I know," Kiara whispered.

"Where is he anyway?" Delani came to stand beside her.

"Who? Harold? Oh. He's outback wit' Ray Ray, fixin' on that old boat of his. They're takin' it out in the morning to go fishin' over at Lake Jackson."

"And Vee?"

"In love," she said with a smirk.

Delani was shocked by this. "In love? Wit' who? Where Vee at?" He made his way towards the kitchen door.

"Now don't go messing up his focus wit' that street mentality perception about women. I know you, Dee. I'm pretty sure by now you've had your fair share of women, wit' your little street status now."

"And what if I haven't?" He replied.

Kiara turned to a curious gaze on her son as he stood there in the kitchen doorway.

"Are you still a virgin, Dee?"

"Just know that a woman is the last thang on my mind, mama," he said. Delani then left the kitchen for his twin brother's bedroom. As far as women went, he was interested in them, but not to the point that he would subject himself to any commitment. He knew how dangerous bitches were out there in them trenches. Delani had witnessed with his own eyes how deadly it could be dealing with a bitch while out there in the streets thugging and getting to the bag.

They couldn't be trusted.

They were worse than most niggas.

Bitches ain't shit.

The only females, other than his mama and Heaven, that he actually trusted were Toby and Dejah. He'd been knowing Monica and LaShonda all his life, and still, he only trusted them to a certain extent.

Vermani was stretched out across his bed on his back, staring at the ceiling, as he talked on his cell phone. Upon his entry, Delani caught his brother in all smiles and looking all dreamily and shit. He then walked right up to his brother and snatched the phone away from his hand.

"Who this?" Delani said into the phone.

"Who is this?" replied a feminine voice from the other end of the phone.

Vermani sat up in bed and regarded his brother with a look of cautiousness in his soft brown eyes.

"This Delani. Vee's twin brotha," he said.

"Oh, hey Delani. This Chasmine from school. Dezeree and Ranaja's home-girl. You know who I am," she said.

"The teacher's daughter, Chasmine?"

"The one and only. Why? You know something I don't know, Delani?"

Delani was staring at his twin and he could tell, without having to ask, that Vermani was smitten with Chasmine. He also knew how tender his brother's heart was when it came to his feelings and how he showed them.

"Okay, Chasmine. I hear you. But I need you to hear me too," said Delani. "Respect my brotha and be about your bizness. Because if you hurt him, I swear on everything I love, I'ma hurt you a hundred times worse. We good?"

A brief second passed before Chasmine answered him.

"We good," she said.

"Your word?" he persisted.

"My word is all I got, Delani. I won't hurt your brotha. Now can you please put him back on the phone?"

Delani said, "Vee'll hit you back later." He disconnected the phone and looked at his brother curiously. "Are you for real about her, brah, or you're just using her to pass time?"

"I'm for real," Vermani replied.

"A'ight," Delani shrugged. Then he slapped his brother's hand in greeting and they embraced one another. Delani sat down on the bed next to his brother and looked over the room. It was clean and tidy, just like it usually was, most of the time. "What's been going on around here?" he asked.

Vermani said, "Not much. Daddy got fired from his job the other day."

"Oh yeah?" Delani found that surprising.

"Yeah. Said he was extortin' all his workers and then he hauled off and punched his boss. I heard him and mama talkin' about his boss bringin' up charges on daddy."

"What he said about the charges?"

A shrug from Vermani. "I think he got a court date coming up soon about that. For now, he's just chillin' and spending all his time out back or in the garage. I think he's back to drinkin' again, too," he said.

Harold's drinking problem had damn near caused a collapse in his marriage, years ago. The twins' mama had given him an ultimatum, stop drinking or get a divorce. Back then, the twins used to hear their parents fighting all the time about his drinking habits. Once, he had laid hands on their mama, and her big brother Ray Ray, the twins' uncle, had to come and put the big man on his ass about that.

That was about six years ago, and Harold hadn't picked up a bottle since. Maybe not to their knowledge, but he had never come home drunk again.

"If he is, mama is gonna leave his ass."

"No she won't." Vermani shook his head. "Mama would never leave daddy, no matter how deep shit gets."

"Well," said Delani. "Just as long as he don't bring any of that bullshit to mama."

Minutes later, while they were kicking it, their mama came to the door and requested that Delani stay home for supper.

He said he would, but also warned her about Harold. She assured him that his uncle Ray Ray would be joining them and Harold would behave himself.

Just before she called everybody in to eat, an hour later, Kiara summoned Delani into the living room.

"What was that about wit' Angie? I can't shake the feelin' that she got something slick up her sleeve. What did she say for you to want to shoot her?" Kiara wanted to know, so she could be aware of what she needed to do about it.

"Don't worry about that bitch, mama," he said.

"Did she threaten you, Delani?"

He kissed her cheek. "Don't worry about it," said Delani. "I'll handle it. I know what to do."

And he did, too. Angie would learn not to ever cross him again. But for now, he would play her game. Then, when he was done with her, he was going to put an end to it all.

Chapter 23

Since Marlon's murder, a whole list of killings transpired throughout the town, making things hot in the area. Apparently, Donte Brown, aka Killa Don, and his crew had waged war against Marlon's whole organization. And from the look of it, Killa Don was leading his crew to a vicious triumph against his opponents of warfare.

Lyonell and only a handful of his soldiers were left, but had gone underground and into hiding. It was a mystery as to where Marlon's chief enforcer had gone.

Dejah found it quite difficult to catch up with Killa Don, so she decided to wait him out. He was going for Marlon's throne, but little did he know, that same throne was already claimed by someone else.

Fortunately, Marlon had trusted Anya more than Dejah gave her credit for. He had trusted her with all his riches and contacts. All the things he had worked so hard to accomplish, he had left it all to Anya, his aunt, and mama. And together, Dejah and Anya saw to it that everything he had going on was revised and reorganized through their new united trust amongst one another.

Basically, Dejah took care of the street side of things, having been acquainted with Marlon's drug connect and contacts. And through it all, she brought her hooliganz aboard and the plan she had in mind would definitely change the game.

If Killa Don had his sights on being king, then he had another thing coming.

Meanwhile, Dejah accompanied Anya to Marlon's funeral, where they both shared the moment of burying the man they both once loved. It was there that Dejah spotted Killa Don, dressed in an all-black tailored suit, flanked by his goons and unmistakably strapped with them tools.

"I see we meet again," said Killa Don, stepping to Dejah as she followed the mourners out of Second Elizabeth Baptist Church into the warm sunshine.

"This isn't the place right now, Donte." She told him.

"Then where is more convenient for you?"

Out of nowhere came Delani and Kahlil, and about eight more, young vicious hooliganz that too, without a doubt, were strapped with them tools. When Killa Don peeped the game and saw it for what it was, he smirked and turned a sharp gaze at Dejah.

"Like I said, Donte." She patted him on his chest right over his heart with her hand. "This isn't the place," said Dejah. Then she stepped around him and allowed her team of wolves to escort her to her car.

Dejah pictured Killa Don in her mind, staring after her in silent fascination, as she distanced herself from him. She knew he knew that she was aware of what he had done. He may have assumed that his presence and the fact that she'd been trying to reach him lately should be reason enough for him to hold her attention.

He thought wrong.

From there, Dejah went back to the hood, where a big block party was gradually becoming a huge event in honor of Marlon's passing. The streets had crowned him king and that's exactly how he was laid to rest.

The blessed life and death of street royalty.

Dejah decided not to attend the burial ceremony, along with the others, even against Marlon's mama's pleading that she come along. Regardless of what Marlon had done to her, Dejah would forever have love for his mama.

Later that evening, Dejah, who was surrounded by her friends and money team, was approached by Marlon's brother, Chad.

His wife, Eboni, fell back to converse with Monica, who was helping serve plates for the people.

"What's up?" Chad said.

"What's up, Chaplain Chad?" Dejah smirked and stood up to hug him. Earlier, in church, she didn't get the opportunity to speak to him, it was too emotional to talk. "You don't even have to say it," she glanced over his shoulder as she hugged him. "I know."

Chad said, "He really did love you, Dej. Real shit. But I know you've heard that more times than you care to even believe. But that's not what I'm here to tell you."

She nodded encouragingly.

"Would you walk wit' me for a minute?" asked Chad. He was a tall, slender built, light skin dude with deep brown eyes. Back in the day, Chad was hell. He was hard to handle, and still was, in a sense. The pain of losing his brother was read in his eyes, and his rage was simmering.

With a head nod, Dejah separated herself from the group and followed Chad across the front lawn, through the crowd of people. Alongside one another, they walked across the street towards the row of vehicles.

"Tell me the truth," said Chad. "Did you do it? Did you kill my brotha?'

Dejah stopped. "Chad," she replied. "If I wanted your brotha dead, I could have done it months ago. No. I did not kill Marlon. I thought about it, though."

"Then it had to be Donte," he replied.

"What makes you believe that?"

"His actions. Going to war wit' my brotha's people. I mean," Chad shrugged, "who else was crazy enough to go against Marlon and his crew?"

Forever Dejah would protect Anya's truth.

"Or maybe it wasn't Donte. He isn't that stupid. But he may have seen the opportunity to take over the streets now, before somebody else stepped up and took it. I don't know. I guess you're gonna just have to keep your ear to the streets," She replied without blinking. "Then again, let the streets deal wit' the streets. What you need to be focused on is being an uncle to your niece, and the child that Anya is carrying of your brotha's."

"Heaven," he said humbly.

"Yes?"

Chad shook his head miserably. "Whoever killed my brotha, I'm gonna find them, Dej." He held her gaze. "I just hope you're tellin' me the truth because I'd hate to have to blow that beautiful face off your shoulders." Chad then turned around and walked away from her as casually as a man unworried.

Dejah whispered. "Only if you know, lil brotha."

Suddenly Delani stepped out from behind a parked SUV with his hand beneath his shirt. In his other hand he was pulling on a blunt of weed he was smoking.

Dejah watched as her young hooligan and Chad walked past one another, sizing the other up. As a sign of fearlessness, Delani blew a stream of weed smoke in his face, as if to dare Chad to test him.

He didn't want no pressure at all.

Just the day before, word on the streets was that Delani had caught Peanut lacking outside of his favorite barber shop and pumped four slugs into him. They bumped into one another coming and going from the barber shop. After Peanut got his usual haircut, he stepped outside the building and got dropped where he stood.

"What're you up to, badazz?" Dejah said to Delani, when he finally made his way to her.

"Checkin' on you."

"I'm good."

"I know," he shrugged.

"One thang I can say about your lil ass, Dee. You always on point," said Dejah. Then she took the blunt away from him and took a pull from it.

"Heaven is going through it right now."

"What's wrong?" Dejah had grown close to her as well, treating her like the little sister she never had. Dejah didn't begrudge the girl because her mama crossed the line, they shared a special bond together. "What's going on wit' my lil boo?" She asked.

"How about you come see for yourself?"

Together they walked back toward Marlon's childhood home, where the repast gathering was taking place. They entered the house and found Heaven occupying Marlon's old bedroom drunk as a skunk. She'd been sneaking beers and cups of liquor into Marlon's bedroom all evening. It was there that she became so drunk she was delirious.

Monica, who had just finished cleaning up the vomit Heaven had polluted the floor with, looked up at them, and shared a look with Dejah.

Also occupying the room was Jamir, Shamar, Veronica and Antwan. They all were there to watch over Heaven as she lay upon the big bed in a fetal position.

Dejah crinkled her nose in disgust at the synch of Heaven's throw-up floating around the room.

"Open up that window, Twan." Dejah knew about his courting Heaven behind her brother's back. She even confronted him about it and told Antwan, in his face, that she would kill him if he so ever harm a hair on her head.

"Try to talk some sense into her before I end up havin' to strangle her hard headed ass," said Monica. In her hands, she held a plastic bag containing the cleaning supplies and the vomit-soiled ruins.

No reply from Dejah. Monica took her leave and Delani shut the door behind her.

"Hev." Dejah walked over to the bed and pulled Heaven up to a sitting position on the bed.

Veronica rushed over to stop her friend from tilting forward or sideways out of the bed.

"Look at you," said Dejah. "I should kick your lil ass right now." She frowned.

Heaven wavered drunkenly with her chin on her chest. "He broke his promise," she mumbled.

"What?"

"Marlon," said Heaven. "He said he would never leave me. He p-p-promised," she slurred softly.

He broke his promise to me too, thought Dejah. But she wasn't going to get into all that.

Heaven slumped against Veronica, and she then laid her back down onto the bed.

"So what's the word on the streets right now?" Antwan replied moments later.

"Everybody's scratchin' their heads," said Dejah. "When I learn somethin' you'll know. Until then, just continue to look out for one another and watch your backs."

"That goes wit'out saying," said Shamar.

She nodded.

After kickin' it with her youngins for a while, Dejah finally took her leave. She had something to go do, and it had to be done alone. She had a meeting wit the devil, and his name was Donte Brown.

One way or the other, he was going to respect her mind, or die in the process.

The throne was for the taking.

There was only one seat.

And it was hers.

Chapter 24

After seeing Dejah off to go handle her business, Delani ordered his latest two regulating recruits, Bush Boy and LJ, to go follow her, but discreetly. She was never to be without her enforcers at her beck, for any reason.

Delani spotted Harold, obviously drunk by the beer in his hand and the way he was walking. Apparently, he had found his way around the block to engage in the festivities to celebrate the passing of Marlon. Harold Taylor was making his way through the crowd of people and headed toward the group of niggas posted up outside of old man Mr. Jake's house.

"This nigga," mumbled Delani.

Also among the group of niggas was Ray Ray and Harold's main man, Omar Pruitt. At least he was around people he knew, or else Delani feared that he would have to intervene and take his drunk ass home, and not even that seemed satisfying.

"I don't like seeing him like that," Vermani appeared at his brother's side silently, like a ghost.

Delani looked at his brother and said, "You really think he could go to jail for what he did?"

Vermani shrugged. "He'd already been there," he answered. Their mama had to bond Harold out of jail for assault on his boss, and still, the boss was pressing the issue. "But I know how to prevent that from happening."

"How?"

The mischievous glint in Vermani's eyes told Delani that whatever he was thinking was definitely along the lines of what he would be down for.

Right then, Jamir appeared before them as Vermani was explaining what he wanted to do, which was go to Harold's boss's house and make him drop the charges.

"I wanna go," said Jamir.

"No," said Vermani.

"Yeah," said Delani, scratching his chin pensively. "We can use him to get inside the house."

"How?" Vermani wasn't convinced of this.

"Pay attention," Delani quickly put a plan together between the three of them. Then, when Shamar showed up, he too was included in the plan of attack.

"Now we need to find out where he lives," suggested Shamar, anxious to do something other than watching Heaven lay around drunkenly and mumbling incoherently.

With his smartphone, Vermani typed in the boss's name, Mathew Donaldson, and then was told by Google search that he lived in the Friendship Community area. Next he put the address in the GPS locator app on his phone and the all piled up into Delani's car.

They were in the Sub-Division (Sub-D) area, which wasn't that far from the Friendship territory. The twins actually had family members that lived in the area.

Kahlil's homie, Jeremy, was from there, but there was no need to include him in what they were up to.

It was almost nightfall outside. Vermani glanced back at Jamir and saw how excited he was to be rolling with them. They always excluded him from being involved in their rebellious acts that seemed too dangerous for someone his age.

Today, Jamir was about to play the wounded kid, who needed help.

The GPS locator led them to Lee Road, which Delani decided to drive past. He wanted to get a good look at the house they were about to invade. It was a brick house with dusty white painting. Two cars were parked out front. But there was someone occupying the front porch.

"You saw that, brah?" Vermani blurted out.

"What?" Shamar asked.

"That girl. She looked like Anastasia,"

Delani, from what his heart was already committed to doing, he didn't care if it was the President of the U.S.A muthafucker had to get dealt with accordingly.

"Anastasia from Mrs. Anderson's class?"

Vermani nodded.

"Fuck her, too," Delani said.

"Change of plan, Jamir. You're staying in the car," Shamar told him.

Jamir bitched and moaned in protest.

The next time Delani spoke up, he said they were about to take it straight to them. Which meant that if it really was Anastasia, then she was about to be used as the tool to get Matthew Donaldson's mind right. No one was spared from their wrath.

Delani parked his car down the street from the house and turned around to look at Jamir.

"Don't make me stay," Jamir whined emotionally.

"You're not. C'mon," said Delani, and got out of the car. The rest of them looked at one another and hurriedly removed themselves from the car.

"What're we doing, Dee?" asked Shamar.

"Just follow my lead," Delani replied, as they made their way along the side of the street towards the brick house. The closer they got to the house, the clearer he could see that it was indeed Anastasia occupying the front porch. She was babbling on her house phone, without a care in the world.

Jamir walked with a purpose alongside Vermani. He had his little bird chest puffed out as he moved. This would be the first time he ever saw that real street gangster side of

Delani. That evening, he was about to learn a valuable lesson, a lesson about true fate.

When the four of them turned onto the path leading to the house, Anastasia glanced up at their approach. Then she bolted to her feet and stared at them in alarm.

Delani snarled, like a venomous creature, when he saw Anastasia turn for the front door. He darted after her and caught her just as she was pushing the front door open. He punched her in the back of her neck, and Anastasia hit the floor, face first.

"What the hell?" bellowed Matthew the instant he saw his daughter hit the floor. He then shot up from where he was sitting on the living room sofa, watching college football on a big sixty-four inch flat screen TV.

That's when Delani drew his pistol, rushed the big bear of a man, and bashed him in the mouth with the weapon. His wife, Gloria, stepped out from the kitchen with another young girl beside her.

Shamar shut the door behind them as he watched Delani pistol whip the father relentlessly. Vermani had taken hold of Anastasia's hair and was dragging her across the floor by her ponytail.

"Get over there and sit down on the couch," Shamar told Gloria, as she watched with panic and fear masking her face, as she held the younger girl close to her. Without being told twice, she went over, took her place on the sofa, and pulled the girl up into her protective arms.

Vermani kicked Anastasia in the mouth to shut up all her screaming.

"Shut the fuck up, bitch," Delani said to Anastasia, as he backed away from her father. He was slumped onto the sofa, bleeding profusely from his face.

Delani then ordered Jamir to go find something to tie them up with. Jamir was so shocked by the act of gangsterism that Shamar had to shove him away to go do as he was told.

With no apparent destination, Jamir dashed toward the hallway to their right. A brief second later, the sound of Jamir's painful cry exploded from down the hall.

Instinctively, Delani, Vermani, and Shamar turned their heads in the direction of the sudden commotion. And that's when a broad shoulder, thick-headed boy, not that much older than them, came barreling out from the hallway.

Seeing the open opportunity to counterattack, Matthew Donaldson lunged for Delani and hit him so hard he was lifted off his feet. He went one way and the pistol went another, and that's where the man's attention was focused.

Vermani snapped into action hastily and jumped on the man's back, wrapping his arms around his neck in a chokehold. Then Shamar went in for the attack on the other older boy, hitting him with all he had to offer.

While they battled it out, Vermani rode the back of the big man, and Jamir was still crying out for his big brothers to come help him.

Shaking away the throbbing pain from the powerful blow he'd taken, Delani climbed up to his feet just as Matthew, despite being choked out, took possession of the pistol. Then Delani watched in tremendous fear as the big man aimed the pistol over his shoulder at his twin brother.

Boom!

A petrified shriek erupted and then the thud of Vermani hitting the floor.

The gun shot blast brought everybody to a halt.

"Get the fuck down on the floor." Matthew swung the pistol in Delani's direction. Shamar then felt the boy behind him wrap him in a bear-hug to restrain him.

Delani stared down at his twin brother, who was not moving and leaking blood everywhere.

"GiGi, call the police," her husband ordered. Then, just because he knew that he could, he swung and bashed Delani across the face with his own gun. Delani hit the floor, and was then kicked in the back of the head.

Jamir was still crying in the hallway.

When the police came, they loaded Shamar and Delani into the back of a cruiser. Vermani was immediately rushed to the ER, clinging to his life, and so was Jamir, whose nose had been broken by the big man's son, MJ. The hooliganz were taken in and processed for a list of violent crimes that would no doubt bring more distress to their young lives.

It was a troubling night for the crew.

Loyalty to a fault did it.

Chapter 25

Dejah had phoned Killa Don in advance and was told if she wanted to see him he would be downtown on the block. He and his crew were up in Doc's Bar, watching the Seminoles battle it out with Clemson, and drinking. Since Marlon's death, this had been the headquarters for Killa Don and his team of goons. He was making it his business to fill the spaces that Marlon and his team had once occupied.

The nigga had some big nuts.

Killa Don was crazy.

When Dejah stepped up into the spot, she was directed to the back room, which was only reserved for Killa Don and whoever he felt was worthy.

Dejah entered through the door of the back room that was guarded by two armed killers positioned nearby. Upon her entry, she was assaulted by a thick cloud of weed smoke. A half dozen half naked bitches pranced about the room, servicing the fellas and looking exotic as hell. To her surprise, Dejah spotted a few of Marlon's guys amongst the others.

"This way," said Fangz, one of Killa Don's shooters, a tall lanky nigga with honeycomb waves.

She took one more lingering glance at Marlon's former goon, Big Duke, and nodded in his direction. If he knew what was good for him, he had better leave.

Killa Don was occupying a table at the back of the room, as one of the exotic women sat perched upon his lap, refilling his glass with purple lean. Two other niggas occupied the table, smoking blunts and drinking, as well. At the sight of Dejah approaching his table, Killa Don slapped the ass of the female, and without having to be told, she got up and left the table.

Dejah sized her up and licked her lips as she walked by, looking all scrumptious and shit.

"Y'all niggaz give me a minute wit' the queen," Killa Don said to the two left at the table.

Both got up, and one of them, Blue Jay, stepped over to pull the chair out for Dejah to sit down.

"Thank you," she took her seat.

Before directing his undivided attention to Dejah sitting across from him, Killa Don ordered one of his people to bring her a bottle of Ace of Spades.

"That's still your drink, right?" he asked her.

"Always," said Dejah.

She looked at Killa Don long and hard. He seemed to quite enjoy the scrutiny. He lifted his glass and tasted his lean, then brought his Cuban cigar to his lips next.

"Did I do well, Dej?" he asked.

"What do you mean?"

"This," he swept his arm around the room. "Marlon and his mark ass. His empire. His pockets. His whole world. I paved the way for you, Queen. If there's anybody that deserves to run this town and make something better of it, it's you. Dejah Cooper. I did this for you. Me and my team. And whatever you choose to do from there, we will honor it and serve you like the queen that you are. We all are in favor of you takin' that throne, so what's it gonna be?" said Killa Don.

At that moment, her bottle appeared in a bucket of ice and was poured for her with genuine pleasure. Dejah looked around the room and saw damn near everybody watching her.

"It's your call," added Killa Don.

"What happened to you, Donte?" Dejah replied, ignoring the urge to taste her drink.

"As you already know, I did go to Georgia Tech and played football for two years. But then I was caught up wit' the wrong muthafuckaz and got shot in the process. Them Georgia niggaz are grimy up there. After I healed up, I said fuck school, I wanted my revenge. And I got my revenge, Dej, all four of them niggaz. From that point on, the streets became my second home, and then my reputation flourished, and now here I am," he said.

"I'm sorry, Donte," she replied.

"It's not your fault," he waved off her comment. Killa Don was not the sentimental type of nigga, at least not now that he was a gangster with street status. "I decided to wait 'til you got home to make my move on Marlon. I wanted you to see all that same pain he had caused you. But let's not get into all that shit, are you ready?"

"Am I ready for what?"

"To take back what's rightfully yours."

Dejah was just about to answer when all of a sudden the door behind her opened and in forced Bush Boy and LJ by three of Killa Don's shooters.

At the presence of her two hooliganz, Dejah bolted up to her feet and demanded to know what was going on.

"Caught these two lil niggaz lurkin' outside the spot, and they was strapped too, my nigga," said Bojangle.

"Is that right?" hissed Killa Don.

Dejah said, "Let them go. They're my youngins. Those two are wit' me, Donte." She turned her gaze on Killa Don and he gave his men the signal. Instantly, Bush Boy and LJ were released and Dejah, still not satisfied with the situation, said, "And give 'em back they guns."

Again, Bojangle turned to Killa Don for direction, and he nodded his head briefly. Bojangle gave the other two shooters the word and Dejah's hooliganz were given back what was taken from them.

Bush Boy and LJ took their places at her side.

"Yeah," said Dejah, "I think it's time to make that call." She turned to Killa Don and said.

Killa Don shot up to his feet and ordered that everybody shut the fuck up. When the music paused and the large screen TV muted, he then moved to stand beside Dejah, taking her hand into his own.

He held everybody's attention.

"The Queen is here," he replied. "From now on, we honor her and protect her for all she is worth. So let the rest of the team know. Whatever she so wishes, you are to command those wishes. No exceptions."

"And as far as my youngins go," said Dejah, "you will respect them equally as you do your own. We are a family now, and family sticks together."

Nods of agreement spread around the room.

"A'ight," Killa Don spoke up again. "There will be some new rules and regulations now. And if anybody is found in violation, the penalty is what?" He looked at Dejah.

"Death," she said.

"Why?"

"Because death rules out all mistakes."

Suddenly, Dejah's phone rang. When she answered, she found LaShonda crying on the other end. Then she got the worst news ever concerning her hooliganz. Dejah rushed for the exit with her two goons in tow. Without hesitation, Killa Don snapped his fingers, and at once, he and his shooters took off after them next.

Twenty minutes later, Dejah was standing in the waiting room of the Quincy Hospital, watching LaShonda pace the floor like a worried lioness. There was also Kiara and a drunk Harold, along with Ray Ray, Tony, Kahlil, Jeremy, and the rest of their team of hooliganz. The facial expressions on the hooliganz were dark with rage and etched with worry.

"What happen?" Dejah asked Kahlil.

"I wasn't there," he answered. Dejah glared at him as Tony stepped forward to explain the situation.

As she listened, Dejah glared over at Harold, as he sat there next to his wife, looking like a lost dog. Kiara couldn't stand the look of him, as he sat slouched in his chair with a dumb look on his face.

The boys had gone to chastise the man whom Harold had assaulted on the job. They had gone to Matthew Donaldson's house in an attempt to convince him to drop the charges, only to be arrested and damn near killed in the process.

Vermani had suffered a gunshot to the chest and was still undergoing surgery. From what LaShonda had added, Vermani wasn't looking too good. And of course, Jamir, who had also suffered a broken nose, was treated already and sent to the Juvenile DOC Center, where he would be transferred, along with Delani and Shamar, to the Leon County Juvenile Detention Center. They all were being charged with home invasion, assault and battery, and possession of a weapon. Delani had owned up to all charges to try and save the others.

"My babies," cried Kiara softly.

"Where's Hev?" Dejah asked next.

Ray Ray said, "At the house, sleepin' off her drunkenness." He looked up at the approach of Killa Don and five of his vicious looking goons. Ray Ray moved to step in front of Kiara to protect her from any possible threat.

"What's the play?" Killa Don asked Dejah. That's when Kahlil, Jeremy, and Youngin stepped forward to flank around Dejah protectively, ready for whatever.

Dejah told her hooliganz that it was all good, that Killa Don and his crew were straight. Bush Boy and LJ added their peace, and Kahlil just shrugged.

"Check this out." Dejah gestured for Killa Don to step over so she could speak with him privately.

"What's up?"

She told him what was up.

"What do you want me to do?" he asked.

"Find Matthew Donaldson and make 'em pay for what he did to my lil niggaz."

Killa Don nodded. "Say no more. Consider it done."

"And Donte?"

"Yeah?"

She kissed him on the lips and gazed up into his eyes. "Don't make me regret this," said Dejah.

"You won't," he promised.

"Go."

And he was gone.

As she watched them swerve around the corner, out of sight, Angie Galloway appeared on the scene, followed by two black cops. When Dejah laid eyes on her, she frowned and returned back to be with the others.

Kiara stood up at the sight of her cousin. "How bad is it?" she asked.

"Bad as it can be, Kiara. A gun was involved and the judge will not let this one slide. Maybe a little time in Juvie, but nothin' too outrageous."

"Is there 'anythang' you can do?" asked Kiara.

"Prayer and patience, cuz. Tomorrow they will appear before the judge to be officially charged. From there, it's up to their behavior to determine how long they will remain there. I could only do so much now that they've gotten caught, if you get my drift," Angie replied.

All Kiara could do was acknowledge her with a miserable nod.

"What about Matthew?" Harold spoke up. He suddenly stood up and didn't waver one bit. "Shouldn't he be charged wit' almost killin' my fuckin' boy?"

"Sit your ass down, Harold. Maybe if you wouldn't have done what you did then we wouldn't be here right now," Angie replied, and Kiara agreed.

Kahlil tapped Dejah on the arm and signaled for her to step aside to speak with her.

"All you gotta do is give me the word and I'll make sure they don't even make it to the tent."

"No," said Dejah. "The last thang we need is for them hooliganz to be on the run from the law. They can handle a little petty time in the tent."

"Jamir? Hell naw," he said.

Dejah said, "It is what it is, Kahlil. Maybe somethin' good will come outta it, who knows. Look at how you overcame your obstacles. Now it's their turn to get a taste of what it feels like to be locked down. It's a motivation in itself, Kahlil. It'll humble them. Until then," she reached up to stroke his face, "It's back to the money."

"What about the other niggaz?"

"Who? Donte and his crew?"

He nodded.

"This is my city now, baby. My hooliganz come first and anythang after that is just secondary. I love you. I trust you. And I'ma need you to be the young boss that you is and help me change the game," said Dejah.

Kahlil nodded and said, "Say no more."

"I shouldn't have to."

Chapter 26

Heaven woke up with a hangover so strong that she could feel her heartbeat pulsating through her migraine headache. It even hurt to blink her eyes too many times.

She sat up in bed and gazed toward the window, where the morning sunshine was shining in.

That's when she felt it. Between her legs, she felt the odd sensation of soreness of her private parts. When she tossed back the comforter that covered her body, Heaven gasped. There was blood on her. It stained the bed sheets. Blood that had apparently come from her private parts.

With a throbbing headache, Heaven tried to think back on what all she could remember from the night before. There were flashes of occurrences, but nothing specific to indicate where her pain transmuted from. The last thing she remembered was Dejah. She had come into the room last night to check on her.

Heaven climbed out of bed and turned to stare at the big red stain on her bed sheets.

She was confused.

Looking down at herself, Heaven saw that she was wearing just her panties and a t-shirt. She felt between her legs with her hand and winced. Suddenly, she felt as though she was about to vomit and rushed across the hallway to the bathroom.

"That's good," said Ms. Connie, moments later, standing in the doorway. "Let it out, honey. You'll feel much better when it's all outta ya' system."

Heaven had tears in her eyes as she hovered over the toilet, puking her guts out.

Ms. Connie stepped away from the doorway and returned a minute later with a glass of water and two Motrins. She handed them both to Heaven and told her to take it for her obvious headache.

"What happen to me?" asked Heaven.

"You had too much to drink last night. Your mama left you some clean clothes to wear. How about you take a good bath and I go see what I can fix up for that belly of yours," said Ms. Connie.

Before she could reiterate her question, the woman had turned away from the door and left again. What her question really meant was what happened to her that made her private parts bleed.

Suddenly, there was a shriek of sheer panic from across the hall, in the bedroom. Then Ms. Connie stormed out of the room back toward the bathroom, where Heaven had pulled herself up on the edge of the tub.

"You on your period, child?" she asked.

"No," said Heaven.

"Are you absolutely sure, Heaven?"

Reluctantly, Heaven shook her head no, and then the woman frowned and took off once again.

Flushing the toilet, Heaven turned the shower water on and stripped down to get into the stall. She felt sticky and bloated for some strange reason. But the hot water cascade down over her was a welcomed feeling. She embraced it and sighed with relief.

Sometime during her bath Ms. Connie had brought in Heaven's clothes and set them aside for her.

Eleven minutes later, Heaven exited the bathroom, refreshed and dressed in clean clothes. When she stepped back over into the bedroom, her father's bed had been stripped of its linen. Only thing remaining was a smaller, dark red stain that had seeped through the bed sheets onto the bare mattress. Heaven felt it in her heart that whatever happened to her wasn't good.

The bang of the front door closing shut was heard. Heaven turned at the sound of her mama's voice and heavy footfalls approaching the room.

Monica entered the bedroom in a rush and hurried right over to her daughter.

"You all right, baby?" she asked.

"Yeah, I guess so," Heaven replied humbly. "Somethin' don't feel right, mama," she added softly.

"What?" Monica reached out to her. "What's wrong?"

Heaven told her about the sensation she felt between her legs and Monica had murder in her eyes.

Taking a brief look at the red stain on the bare mattress, Monica took her daughter by the hand and led her out of the room.

In the living room, Monica sat her daughter down on the sofa and joined her.

Ms. Connie was busying herself in the kitchen.

The TV was on mute, but also showing the latest top story news of a local massacre out in the Friendship area. Sometime during the wee houses of the night, Matthew Donaldson and his whole family were murdered in their family home. It was a sure sign of more hell to come.

"Last night," said Monica, "I left you wit' Veronica and Antwan…"

At the mention of his name, Heaven was struck with the remembrance of his existence.

Whatever her mama was saying at that point was lost on Heaven, as she thought back on her experience with Antwan. A flashback of him on top of her came to mind. She didn't remember the initial experience, but him on top of her was something that couldn't be denied.

Had Antwan raped her while under the influence? Wondered Heaven, as tears welled up in her eyes.

"Heaven?" Monica shook her by the shoulders.

Heaven turned to look at her mama.

"Did you have sex wit' Antwan last night? Huh? Did you?" she demanded.

"Yes," she answered. "I did, mama."

"Was it willingly, or don't you remember?" The look Monica was giving her daughter was a look that meant, if she said the wrong thing, she would be definitely going to prison for killing somebody for violating her baby.

Of course, Heaven read the look in her mama's eyes and understood the dangers of the situation.

"I agreed to it, mama. I wanted it to happen. I was conscious of what was going on. I really was," Heaven said, lying through her teeth.

"You being honest wit' me, Heaven?"

"Mama," Heaven frowned. "Stop it. Please," she said.

From the kitchen doorway, Ms. Connie looked in on them and frowned. She knew Heaven was lying, she could feel it in her heart. Ms. Connie didn't know why the girl was protecting Antwan, but could only hope that it didn't come back and bite her in the ass.

"Okay, Heaven. Okay," said Monica. Then she let the matter go, for now. "But there's somethin' I need to tell you about your brothaz." she added.

Alarmed, Heaven said, "What is it, mama?"

She told her the bad news.

Heaven cried and pulled away from her mama, running back down the hall in search of her phone. She needed to call and check up on her brothers.

Monica followed with her own phone and showed her the full story, which was circulating through social media.

Heaven cried some more. She felt so alone all of a sudden.

Later that day, she was standing outside of LaShonda's house, at the curb, alongside Porchia and Veronica. She had told them both the truth about Antwan and what she planned to do. Her girls were both down with a dirty game, and Antwan had no clue what was coming.

As she waited outside at the curb, across the street from her house, Heaven toyed with the box cutter in her jacket pocket.

When Antwan pulled up in his Land Rover truck, she stepped off the curb and opened the passenger door. Heaven got in and slid onto the seat next to him.

"What's up, baby?"

"You," she smiled sadly at him.

"I see you're lookin' better today," Antwan said, as he leaned over to kiss her cheek.

"Why did you do it, Twan?" Heaven asked with a sad expression on her face.

"Why did I do what?" he replied.

"Take advantage of me while I was intoxicated."

"What?" Antwan looked at her in disbelief. "Why the fuck would I do some stupid shit like that?"

"I thought you loved me, Twan," she expressed.

"I do love you," he declared.

Heaven shook her head and drew the box cutter. Then, before Antwan could understand what was happening, five slashes across his face sent him into a panic. Then the driver door opened and Porchia and Veronica began to slash him up with their own razors.

Antwan was hollering like a madman.

Blood was everywhere.

Somehow Antwan tumbled out of the truck, and both Porchia and Veronica were on his ass like a tic on a dog. They beat, kicked, and slashed him repeatedly.

From the passenger seat, Heaven just sat there watching, with dark pleasure, as her girls did Antwan in. That was when she spotted the gun on the floor just beneath the driver seat.

By this time, more than a dozen witnesses were watching along the neighborhood street. Children and all were witnessing this act of savagery.

Heaven reached for the gun and crawled over the seat to get out from the driver side. She watched in silent malicious intent to do Antwan greater bodily harm, as her two best friends stripped him of his shirt and pants in front of everybody. Antwan had no chance of recovery.

"Don't do it, lil mama," said Amp, one of the older gangsters in the hood. Behind him Porchia and Veronica were doing Antwan dirty in the street.

LaShonda and Tony came out the house and hurried over to where Heaven was.

Heaven, with the .9mm Glock in her hand, stared down at Antwan, who was now rolling around on the ground writhing in pain and agony. The girls had stripped him down to his boxer briefs. Antwan was shivering, like he was cold, and cut to ribbons, as he lay there bleeding in the street.

"Give me the gun, Hev," said Tony.

Heaven moved to stand over Antwan, whom she no longer could recognize due to his damaged face.

"Think about your future, Heaven. And your brothaz. Your mama. You don't wanna disappoint them by throwin' your life away for that boy," LaShonda replied, stepping alongside Heaven and touching her arm tenderly.

"Hev." Monica came bolting from the house across the street, like the mama bear that she was. Seeing her daughter with the gun in her hand brought raw fear to her heart.

At the same time, three hooliganz came running up the street towards the scene.

When Monica made it to her daughter, she hurriedly snatched the gun away from her. Then she turned around towards Antwan and aimed it dead at his head.

"Monica, no," LaShonda lunged forward instinctively.

Boom!

At the sound of the gun exploding, everybody startled and stared at Antwan in horror.

Luckily for Antwan, the bullet only grazed the side of his head instead of going through it. LaShonda had grabbed Monica in the nick of time of her committing murder.

"Lemme go. Lemme go." Monica fought against LaShonda as Tony intervened to wrench the gun from her hand. "That muthafucker raped my daughter. He hurt my baby," she screamed and tried to get at Antwan.

"He did what?" Tony turned to Heaven and looked at her. He saw the truth in her eyes. "Baby girl," he murmured.

JoJo, Blaze, and Quan made it to the scene just in time to hear that Antwan had raped Heaven. Without having to be told what to do, the three hooliganz loaded Antwan into his own truck and peeled out. They were about to take him on that gangster ride. Antwan had a deadly price to pay for his actions.

"C'mon, baby." Monica wrapped her arms around her daughter and led her over to the house.

"Porchia. Veronica. Y'all gimme those razors," LaShonda said to the two girls. "Hand 'em over b'fore the police come."

"Ok," Veronica said. Then her and Porchia followed Heaven and her mama, and went inside the house, without a backward glance.

Chapter 27

The Leon County Juvenile Detention center was nothing like the images Shamar saw on TV of jails and prisons. The thought of being caged in with dangerous grown men and baby rapists and murderers had been a very sobering experience. Come to find out, he was surrounded by children and teenagers. He was content with being suited with those of his generation.

It had been a week now, since the incident at Matthew Donaldson's house. He only had to do twenty-one days in detention, and then he could go home.

The day before, Dejah, Sassy, and Kahlil came to visit him and told him everything that was going on. Sassy brought him a pair of brand new high top Air Maxes. Having them come to visit him made him feel much better.

Jamir and his parents were there, plus Delani and his folks as well. To see his friends made Shamar happy and sad, at the same time. He wanted to be housed with Jamir and Delani, but the administrators were against it. They figured with them together shit was bound to pop off.

Speaking of which, Delani appeared to have already started raising the roof up in the place. It was said that he'd already assaulted four inmates and a staff member. The only reason he was allowed a visit was in hopes that his parents talked some sense into him. Harold was good buddies with one of the high ranks and was permitted a visit with his son.

Vermani was still in the hospital, in the ICU ward, recovering from his near death experience.

That's why Delani was acting a fool, because he was worried about his twin brother. Plus, he wanted to be with Jamir to protect him, and with Shamar to chill and politic with.

After visitation was over the day before, Delani went against all facility rules and hurried across the basketball court (the visiting area consisted of a court sectioned with plastic chairs for visitors) and hugged his brothers. Jamir clung to him and cried, which only made Delani want to break something, out of anger.

Seeing Jamir cry, with his broken nose bandaged and his face all swollen, made Shamar livid. He wanted to hurt somebody.

Delani certainly did, just as soon as they locked him back up in his housing pod. Not long afterwards, a Code Red was announced and a team of enforcers arrived. Delani had to be restrained and put away in solitary confinement.

Having already been housed alone, due to his status, Shamar embraced solitude. He felt it was better to be alone than go out to be with the other inmates. But he was assigned to attend all the educational classes, where he sat at the back of the class. He didn't want to be a part of the group. From one class to the other, throughout the day, he maintained his solace. Until one of the teachers, Mrs. Murphy had taken a little interest in him. It was after singling him out one day to answer a challenging question, and he did so without any difficulty. Mrs. Murphy challenged him again the following day, and he made her believe, once again, that he was way smarter than he looked.

Shamar also had a way with words. Once Mrs. Murphy caught him jotting down his thoughts and feelings on paper, when he was supposed to be doing his school work. When she read what he had written, the lady was greatly surprised.

"Shamar, you have a very unique style of writing," she complimented him afterwards, seeing something special in him that she didn't see in the others.

That was when Shamar was introduced to the love of spoken word and poetry. Then he was provided a dictionary to build his vocabulary and sharpen his mental. By the second week of learning and studying his new craft, Shamar had grown fond of the creative writing skill and utilized it to escape from his own current reality.

Mrs. Murphy had even went against her own rules and regulations and became personally attached to Shamar. She even went to the trouble of taking out personal time to tutor him and got to know him on a deeper level.

His story was so surreal that it affected her, even when she laid in bed at night.

Meanwhile, Jamir was becoming something of a wild animal over in the housing pod with the younger inmates. He'd broken one kid's nose, gave another a concussion, after bashing him in the head with a metal stapler machine, and even attacked a boy for looking at him in the shower.

Things had gotten so bad with Jamir that, once it got around to Delani, he raised so much hell that the only way he could calm down was to see his little brother.

Delani was turning the place upside down.

The Tent had never seen someone as viciously dangerous as Delani, and he was becoming a young legend. He became such a menace to his environment that he was forbidden to be around the other inmates. His violent behavior made him a threat to others.

On his seventeenth day in, Delani had stabbed one of the male staff in the eye with a pencil for disrespecting him. He had just finished talking on the phone with his father and was informed of Vermani's speedy recovery. Delani had cried in happiness over the good news and the male staff saw it as something else.

Denali was charged with assault and it wasn't looking good for him. His first rodeo was about to lead him to a bigger predicament.

The judicial system wanted to make an example out of him, and Delani was about to have his time extended due to his violent, predatory offenses.

Then, suddenly, another hooligan came to the Tent the day before Shamar was to be released. It was Nook, from over by Betsy Funeral Home, with the buck-teeth. He was housed in the same pod with Shamar, two cells down from where Shamar's room was.

"What you doing in here, Nook?" Shamar asked him as the call for chow time came. They all formed a line leading from the door to the back of the main pod area.

Nook observed his surroundings for a brief moment before answering. He was a chubby fifteen year old hell-raiser, whom Delani had recruited to join his money team. He was the son of a pill head mama, and no father to mention.

"Arson," said Nook. "They say I burnt down Mrs. Baby's shed behind her house."

"Did you?"

After a brief second, Nook said, "Hell yeah, I burnt that shit down, Shamar." He chuckled.

"Why?" Shamar asked.

"Shoe Shine base-head ass stole my dope from where I hid it behind the pay phone at Mike's store. I was servin' Peggy-Ann and he stole my shit. I chased him up Key Street all the way to Mrs. Baby's house. He hid in that big old shed behind the house. So I set that muthafucka on fire while he was in it."

"Did he get burnt, too?"

"I don't even know," said Nook. "I hauled ass when Mrs. Baby came out the backdoor wit' her husband's shotgun." He laughed at the memory of her facial expression.

Shamar shook his head amusingly.

The guard called a head count and one by one, from front to back, each inmate said their numbered spot. Then, when it was confirmed, they all left the building for the cafeteria across the way.

Today it was pizza and French fries, and both Shamar and Nook had to sit at the table with two other boys, for the time being.

"What about Hev?" Shamar questioned. He had been keeping tabs on Heaven through Dejah and Monica, and Shamar didn't like what he had heard. He wanted to see what Nook had to say about her.

"Hev ain't the same, bro."

"What do you mean?"

Nook munched on his fries. "She ain't going to school no more," he said. "She done started messin' around wit' LJ now. She smokin' a whole lot of weed and poppin' molly now. Her and Porchia done fell out about that clown Sonny Boy."

"What?" Shamar found that shocking. "What happened between them, Nook?" he asked curiously.

When it was said that Heaven had fucked her best friend's boyfriend, Shamar knew she had crossed the line. Then Nook informed him that LJ had been trying to help Heaven shake back from her new attitude, but to no avail. Heaven was going down a dark path and that scared him.

If Delani knew what was going on, he no doubt would go off the deep end about his little sister.

"I know Heaven," said a kid named Kiontay, who was sharing the table with them.

"Who the fuck asked you, pussy?" Nook grilled the boy.

Kiontay grilled him right back. "I'm just sayin', she ain't all that anyway." Kiontay didn't get the opportunity to finish his statement before Shamar went across his face with is fist.

Nook sprung forward and went after him next.

The guard hit the panic button immediately. By the time re-enforcers came, Kiontay was stretched out on the floor, bleeding and crying out in pain.

The boy didn't even stand a chance.

And Shamar didn't get his chance to go home the following day because of his violent actions.

Such a pity.

He was mad as a muthafucker.

Chapter 28

When Jamir was released, after twenty-one days, he left with a heavy heart. He wanted Delani and Shamar to come home with him. In the car, on his way to the hospital to see Vermani, he cried silently in the backseat.

His nose was still hurting, but the physical pain wasn't as strong as the emotional pain.

At the hospital, Jamir was welcomed home by all his loved ones, including Vermani, Jeremy, Junior, Kahlil, Stacy, and everybody, except for Heaven. When he asked about his sister, all Jamir got was a lot of weird looks.

"Where's Heaven?" He demanded.

On cue, Heaven walked through the door into the room, looking fabulous as ever in her Prada outfit, thousand-dollar sandals and sparkling jewelry.

Jamir ran to her and threw his arms around her. When Heaven looked around the room and didn't see Shamar, she inquired about his whereabouts.

"He had to stay back," said Kahlil.

"For what?" she asked.

Dejah recounted what took place and what the judge ordered for Shamar to do should he violate court order. He violated and now his time was extended.

Both Jamir and Heaven looked at one another, and she just wrapped him in her arms tightly.

In the bed, Vermani lay there in his hospital gown with a sullen look on his face. He was ready to go home. For the last twenty-one days he spent in the hospital, he was glad that he hadn't gone to the Tent. He already knew he would be right along with his brother, if he'd gone.

Having Shamar and Delani left back in the Tent was not a comforting thought.

"Are you coming home now, too?" Jamir asked Vermani.

Vermani told him not today. He had been shot in the chest and the doctor ordered for him to remain in-patient until he was comfortable with him without urgent care.

Jamir just let out an exasperated breath.

If it isn't one thing it's another, and Jamir hadn't planned to come home to hear all this bullshit.

From the hospital, Jamir was taken home, where a homecoming party awaited him. He dressed in the brand new Polo outfit that Heaven had bought him. All his friends and loved ones were there to welcome him back. There was BBQ chicken, ribs, and fish on the grill in the backyard. They were doing it big for him, and doing whatever it took to make him feel better.

In the process, to Jamir's curiosity, he observed Heaven closely and saw that she was acting a little strange. There was something about her that didn't sit right with him. She was always sniffing like her nose was constantly running. She was cussing more now, flirting, and even Jamir noticed that she had darker lips now from smoking so much.

"What's that you keep on eatin', Heaven?" Jamir walked up to her later on that day, alongside the house.

Heaven looked from left to right to see if anyone else was in earshot. "It's nothin', Jay," she answered.

"You eatin' somethin' 'cause I saw you do it three times already. And every time you do it, you be hiding to do it. So what is it?" Jamir demanded to know, and he wasn't accepting no bullshit.

"It's Molly, Jay, now you happy?"

"What is Molly?"

She frowned. "It's somethin' you don't need to worry about and better not lemme catch you doing it."

"You doin' it," he retorted.

"That's because I'm grown, boy."

"You ain't grown. You only thirteen, Hev."

She mushed him in the face and walked off, but not without hearing Jamir howl in pain. She halted and spun around to see Jamir holding his face as blood begin to drip from his wounded nose.

Heaven panicked.

"Get away from me," he screamed, and kicked her in the leg when she reached out for him.

"Jamir?" Heaven called after him as Jamir turned around and ran away from her. He dashed around the back corner of the house, out of sight.

Minutes later, Jamir was in the bathroom with Vermani and Delani's mama tending to his wounded nose. His nose was still sensitive from its recent injury.

"What did you do?" she asked.

He didn't reply.

Jamir would never tell on his siblings, no matter what they may go through in life. Although he didn't like the person whom Heaven had become, he knew she didn't mean to hurt him intentionally.

"You just need to be careful, Jamir, Okay? I love you and be good," she stroked his curly hair and sent Jamir on his way.

Outside on the front porch, Jamir watched as Heaven got into a red and black car at the curb outside her house. For a minute or two, the car just sat there at the curb, and Jamir stood there watching.

The front door opened behind him and his stepfather, Tony, stepped out on the porch.

"Wanna ride wit' me to the store real quick?"

"Yeah." Jamir nodded.

They got into his Cadillac Escalade truck and hit the streets. The sound system was playing some Oldie Goldies and Tony was humming along. He was obviously in a good mood and Jamir was loving his energy.

Since he was four-years-old, Tony had been in Jamir's life, doing whatever he could to provide for him and his mama. He wasn't perfect but Tony was real, the closest thing to a real father Jamir would ever have.

Men like Tony were rare in this world.

He was solid as they come.

"Can I ask you a question, son?" Tony spoke up as he reached to lower the volume.

"Yeah. What's the question?" said Jamir.

"What if I told you I might be going away for a while, Jamir?" he asked. "How would you feel about that?"

"Are you coming back?"

Tony didn't answer right away. "Maybe. That all depends on whether I survive or not," he said.

"Survive what?" Jamir asked.

"Prison."

Jamir felt his heart skip a beat.

"Prison? What're you talkin' about, daddy?" Jamir's eyes welled up with tears.

"Not too long ago I was caught doing somethin' that I wasn't supposed to be doing."

"What did you do?"

"Fraud," said Tony. "It's how I've been takin' care of you and your mama all these years. My bullshit caught up wit' me and I must pay a penalty for it."

"I thought you had a job."

"I did." Tony told him. "But one job wasn't enough to give you and your mama what y'all wanted and needed. And your mama is a very expensive woman. Me doing what I did made life a whole lot less complicated. It'll only be for three years, though."

"Three years ain't that long, daddy."

Tony nodded.

"You can survive three years," said Jamir. "You the toughest person I know."

Hearing that made Tony happy, and he reached over and pulled him to him for a brief embrace.

Quincy Liquors was the store that they arrived at minutes later. Tony told him to wait inside the truck while he went inside to handle his business.

A whole bunch of dope-heads, drunks, and winos occupied this area on a daily basis. The spot was known for violence and drug activity. Several months ago, an old drunk by the name of Sporty was killed behind the liquor store by another dope head. Since then, the authorities stopped all activity from going on outside the store. If you wasn't shopping inside the liquor store, there was no reason for anyone to be hanging around outside.

After a couple of days, the spot resumed its normal daily activities.

From where he sat, Jamir watched the movement going on about the area. As he observed the activities, he thought to himself that he would never grow up to be like them.

Then he thought about Tony going to prison for three years, and wondered what life would be like for his family now, without him.

Jamir was very familiar with his mama's expensive taste. He knew if Tony could, he would give his mama the stars from the sky, if she wanted them. It was time for him to pick up the slack.

He needed to do something.

What could an eleven-year-old boy do to help provide for his family? He wondered.

He would have to have a talk with Kahlil or Vermani. Maybe work as a block runner, or hustle for them. One thing was for certain, Jamir was not going to allow his mama to need for anything, at least until Tony came back home and picked up where he left off.

Chapter 29

Five years later.

Delani stepped out from beyond the prison gates and breathed in the fresh air of freedom. He stared up into the bright lit sun in the sky and said a silent prayer to the heavens above.

Dressed in a crisp, all-white Balenciaga outfit, with a pair of five thousand-dollar white LV X Nike Air Force One, low-top sneakers, Delani looked like brand new money. He didn't even glance behind him, out of caution, as he unzipped his pants, pulled his dick out, and pissed on the prison grounds.

Moments later, a shiny black 2017 Bentley Continental GTC GT V8 pulled up to a halt in front of him.

Vermani hopped out from behind the wheel of the car and burst out laughing. Then he ran over to his twin brother and hugged him, long and hard. It had been a long time coming, and their reunion was a much needed one.

Five years of hard time and finally, Delani was blessed with another shot to do it all again.

He would have been home a long time ago, but Delani was like an untamed animal that needed to be caged. The system couldn't break him for nothing. Their attempts only made him wiser, stronger, and more vicious than ever. But he played his position and made it out.

Nineteen years old and realer than ever, he was back, the King of the Hooliganz.

"You ready for this shit, brah?" Vermani said happily, when they finally released one another.

At two hundred two pounds of solid beast-mode and fearless as a den of lions, Delani was ready for whatever.

That's when Vermani raised a hand towards the car, and Delani's eyes bore into its dark tinted windows. He waited patiently to see what happened next.

Then the passenger door opened and Heaven stepped out in her eight hundred-dollar Autumn Adeigbo Camille dress and thousand-dollar Jimmy Choo pumps, looking like a movie star. She looked like a grown ass woman, and flawlessly gorgeous.

Then Shamar climbed out of the car, dressed fresh to impress in an Amiri pair of pants that ran him a cool fifteen hundred dollars and a five-thousand-dollar Jeff Hamilton leather jacket, over a fresh, white, hundred-dollar Vintage t-shirt. On his feet, Shamar stepped out in the same black and gray Amiri shoes that Delani, himself, had fantasized over. The nigga had a full beard and all, tapered and clean as a whistle.

But it was when Jamir presented himself next in an also all-white thirty-five-hundred-dollar Chrome Hearts outfit and Cartier black buff glasses that brought tears to his eyes. Each one of them had a bottle of Rose and Ace of Spades in their hands, and they saluted him with them all.

The whole view was breath taking.

Delani was overwhelmed with growing excitement.

Then he hollered as loud as he could in total happiness and ran toward his crew. They hugged and welcomed him home in pure style.

"We gotta do this for the Gram," said Vermani as he recorded the whole initial experience of Delani's joy of being welcomed by his loved ones.

"Oh shit, Jay, my lil nigga." Delani couldn't believe it as he looked at Jamir and was shocked at how much he'd grown over the years.

Although he had received hundreds of photos, via email, to his prison issued tablet, of them all, it was nothing like seeing them all in person.

The whole scenery was so uplifting.

It was remarkable.

"Man, let's go. Why the fuck are we still here right now?" said Delani.

"Say no more," Vermani responded.

They all got into the Bentley Continental and got the hell out of dodge.

On the road, they didn't have that far to travel to make it back home. With good behavior, Delani had gotten transferred to a prison closer to home. It was called Jefferson C.I. which was just outside Leon County, about an hour or so from Quincy. Back at the prison, Delani left a lot of homeboys he had love for and would keep in touch. He had big plans for the homies behind the wall.

It didn't take Delani long to figure out that prison was a million-dollar enterprise, and he wanted a piece of the pie. He would make it his business to do so.

Loyalty was a must.

As they made their way back home, Delani was filled in on what was going on, on the home turf.

Dejah was running the streets of Quincy, and pretty much all of North Florida, and even South Georgia. With a Mexican plug and a Cuban plug on her team, Dejah was flooding the streets with product, and had the strongest team in the game behind her.

With Killa Don as her 2nd-in-command, Kahlil as her street chief, and Vermani, the Captain of his own crew, the empire was strong and dedicated to the game.

Jamir, at sixteen-years-old, was about to be a father to his first child by his girlfriend, Harmoni. She was two years older than him, but loyal and cherished by the family.

Heaven was attending FAMU College, studying psychology, and living her best life with LJ and their one-year-old baby girl, Aliyah Renee. She was loving her new status and security, and Delani told her that he was happy for her.

Then there was Shamar, who turned out to be quite the business man and certified goon. About two years ago, Shamar was on trial for a double-homicide. He beat the case, and a week later, he became the prime suspect of another murder of a local business owner out in Tallahassee. The streets were saying that Shamar had approached business owner, Reginald Reliford, about investing in his coffee shop, and Reggie pretty much told Shamar to go fuck himself. Two days later, Reginald was found shot to death, parked in his own driveway. Now that same coffee shop was a bookstore and lounge-cafe that was being run by Mrs. Sandra Murphy, herself.

Over the next couple of years, Shamar had opened up a car detailing shop and a game arcade for the youth. With Dejah financing everything, he was just making it happen and creating opportunities for others.

Delani had been gone all these years, just to get out and see that all his people were still good. He was proud of their accomplishments, and would be very supportive. But he had his own thing that he wanted to do.

"How many people you got on your squad, twin?" Delani asked his brother. He was nursing his second cup of champagne and loving the effects from it.

"About forty," he said.

"Forty-three," Heaven corrected from the back, behind the driver's seat. "Three was just recruited over the weekend: Skinny, Brodrick, and Wank Wank," she said.

"Oh yeah," Vermani added with a glance. "That headache behind me is the crew's secretary, too."

She thumped him in the back of the head with her finger.

"And I'm good at what I do," she said. Then she materialized with a miniature duffle bag and handed it up front to Delani, along with a smartphone, equipped with all the important numbers he may need in his contacts.

When Delani unzipped the bag, he was taken aback by the sight of bundles of cash money.

"That's a hundred thousand, a box of condoms, your jewelry, and a present from Kahlil," said Heaven.

The present was a chrome Glock .23 pistol with two extra fully loaded clips.

"This muthafucka is beautiful," said Delani. A sense of power awakened inside of him as he admired the weapon and its brilliance.

"Figured you would like it," Shamar grinned.

Next, Delani draped over his gold Cuban link chain with the diamond-emerald encrusted medallion of the two HCG (Hooliganz Crime Gang) badges of honor. The diamond gold Presidential Rolex came next, the matching bracelet and pinkie ring all customized by NYC Luxury.

Flipping down the sun visor to look at himself in the mirror, Delani grilled himself and growled like a pit bull at his own reflection. The day before, he had the big homie Jimbo Blue hook him up in the barber shop. His shit was on point and his wave game would leave you sea sick.

The nigga definitely looked like money now, like a true boss.

Real shit.

By the time Delani made it home, the block party was already in full swing, and everybody welcomed him. Another young street legend was back in the mix, and by any means necessary, he was going to uphold that title.

That day, Delani partied hard, and even danced with his mama in the middle of the street. He and Harold shared a moment, and it was nothing but love there. He joined a dice game and lost money, got some head from one of Dejah's trick bitches behind his house, and slap boxed with some of his old hooliganz crew members, to see if their hands were proper. Killa Don had a sit down with him and talked business. Delani was there in his true element.

He was back.

Later on that night, a private party was thrown for him up in Club Gems, a low-key strip club that one of Killa Don's men owned out in Havana. Some of the baddest strippers in the dirty south were brought in to show the HCG clique a good time. The team did it big for Delani, and he made a movie out of it.

That night, Delani partied until about 2:00 a.m. and then went to the Four Seasons with three bad bitches, who fucked and sucked him dry.

When the sun rose the next morning, Delani woke up with his dick in a Spanish bitch's mouth, and a juicy pussy on his face, while Kevin Gates played in the background. By noon, he was sitting in his mama's kitchen, watching her prepare his favorite dish.

Delani was grinning like a cat.

"What's so funny, Dee?" Kiara asked, looking not that much older than her forty-seven years. She looked damn good, and Delani told her so.

"All those years I did locked up, this was the most important thang I missed the most."

"What?" she said curiously.

"Being home, in the kitchen, watchin' you cook and look pretty," he replied.

"So you miss my cookin'?"

"And I missed how you used to sang to us."

"What else?"

"And your beautiful smile."

"And?"

He grinned. "Don't get the damn big head, mama."

She laughed, and it was music to his ears.

Delani knew he couldn't disappoint this woman again, nor his crew. So this time, he would go harder than hard.

No more bullshittin'.

Chapter 30

Two weeks later, Shamar entered Horizons Bookstore & Lounge Cafe at the bloom of its full potential. Today, one of the new, local, urban book authors, by the name of Trigger, was having his book signing event. He actually had quite a crowd outside his section. Trigger was one of them young street niggas, who decided to try his hand in something positive for a change. As he made his way through the spot, Shamar saluted the author and approached the service station.

"Can I get a cup of your beautiful smile and an extra dose of your essence?" said Shamar.

"Will that be all, sir?" smiled the pretty redbone female standing behind the cashier counter. Her name was Danielle Wilfred, five-foot-nine, petite, and with the most dazzling pair of brown eyes Shamar had ever seen.

"How about a taste of those sexy lips, too?"

"Sounds good to me," she said.

He grinned and leaned forward to kiss his woman. The taste of her lips made him feel warm all over.

At that instant, the door behind Danielle opened as Mrs. Murphy emerged from the back storage room. She saw them lip-locking and broke it up immediately.

"You two know better," she chastised Shamar and her niece, Danielle. "This is a place of business, not some damned lover's lane." She had a box of pastries in her hand and a testy look in her eyes.

"You didn't say that to Ira when he swept you off your feet in the middle of your high school graduation," said Shamar.

"That was then," Sandra handed him the box of pastries and continued, "this is now. Go put these on the refreshment stand for the people."

"Just gon' boss me around and shit," he muttered.

"I love you, too, Shamar." Sandra smiled and waved mockingly after him as he carried the box away.

Halfway across the room, Shamar glanced in the direction of the entrance as the door opened. He watched as three dudes entered and approached Trigger's table.

Something was up.

Shamar watched as the three dudes moved towards the front of the line of people standing in front of Trigger's table. One of them boldly interrupted the moment between Trigger and a fan and slapped his palms down on the table. He then leaned towards Trigger's face and was saying something that obviously made Trigger glower up at him.

Shamar glanced toward the front counter and saw the troubled expressions on Sandra and his girl's faces.

He had to do something.

Sitting the box down upon the refreshment stand, Shamar made his way over to the table.

"We got a problem here, my nigga?" asked Shamar. At a hundred ninety pounds of pure pressure and ruthlessness, Shamar had no problem pushing his weight around when need be.

"Do you got a problem, lil nigga? You better find you some business," said one of the two behind the leader.

"You're 'in' my business, potna," Shamar growled. "Matter of fact, you niggaz need to leave like right now."

"Or what?" challenged the leader, sizing Shamar up.

There were children in the spot and Shamar didn't want nothing popping off in there around them.

"Let's do it," without another word, Shamar moved towards the exit while intentionally bumping into one of them in the process, to let them know he was on that demon time.

Next, Trigger got up and followed Shamar outside, with the three goons in tow.

By the time the three dudes exited from the building, they were instantly shocked to see, not only Trigger and Shamar, but about seven hooliganz posted outside, looking like they wanted some action.

What they didn't know was the barber shop that was adjoined to the bookstore belonged to Kahlil. And that muthafucker was always equipped with a team of hooliganz moving around the spot, holding shit down.

Hooliganz Crime Gang ran the city, and if a nigga didn't know, then he would find out with the quickness.

"This nigga No Good?" said Spud, one of the hooliganz standing amongst the group. "Man, this pussy nigga is a bitch. He don't want no smoke wit' the team."

"No Good, huh?" then he approached No Good, who was a nigga of about twenty-five years old, stocky built, and actually looked like he was about that life. "You asked me 'or what', right? Well guess what?" he replied.

No Good sneered. "There ain't no bitch in my heart, lil nigga," he countered aggressively.

"My nigga Spud said you a bitch," he said.

"He is a bitch," Spud replied.

"However you niggaz wanna do it, let's do it," No Good barked.

"I see fear in your eyes, No Good."

No Good stared at Shamar and wondered if he could hear his heart pounding in his chest.

"But I'ma spare you today, potna." Shamar reached up and squeezed No Good's shoulder. "How about you and your little crew bounce up outta here. A'ight? Becuz I don't wanna have to create a crime scene out here."

"That muthafucka owes me money." No Good gestured at Trigger.

"Consider it paid wit' your life for coming up in my place of business, disrespectin' me and my people." Shamar didn't give a fuck if God owed him money, he crossed the line and had to be handled accordingly.

Next to No Good, one of his homeboys shrugged in the way that he saw the matter as phony.

That's when White Boy Ty drew his gun and eased up on the nigga with that look in his eyes. White Boy Ty asked him if he wanted some smoke. No Good stepped between them and claimed that everything was good.

"Ain't shit good," said Spud. "Go or get smoked."

No Good nodded and said, "You got that." Then he acknowledged his crew, and they got into their SUV and left.

"Spud, Chili Willie," Shamar turned to his two shooters. "Y'all know what to do. Sleep time. I don't trust them fools," he announced, and they hurried off to go catch up with No Good and his crew in traffic, to wipe 'em down.

Shamar was considered one of the generals in the gang, and his position was as respected as any other.

He then turned to Trigger and demanded to know what that was all about.

"I used to hustle for No Good and his brotha, Dale, before I got knocked on that petty dope charge that rode me out in the county. The nigga feel as though I owe him for gettin' the trap kicked in and shut down. Me and Dale got an understanding, but that nigga's on some other shit." Trigger was twenty-two years old, and about that life for real. He just humbled himself to keep from having to get his hands dirty again.

"Well," Shamar replied. "You don't have to worry about that shit no more."

"I appreciate your loyalty, lil brah, but you know I can handle my own shit."

"I know."

"I'm humble now, for a reason." Trigger held his gaze intensely, and Shamar told him he understood.

"I know, my nigga. Get back to your people in there. They're waitin' on you."

Trigger nodded, gave the young hooligan general some love, and went back inside the building.

For the next few minutes Shamar hung outside for a while to kick it with his crew. He then entered the barber shop to see who all was up in the spot. It was there that he saw the last person he expected to see.

It was Lyonell, Marlon's former chief of enforcers, the very same nigga that Killa Don and his people ran out of town when the pressure was on. He was a killer with no conscience, a goon who knew no boundaries.

He was back in town.

But for what? Thought Shamar as he claimed the barber chair next to Lyonell, when Big Bob was finished with another loyal customer.

"Long time no see, Ly," said Shamar. "Heard you was back in town."

Lyonell was in the process of getting a trim and his beard tapered by old school Melvin. Shamar observed him closely and knew, without a shadow of doubt, that beneath his barber cape, Lyonell was in possession of a weapon.

"I'm back," he replied.

"You know the streets ain't the same no more, Ly."

"Trust me, I know. But I'm back, lil homie, and not a damn thang nobody gonna do about it. I'm mad at myself for waitin' this fuckin' long to come back."

"You talked to Dej yet?" asked Shamar curiously.

"Why should I wanna do that?"

"She's running the show now," said Shamar. "You know she always spoke highly of you."

"If you're insinuating that I join your lil' money team, I'ma pass on that. I got my own squad now, lil homie. My shit is poppin', we gon' get it poppin'. Not to fail," Lyonell answered.

No reply.

"Good day, lil nigga." Lyonell rose up out of his chair, when Melvin removed the barber cape. In his hand, he clutched a gold-plated FN 5.7mm pistol, which held a total of twenty-one shots. "We out," he said.

Suddenly, four more people stood at his beck, and together, they exited the shop in a formation that indicated that their presence was not to be taken for a joke.

"What's the word, Mar?" said Bizzy, coming to stand next to Shamar. He was seventeen and vicious, always ready to sling that iron.

"I don't even know," he told his eager shooter.

"Should we move on 'em?" Bizzy asked.

Shamar thought about it for a moment and got up out of the chair. He walked over to the window and looked outside, just in time to spot Lyonell getting into the passenger side of a Rolls-Royce Wraith. *How did I miss a car like that?* Wondered Shamar.

Whatever Lyonell had up his sleeve, it wouldn't be good. He was run out of town, and now he was back, bigger and badder than the day he left.

Without waiting to see what happened next, Shamar pulled out his phone and called Dejah.

Shit had been going so well for the team. Now with Lyonell back there was no telling what was about to go down. Whatever his plan was, Lyonell's intention was to not fail. He made that point loud and clear.

And so Shamar would share that same sentiment, not to fail, especially not fail the Queen.

Chapter 31

Speaking of the queen, Dejah was sitting in the back of her bullet-proof Bentley Azure, smoking a blunt of Runtz weed and sippin' Rose Black, while her driver cruised through the city streets of Tallahassee. Next to her was her down-ass-bitch Redd, curvaceous and lethal as a pit full of vicious rattlesnakes. Redd did not play any games, she would smoke your ass.

Two and a half years ago, Dejah flew Redd in from the stomping grounds of Baltimore, Maryland to come hold her down and get a taste of the good life.

It was just ten years ago, when Dejah met Redd back in the penitentiary. When three other bitches tried to step down on Dejah for making moves in their housing unit, Redd was right there to back her up. Together, they thrashed them bitches and were bound by blood and loyalty forever.

Then Amelia came into the picture and made their three-woman team one to be reckoned with.

Dejah couldn't wait until Redd got released from the pen to show her true appreciation.

Not even two weeks in, Redd had slumped three niggaz and established a murder game that the streets of North Florida had never seen. Since then, her and Dejah had become thick as thieves, and almost inseparable.

A minute ago, Dejah had disconnected with Shamar, after being informed of Lyonell's presence in town. Shamar sounded very concerned for the sake of the team, and wanted to know how she felt about it.

Last she heard of Lyonell, he was up in Atlanta making major moves. Apparently, when he took off, he did so with a whole lot of Marlon's product and money. He'd also took with him a handful of his men, and went to set up shop in Georgia. Throughout the years, Lyonell had gotten his weight up on some boss shit. He also commanded one of the most deadly kill teams in the streets.

Lyonell was back home now.

He was a threat.

"I can make it happen if you want," said Redd. She was ready to utilize her enticing game of a temptress to lure Lyonell into a trap of death.

The bitch was good at what she did.

"Not just yet," said Dejah. "I wanna see what he's up to first, before I press play on that."

"Which means I need to stay in the shadows for now." Redd didn't mean it as a question, she understood her position. If Lyonell is watching Dejah for any reason, it would be wise for Redd to play the backfield, to be the ghost.

"If that's the case, then let me gon' and get my shit right now," Redd said, before taking the cup away from Dejah and downing the rest of its contents.

Moments later, Dejah watched as her jeans were pulled down to her ankles, along with her panties, and Redd buried her face into her pussy with vicious intent. Dejah was stretched out across the backseat, stroking the back of Redd's head, as she feasted on her like the Last Supper.

"Stick your finger in my ass, too, baby." moaned Dejah, then pulled on her blunt while enjoying the pleasure.

Redd did as she was told.

"Damn," Dejah panted. "Just like that."

After a while, Redd drunk every last drop of her love juice as Dejah climaxed with a shudder.

Then her cell phone rang, and when she checked the number, she saw that it was Killa Don calling.

"What's up, boo?" she answered.

"Dej," said Killa Don, before what sounded like his phone dropping somewhere and he had to recover it. "My bad, my bad. Hey, I know you heard the latest news."

"Ly is back in town."

"Yep," he said. "We need to meet up."

"Put the rest of the team on alert. I want all top ranks at the spot in one hour. An emergency meetin', mandatory, no exceptions," Dejah said as she straightened herself up.

"Say no more," said Killa Don.

"Enough said."

Fifteen minutes later, Redd was dropped off at the condo apartment out in Woodville, away from the city. That's where she would remain until further notice.

Dejah fucked her good for about twenty-minutes and got back in traffic, after switching cars. This time, Dejah was riding in a blood red 2010 Shelby GT500 with her young hooligan, Booby, behind the wheel again.

Booby was deaf, but loyal and ruthless. Her communication with him was beyond remarkable.

He, too, was just as fierce as the rest of them.

The meeting location was in the East Quincy area, where one of the crew members ran a paint and body shop in the warehouse he operated. When Dejah arrived at the location, there was a total of fifteen people awaiting her presence, four bitches and eleven niggaz. Everybody was strapped and ready for whatever the universe presented.

"What's poppin', family?" She greeted them all the second she stepped into the big room.

Everybody responded and saluted her.

Dejah went around the room dapping up her people and hugging them in turn.

"When the meetin's over, we need to talk," she said to Delani as she made her rounds.

He nodded, but said nothing.

"A'ight." Dejah took the floor alongside Killa Don and Kahlil, her two top dawgs. Vermani would have been there, but he was attending school over at FSU and was not to be interrupted from his education for any reason.

Vermani and Heaven were the two scholars on the team, and the future of their successes.

"As you all may already know, we have a problem on our hands by the name of Lyonell Roberts, aka Ly. Years ago, after killin' his commander, Marlon Jones, he was run outta town by some of y'all that's present. However, Ly is back now, and whateva his intentions are, they ain't good." Dejah paused to look at her people, seeing the grimness on all their faces. "Before Ly was run off, he was chief enforcer for Marlon's team. Therefore he is a thoroughbred killa, and considered a serious threat to our organization. So I'ma want all of you, and the rest of the family, to stay on your P's and Q's. Remain vigilant and watch one another's backs for all we're worth. I love y'all, and always will," she said.

"What? So we're not gonna go after this nigga?" Jeremy replied from the back of the group.

"If you know Ly like I know him, today was the last time any one of us will see his face," said Dejah. "The move he pulled earlier was just to let us know that he's back and ready for whateva."

"What's the current stats on this nigga?" said Trill.

That's when Dejah shared with them what all she knew about the nigga who had become the renewed enemy.

"So he's a big dawg now?" asked Lil LuLu.

"Larger than he was before," she said.

Killa Don stepped forward. "To sum it all up, this muthafucka's been preparing this moment for years. And I'm his prime enemy becuz I'm the one who ran him off. He wants blood, no doubt about it."

"Then it's wartime," said Delani.

The reason why Dejah didn't correct his exclamation was because she knew he was right.

The rest of the crew responded to the statement, and some of them even drew their guns.

Dejah said a few more chosen words, and ended the meeting with one last statement: "This is our world and nobody's gonna take it from us."

When the group dispersed, they moved towards the exit and wherever they chose to go. Dejah pulled Delani aside to speak with him more privately. She even put Killa Don on hold to share a moment with her young hooligan.

Dejah had two whole different organizations under her leadership, but they were all one big family. Delani and his HCG clique and Killa Don and his Gutta Boyz Movement crew.

Both organizations teamed up for the sake of Dejah, making her who she was that very moment, the Queen of the streets.

"What's up, Dej?"

She tossed an arm over his shoulders. "I want you and the crew to take that trip up to ATL. Move in the shadows, but find out what all you can on Ly. I need to know his weakness," said Dejah.

"I'll round them up right now," he said.

"Don't make a mess, unless you have to, but stay in the shadows, Dee," she reiterated.

He kissed her cheek. "Like a phantom."

She nodded.

And Delani was gone.

"We need to get the rest of the family somewhere safe until we find out what Ly's next move is," Killa Don announced.

"I'm about to find out," said Dejah.

"How?"

"I'ma set up a meetin' wit' him."

"Of course not," said Killa Don. "That nigga'll kill you the second you show your face."

"No he won't, Donte. You, he will kill, but not me. I got this under control," she assured him.

"And how do you expect to do this?"

Dejah wrapped an arm around his waist as she led the way towards the exit of the warehouse. She appreciated his love and concern, his shit was nothing less than genuine. Over the years, she and he had fought a hard battle over the control of their hearts. Their closeness was like no other. She adored Killa Don immensely.

The nigga was real as the come, so real it was scary.

"I love you, Donte. You know that, right?"

"I love you, too," he said. "But I'm not gonna just allow you to put yourself in jeopardy like that."

"Do you trust me or not?"

"You know I do."

She said, "Then trust me to handle Ly, like I wanna handle him. We got history. He won't hurt me, at least not if I don't give him a reason to. But I got this, Donte. And if I can't get through to him, then we're gonna turn the pressure up."

"If you say so." Killa Don let out a troubled breath.

"I know so," she replied. "I got this."

Chapter 32

When the final bell rang, Jamir was up on his feet and slinging his backpack over his right shoulder. By the time he made it out into the noisy hallway, Hollow and Zamon were already waiting on him. He dapped up his two friends and HCG members and they moved towards the building's exit.

"You heard about the new memo?" asked Hollow, seventeen years old and thuggin' hard in the streets.

"What memo?" Jamir asked, pulling out his cell phone to see if the notification came through his connection.

"Operation lock and key," Hollow replied.

"The superiors want us to report to them. We got trouble lurkin', shit ain't safe," said fat boy Zamon. He'd already had his phone out and had spoken with his superior already. Blocka didn't say too much on the phone, but he made it clear that some shit was about to go down.

Jamir read the new memo personally from Delani himself, telling him to get home to his family.

At the entrance gate of East Gadsden High School, a 2020 Camaro 2 SS was awaiting Jamir. He embraced his two homies and promised to get up with them later. Jamir got in on the passenger side of the sparkling burgundy Camaro and kissed Harmoni tenderly on the lips.

"What's up, green eyes," he greeted his girlfriend.

"How was your day, baby?"

"Progressive. I missed you and my son." Jamir grinned as her bloated belly just begged for a good rub. He reached

195

over, laid a hand upon her belly, and instantly felt the light thump of the baby's kick from inside.

Harmoni was seven months pregnant and barely showing, except for the bump of her belly. She still maintained her petite frame, still sexy as the day he met her, which was the day he first stepped upon high school grounds. Since day one, it had been them against the world.

When Harmoni's parents realized she was seeing a young hooligan and had become pregnant by him, they gave her an ultimatum: an abortion or get out of their house. She chose to keep the baby and LaShonda welcomed her into her home. It had become the best moment in their lives.

Months later, they all but crashed and burned. Jamir became the young man that he was destined to be.

Years ago, after his stepfather went off to prison to do thirty-six months for fraud, Jamir stepped up to the plate. He went from being an errand boy for Delani's cousin, Kahlil, to saving up his money to invest in Toby's hustle game that made him a young investor. When he saw his first one thousand dollars, he blew it all on his mama. Since then, all he did was go to school, collect from Toby, and now LJ, and just focus on building his own family's foundation.

At sixteen years old, Jamir had become quite the young go-getter, but his big brothers were always getting on him about indulging in the affairs of the streets.

For example, one day, not too long ago, Jamir caught one of the HCG members tricking off with a dope head with the product he was supposed to be serving. So instead of alerting Kahlil or Delani about it, he took the matter in his own hands. Jamir chastised the hustler, then demanded that he give him all money and product. When he refused to do so, Jamir attacked him with a lead pipe he found nearby and sent him straight to the ER with a fractured face and a bruised ego.

Delani banished the hustler from the organization, instead of killing him, which surely was his intention. But it caused a confrontation between him and Jamir that pretty much made things bitter for a while between them.

He only wanted the best for his little brother. The game they were playing was in the major leagues, niggas were getting killed every day.

Jamir felt like he had something to prove. He wanted to make his big brothers proud. After a while, Delani and Jamir settled their differences, and now Jamir was a young captain of his own inner squad within the HCG. They were a bunch of hooliganz that brought absolute fear to many.

"I went to the doctor today," said Harmoni.

"Oh yeah? What he talkin' about?"

"The same, me and the baby are healthy." Harmoni was taking online classes to finish her senior year and graduate. Jamir wanted her as comfortable and stress-free as possible. "LaShonda and my mama was there," she said.

At the mention of her mama, Jamir nodded. Just recently, he and Harmoni's mama, Lisa, had made amends for the trouble she caused their relationship. Now, she saw with her own eyes how happy and secure her daughter was with him.

"Anything else new?" asked Jamir.

Harmoni shrugged. "Should there be?"

He told her about the new memo and wanted to know if she had seen anything strange or out of the ordinary today. She said she didn't and Jamir took it as law.

Harmoni was very observant of even the smallest things, and her sense of direction had always been on point.

When they made it to the house, Jamir helped her out of the car. He was escorting her to the door when he noticed Shamar standing outside his crib on the phone. He saw him and waved Jamir over.

"Where you going?" Harmoni asked, once he opened the front door for her and turned away.

Jamir turned towards her. "I gotta go see what Mar talkin' about real quick."

"I wanna do somethin' wit' you before LaShonda gets back home," she said. Harmoni meant in so many words that she wanted to fuck. She was horny and he knew just what to do about it.

"When I get back," he promised. "I'ma take care of you when I come back, okay?" Jamir climbed back up the two steps to her and kissed her cheek.

"Hurry up, Jamir."

"I will."

Jamir hurried across the street, over to where Shamar was standing in front of the house. The front door was wide open and Jamir could see Shamar's wifey, Danielle, and young Rikah in the living room. Rikah was from the High Bridge area and one of the few female HCG members. Toby was her superior and under her leadership, Rikah was not only a go-getter, too, but she was also a feminine goon.

Rikah was a pit bull in a skirt.

She was certified.

"What it do, brah?" Jamir dapped his big brother up in their signature handshake greeting.

"Check this out," Shamar beckoned Jamir over to the porch steps, where he sat down and Jamir did the same. Then he operated the video call with Kahlil, whom he was already on the phone with. "I got Jay wit' me now."

"What's good, my nigga?" Kahlil saluted Jamir from the screen of the phone and he returned the gesture.

"We good," he acknowledged.

"A'ight. By now you should already be aware of what's goin' on out here in these streets, Jay."

"I got the memo."

"Okay. Then you know your family has to be moved to a more secure spot for safety purposes. Today. Whatever this nigga Ly got goin' on, we must be ten steps ahead."

"Ly?" Jamir appeared confused and turned his gaze over at Shamar for an explanation.

Shamar explained to him who Ly was and the reason he may have come back to town.

"Watch your backs and stay strapped. You can't sleep on this nigga. He's militant and way too dangerous."

"Where is Ly now? What's his position?" asked Jamir.

"That's being investigated as we speak," said Shamar.

Then Kahlil informed them of Delani's mission to Atlanta to dig up what he could on Ly and capitalize from it.

After hanging up with Kahlil, both Jamir and Shamar spoke on the matter and strategized a plan.

Within the next couple hours, Jamir had his family were secured within the living area of a 5-star hotel, equipped with a small kitchenette, walk-in shower stall and Jacuzzi, spacious bedroom with an adjoining room, and living room. Jamir wanted his family comfortable, and with Tony keeping house, he was sure all would go well.

"We good?" Jamir asked them once they were all settled in and secured.

Just down the hall, Heaven and her mama and Monica's boyfriend, Ced, were already settled in.

"Do you have to go out there, Jamir?" Harmoni asked. She was concerned about his well-being, although she knew that Jamir could handle his own.

"No. I don't," Jamir replied. "But I gotta go make sure the rest of the crew is straight."

"The crew can handle themselves, Jay." LaShonda wasn't keen on being run off away from her own home to feel safe. She agreed to it only because of Harmoni and the baby. Other than that, she would have never left her home.

"Of course they could, mama." Jamir approached her, and his mama just glared at him. "Don't fight wit' me now, okay? I got too much on my plate that needs to be handled."

"You got a family to look after, too, Jay."

"And that's what the fuck I'm doin', mama," Jamir said, and LaShonda slapped the taste out his mouth.

"You watch how you talk to me, dammit."

Jamir rubbed his stinging face. He was livid. Without another word, he took his leave and slammed the door behind him.

When he left, Harmoni broke down and cried.

On his way out, a door to his right opened and Ced stepped out into the carpeted hallway. He and Jamir looked at one another, and a silent communication of understanding passed between them.

"My sista and Monica good?"

Ced nodded. He was a jet black nigga, who retired from the streets and owned his own trucking business. "Everything copasetic," he said.

"Where you headed to now?"

"Got a few loose ends to tighten up out there. You?" him and Jamir stepped onto the elevator.

Jamir liked Ced, he respected the OG, but there was something about him that was off a little. He believed Ced was using drugs, the hard kind, but he just couldn't figure it out.

Whatever was done in the dark would eventually come to light, that's what Aunt LaVetra said.

On the elevator down, Ced retrieved his phone and made a call. Almost instantly, Jamir caught on to the fact that he was speaking in code to somebody. Maybe the nigga thought Jamir was too young to peep the play that he was on some secretive shit.

Little did he know, minutes later, Jamir exited the hotel and headed for the car that he had bought Harmoni. He got in and waited until he spotted Ced's truck on the move. That's when he decided to tail him at a safe distance.

It was about to be nightfall, and Jamir knew that's when them hooliganz came out to play.

It was war in the streets.

Being the protégé of some of the most feared and respected hooliganz in the game, Delani, Shamar, and LJ, he understood the strategies of war. Jamir knew what actions to take if ever there came a time when he sensed something unrighteous was amiss.

Like now, he felt Ced was up to something grimy, so he wanted to find out what he had going on.

About twenty minutes later, Jamir was led just across the Florida-Georgia line on Hwy 27 outside of Havana. Ced entered the lot of a nearby bar, got out, and went inside. Jamir had driven past the bar and bust a U-turn when he scanned his surroundings and saw that no patrol unit was in sight.

It was said that Georgia's law patrol was very strict, so Jamir had to be careful how he moved.

Across the street from the bar was a family owned diner. Jamir pulled his car into its lot and parked. Then he slipped across the street, over to the bar, to see what Ced drove all the way out here for.

He peeped in through the window and surveyed the scenery, then he spotted Ced sitting at a rear table across from someone else. And that's when Jamir gasped in total shock, because that someone else was none other than the last person he expected to see.

It was like seeing a ghost.

It was the wickedest thing Jamir ever seen.

In the flesh, it was Marlon Jones.

Chapter 33

At ten minutes to eight that evening, the big black Lincoln Aviator carrying five Hooliganz Crime Gang members rolled to a stop outside a white house on Glenwood Drive. From the passenger seat, Delani pulled out his iPhone and called his Atlanta contact.

In the back, White Boy Ty, Wank Wank, and Skinny were strapped to the tee and ready to put in some work. They were rotating a blunt between them, while MO3's "Round and Round" played low in the background.

"I'm here. Where you at, my nigga?" said Delani into the phone as he surveyed the night's surroundings outside the SUV. Behind him Wank Wank laid his Mac-11 across his lap.

"I had to step out for a minute, Dee. I'll be there in five minutes tops," said Koenisha Pittman. This was one of Dejah's people, whom she met in the joint and eventually brought her aboard the gravy train, when she touched down a year ago. Delani met her a few times already and the impression she had made on him was nothing less than respectable.

"Okay. Get here," Delani answered.

"Say no more."

The line disconnected, White Boy Ty opened his side door, and said he had to take a piss.

"Shiiddd. Me too," said Bizzy from behind the wheel. He then opened the door and got out next.

"Think we gon' catch this nigga t'night, cuz?" Skinny spoke up from the back seat.

"If what Dej said was accurate, then Ly is a big dawg up here in Atlanta. But she also said he keeps below the radar, too, which doesn't mean shit because regardless if he lays low or not, somebody knows something. All we need is one good clue and we go from there."

Delani felt his phone vibrate as he glanced down at the screen to read the incoming text message from Vermani, his beloved identical twin brother. Vermani was notifying him on the new developments with what was going on black at home in Quincy.

No word nor presence from Lyonell yet, which made the situation all the more alarming.

He was plotting.

To have shown up now, after five years of being run out of town, Lyonell, the chief enforcer of Marlon Jones' drug empire, did not return to make amends.

He'd come back for blood, which was why Delani and his crew were there in Atlanta that evening, to learn all they could about Lyonell and try to use it against him to gain the upper hand. Suddenly, the back passenger door swung open and Bizzy stood there in the doorway looking grim.

"We might have a problem, y'all," he said.

Wank Wank said, "What problem?"

Right then they all heard the unmistakable sound of White Boy Ty's Glock .40 click-clack just beyond the doorway. Then at once, Delani and the others bolted from the SUV to find three other niggaz advancing on White Boy Ty.

"What it do, Ty?" said Skinny, walking up to stand next to his HCG brother.

"That's what I'm tryna find out now," White Boy Ty responded without taking his eyes off the Atlanta-crew. Bizzy came to post up on the other side of him.

But it was the big gun that Wank Wank was clutching in his hands that spelled out the word "danger" for the trio, and made them come to a halt.

Instead of taking a piss behind the SUV, like Bizzy had done, White Boy Ty decided to do his business alongside the house that belonged to Koenisha. Apparently, one of the three niggaz saw this, and noticed that he was white. They exited from their house next door to confront him about it.

Obviously, they had no clue of White Boy Ty's gangster and were now witnessing it firsthand.

"Who the fuck are you niggaz?" demanded the shortest one of the three, stocky built and noticeably fearless towards their artillery and being outnumbered.

That's when Delani stepped up and came to stand before the short guy. "What's your name, dawg?"

Reluctantly, he answered. "Gunz."

"A'ight, Gunz," Delani smirked wickedly. "We don't want no problems, because as you can see, we don't have no problem solving them. Koenisha sent us," he said. "We just waitin' on her to pull up."

"Y'all strapped like that? What do Koe got to do wit' all that?" Gunz replied warily.

"She's family," said Delani. "You don't need to worry. Matter of fact," he pulled out his phone and hit Koenisha on speed-dial, spoke to her for a second, then handed the phone towards Gunz for clarification.

Moments later, Gunz handed him back the phone. "They good," he said to his crew.

One look at White Boy Ty, and Delani could see that he was itching to bust something.

Avoid making a mess unless there was no other choice was what Dejah advised him to do, so he would honor it.

Before long, Koenisha pulled up on the scene in her 2021 Audi RS 7 and turned into the driveway of the house in question.

"Everythang copasetic?" Koenisha exited her vehicle, along with another female and a young nigga, who was probably no older than Delani. She was a mulatto bitch, chunky thick and in her mid-thirties, serious looking and dressed like a "dope boy" would.

Both Delani and Gunz assured her all was well.

"You said five minutes tops." Delani replied. "That was twelve minutes, my nigga."

"Don't be clockin' my shit, Dee, Damn." Koenisha acknowledged her other two homeboys and beckoned Delani and his crew to follow her inside the house.

Inside the house, the HCG crew was introduced to Shaunta and Lil Cam, both of whom Koenisha confessed to being the only two people she trusted next to Dejah. Lil Cam was not only her nephew but her young hustla, while Shaunta, her childhood friend, was only present in regards to her loyalty and street connections.

Shaunta was the big sister of one of Zone 6's most respected street niggaz.

Koenisha entered the kitchen and fixed them all drinks of Grey Goose and sparked up two blunts of Runtz weed to put in rotation around the living room.

"I didn't come here for all this," said Delani.

"I know why you're here, Dee. I spoke wit' Dej earlier about the whole situation. And that's why I brought my nephew here wit' me t'night," said Koenisha, having perched on the arm of the plush sofa next to Bizzy. He couldn't help but stare at her thick round ass, but at the mention of her nephew all eyes swiveled towards Lil Cam.

"What's up?" White Boy Ty replied, who was sitting directly across from Lil Cam. Lil Cam was putting fire to the second blunt and sat upright in his seat.

"I know him by a different name than what y'all know him as," Lil Cam said, looking at Delani. "Up here, they call him Lion."

"Lion?"

Lil Cam nodded.

"Okay. What do you know?"

"I know he has a son. His name is Ezekiel. The streets call him Zeek. And he's the truth," said Lil Cam, passing the blunt over to Wank Wank.

Delani leaned forward. "What do you mean by that?" he inquired curiously.

With a troubled breath, Lil Cam told him.

As he listened, a dark scowl crept upon Delani's face, as well as the rest of his crew. From what he was hearing, Delani compared the information to what Dejah had given him on Lyonell and his habits and lifestyle. He knew, without a shadow of doubt, they had their man.

Apparently, Lil Cam was more knowledgeable than what the crew expected. But the obvious thing was Lil Cam's sudden troubled spirit where Zeek's reputation was concerned. Whoever this Zeek character was, he was surely about to have a rude awakening.

It turned out that Lyonell had had a bastard son all along, no wonder why he chose to run to Georgia. If that was the case, then both of them could die tonight.

Little did the hooliganz know...

Chapter 34

For a long moment as he stood outside the bar looking in through the window, Jamir contemplated what should he do about the situation. Just the thought of Marlon Jones being yet alive was scary in itself.

Unfortunately, Marlon had survived the gunshot to the head as Anya had described. After being beaten within an inch of his life, Killa Don made his cousin Anya finish him off with a bullet to the head. Now as Jamir peered into the window, he was witnessing the resurrection of the very same nigga, who once ruled the streets before Dejah.

Marlon was not dead.

He was very much alive, and with this revelation, there was a bad storm coming in its wake.

Without a second thought, Jamir pulled out his smartphone and hit Dejah's number. If there was anybody who should know about this first, it would be her.

"What's up, Jay?" she answered on the first ring.

"He's not dead," he replied.

"What are you talkin' about?"

"Marlon," he said. "He's not dead, Deja. I'm lookin' at him right now." Jamir's adrenaline was racing through his body, like a warm surge of electricity. "Hold up." He then activated the camera app on his phone and took three pictures of Marlon, before sending them to her phone. "You see that shit?"

"I see," her voice was surprisingly calm.

"Crazy, huh?"

"Where are you, Jay?"

He told her.

"Stay where you are, and don't let him outta your sight. I'm on my way," said Dejah.

Jamir nodded his head and ended the call with her. Then he made his way over to Ced's truck to see what he could learn.

The truck was a dark colored 2017 F-150 Lariat, and to Jamir's surprise, it was unlocked. After another glance in the direction of the bar entrance, he opened the door and rummaged through its cabin.

"Oh shit," muttered Jamir a minute later, after opening the glove compartment and discovering what appeared to be a black leather wallet containing an FBI shield and credentials inside, naming Cedric Anderson as Michael Phillips. "Oh no. This muthafucka is the Feds," he said.

After pocketing the evidence, Jamir reclaimed his earlier position to keep watch on Marlon, and now the perpetrator, whose cover had just been blown.

Heaven couldn't catch a break for nothing, thought Jamir, as he dwelled on the matter concerning his big sister's situation. First she learned, after thirteen years, that Marlon was her father. Then Marlon was suddenly taken away from her by a bullet. Now here it was her step-daddy of two years was not the person Heaven saw him as. The man was a field agent for the FBI. Now he was in the company of Marlon, whom just five years ago was considered dead.

"This shit is crazy," Jamir whispered. When Dejah finally arrived with her goon squad of young killers, it took everything in Jamir not to blurt out his findings. He had always suspected Ced of treachery, and that evening proved just how right he was.

"Where's Donte?" asked Jamir, referring to Killa Don, the second-in-command next to Dejah.

"He's doing his part."

"Look," Jamir humbly dug into his front pocket and revealed his discovery to her.

Taking possession of the evidence that found Ced guilty of betrayal and manipulation, Dejah, flanked by eight of her men, frowned menacingly. "I figured that muthafucker was up to no good," she said.

"Me too," said Jamir.

Several others voiced their opinions.

Without further ado, Dejah made her way toward the entrance door of the bar. Jamir took off after her, like a loyal puppy, and they all entered.

Upon their entrance, all eyes were on them. They stepped through the door like a pack of wolves on the hunt for their prey. In the back of the room, Ced turned a glance over his shoulder and gaped in shock. He bolted to his feet, as if he was contemplating fleeing.

"Sit your bitch ass down, nigga." Dejah approached the table, pulled out a chair, and sat her thick ass down. Across the table from her sat Marlon, whose placid expression seemed to irk her with every growing second.

The rest of the team circled around the table and took position around the bar. One of them, Youngin, ordered Ced to sit down, and he complied. Jamir took up his position, standing next to Dejah, and stared daggers in Marlon's direction.

Marlon did not appear worried one bit.

He seemed intrigued.

"Okay. Lemme take a good guess," Dejah said before placing the FBI's shield upon the table before them. Ced looked at the gold badge and slunk down in his chair. "You survived the bullet to your head and went under federal custody. They placed you into protection management and gave you a new identity, in exchange for you providing them with critical information for compensation of them saving your life. Then as time passed throughout the years, you learned to trust this nigga over here," she glared in Ced's direction and he looked as though he was about to be sick. "Somehow you managed to convince him to connect with Monica in order to watch over Hev and give her what you couldn't. Playin' games like that could get someone hurt, Marlon, and now maybe this creepy muthafucker gets killed in the process."

"And you're absolutely right, Dej. I took that chance, even if it brought just a little happiness and comfort to her life. He was just doing his job," said Marlon.

"At the risk of his cover being blown and possibly gettin' his ass murdered for being stupid?"

"Tell me what's going on out there," he said.

"And yet you're still playin' a dangerous game." Dejah wanted to blow Marlon's brains out right then and there.

"Is my family safe, Dej?" he asked.

"You don't have no family, nigga." She had to catch herself from spazzing out on him. Then suddenly, she told Ced to rise up and leave her sight. Booby, one of her goons, who was vicious but deaf, snatched the man up by his shirt collar, and together, he and two other hooliganz escorted him towards the exit door.

"He's a good man, Dejah. Don't kill him."

"I don't give a fuck," she replied.

Jamir remained where he stood and watched as Dejah and Marlon glared at each other.

"Where is Lyonell?" demanded Dejah.

The question astonished him. "I don't know where he's at," said Marlon.

"Okay. Where can I find him?"

He shrugged. "Don't know,"

Dejah frowned. "You bullshittin' me, right? I'm serious. Hev could be in danger right now, Marlon. Ly is here and he's up to something. After all that's happened all those years ago, I very much doubt he's back for a fuckin' picnic," she said earnestly. Then her phone rang, sounding off the alarm.

That was when it happened, the first blow, one that shook the grounds beneath them as bodies began to drop all at once throughout the whole entire area.

Chapter 35

After years of planning and dreaming of this moment, Lyonell felt as though he had accomplished his mission way before he gave the order to attack.

There were twenty-three of his men, certified killers, all of whom Lyonell had positioned throughout the surrounding areas of Gadsden county. Each one of his men was ordered to pick a man from Killa Don's Gutta Boyz Movement (GBM) crew and stick with them, but discreetly. For the past several hours, the BGM crew members were being followed, watched, and stalked without any of them being the wiser.

One call was all it took to do certain things of this nature, but this massacre was prompted by a set time. The instant their time read 8:30 p.m., them killers sprang into action and made the world stand still for that moment.

The element of surprise, total chaos.

Within a brief moment, twenty-three of the GBM crew members died in various ways. The additional casualties affiliated with them just made the vengeance taste even more delightful. Some were gunned down in traffic, others within a local gas station and outside the store. Three of them occupying a trap house, one parking his car in the driveway, more hanging out inside a nearby diner, awaiting their food to go. It was as though the Grim Reaper had come and saw to it that they all died at once.

Even Killa Don himself, along with Big Duke and Fangz, all three of them were murdered by three bitches, whom they hadn't a clue were thoroughbred killers. They were just leaving the building of Doc's Bar when the three females approached them in the parking lot. Right there, with two knives and one gun, Killa Don and his men died before they even realized what was going on.

You could smell the death in the air all throughout the old black town, the stench of revenge, pure savagery.

"What's the status?" asked Lyonell. Next to him, behind the wheel of the dark sedan, was Fat Boy. This was one of the original crew members that Lyonell had run off with five years ago.

Fat Boy gazed down at the Samsung communicator in his hand. Behind them sat CJ, another one of the originals, while the other three commanded the kill teams that were out there in the field.

"As of right now, there's a total of thirty-one of them clown ass niggaz dead. Thirty-one outta the confirmed forty is damn good, homeboy," said Fat Boy.

"Damn," was all Lyonell could say. He had been confident that his team could pull it off without risking being compromised, but hearing the outcome was overwhelming. In a matter of sixty seconds, thirty-one niggaz paid the price of death for Killa Don's actions.

By this time, the rest of Dejah's team was in a panic, and soon to be raising pure hell.

After careful planning, Lyonell had been studying Killa Don's pattern and his daily routines, and appointed GBM members to know where and who to target. He knew who was who, and that the HCG members were a whole different team. Lyonell understood their positions, he knew who to touch, leaving all the youngsters alone to focus on Killa Don.

Though they weren't exempt from his malicious kill game, they were safe as long as they stayed the fuck in their place.

"That many murders at one time in this small town will definitely bring the Feds in," said CJ, whose cousin Mane Mane had died tonight by his own men's hands.

"All the reason to load up and head back to the A," said Fat Boy.

"Not just yet," Lyonell replied.

"What's next?"

"Send the rest, but we will stay." Lyonell wanted to visit somebody before they took off. Plus, he knew the rest of his closest homies wanted to see their loved ones, even if it was just for a moment.

CJ sent the word out to gather up the troops and send them back to Atlanta.

Fifteen minutes later, their vehicle pulled up outside a Circle Drive residence with an old '71 Chevy truck parked out front. Of all the places Lyonell could have chosen to visit during this crucial hour, it was this one, the home of his beloved brother, Aaron. Aaron wasn't like him, he was one of the decent men left.

"Y'all know what to do," said Lyonell to his men. Then he got out and made his way to the door.

Both Fat Boy and CJ got out of the car to stand guard outside the house. Anything suspicious while Lyonell was visiting his loved one, they knew to shoot first and ask questions later, when the smoke cleared.

Lyonell took a deep breath and knocked on the front door. This was his older brother. Aaron would be fifty-five this coming August, still fairly young enough to enjoy life. Over the course of the past five years, Lyonell had managed to send his brother money and make sure all was well with him, without giving up his whereabouts. He knew Aaron was receiving the money because he'd used some to fix up his fishing boat, restore their father's old Chevy truck, and even managed to rebuild the old work shed behind the house. Lyonell checked on his big brother from time to time, just not within the past several months.

That time was spent on plotting his revenge to take the GBM down.

After knocking a second time, the voice of Aaron Copeland spoke from the other side of the door.

"Who is it?" he asked.

"It's me, Bernard," said Lyonell. Bernard was his brother's middle name and not many people besides Lyonell, their dead mother, Gina, and Uncle Jacob called him that. Almost immediately, the door swung open and there stood Aaron, with an astounded look on his face.

"Lyonell."

"Hey, brotha."

"Get in here, quick. You know how Ms. Tami likes to be all nosey and stuff," said Aaron. With a quick glance over at the house next door, Lyonell smirked and stepped over the threshold into the house. For a long second the two brothers looked at one another, then Aaron pulled him into his arms for a long overdue brotherly hug.

"I can't stay long. I just stopped by to check up on you, big brotha," said Lyonell.

"Check this out." Aaron beckoned him to follow as he led the way through the house. Lyonell followed, noticing its tidiness and cleanliness. This was their childhood home that Aaron decided to keep after the death of their parents. After being gone so long, Lyonell felt a sense of familiarity as he moved through the house.

Aaron led the way to the backdoor. He switched on the porch light and opened the door. Instantly, a big black Rottweiler lifted its large head and stood up at attention, when they stepped out onto the back porch. The big dog was secured with a long thick steel chain to a heavy stake in the cemented ground beneath its living area.

"He looks just like-"

"Cano," Aaron cut in and said. "Damn sure does, brah."

"I got him about a year ago. I was missing you, brah. Then I saw him at the pound when I went wit' my old lady. The second I saw him, he reminded me of your old dog, Cano, when we was little. I named him Cano, too," said Aaron.

When Lyonell decided to approach the big dog, Cano growled and snarled viciously at him.

"He ain't friendly," said Aaron.

"Neither was Cano." Lyonell didn't go any farther.

"All the reason why I kept him. Having him here was the closest thang I can get to you, brah." In the distance, the sound of gunshots was heard in the night. Both brothers looked at one another and Aaron shook his head wearily. "When will it ever end?" he grumbled.

"It's a war going on out there," Lyonell exclaimed.

"I know," said Aaron. "Yours."

Chapter 36

Kahlil was panting and on the verge of panic as he floored the Pontiac Grand Prix up Stewart Street headed back toward the Old Projects. He glanced over at his right, where Tank sat slumped in the passenger seat. He was dead as a doorknob. His brains blown out and splattered all over Kahlil. Why he, himself, wasn't dead, too, Kahlil didn't know, but he knew what was about to happen next.

As he drove Kahlil's cell phone was blowing the fuck up. He spotted several of his hooligans' numbers calling his phone in a matter of seconds. That's how he knew something was up and his people were in trouble.

Lyonell. Kahlil figured it had to be him somehow. It was only just a matter of time that he struck the first blow. He were Tank were in traffic at a stoplight when it happened. One second, Tank was telling him about some bad, thick snow bunny that he bagged after the club not too long ago. The next moment, a nigga snuck up on him outside the passenger door and dumped a half dozen slugs into the car. The third bullet is what did him in, pushing his top back like a convertible. Without hesitation, Kahlil punched the gas pedal and got missing. Confusion overwhelmed him when he realized no one was chasing after him to finish him off.

When he made it to the Old Projects, a minute later, Kahlil swung the car to a halt outside a low-rise apartment building. Kahlil jumped out, pulled off his ruined shirt, and wiped his bloody face with it.

"These muthafuckaz done fucked up," said Kahlil as he reached for his cell phone.

Three minutes later, a group of hooliganz came running toward Kahlil as he paced back and forth behind the Grand Prix. He was now clutching his .45 Caliber and on the phone with Jeremy, who was Tank's young cousin, and one more nigga whose wrath was surely about to unleash.

"What the fuck is going on right now?" Kahlil demanded to know. Also roaming the premises were some of the Old Projects' own gangsters and dope heads and family alike.

"We just heard what's going down."

"Heard what?" Kahlil snapped.

It was HCG Lil Monsta, whom Kahlil directed his attention on when the four of them arrived.

Lil Monsta said, "There's been an attack on all 'em GBM niggaz just now. Killa Don's dead, Big Duke, Fangz, Bush Boy, Amp, all of 'em."

"They whole muthafuckin' crew gone," said young Rocko.

"What?" Kahlil blurted out.

"It's true," Jeremy interjected from the other side of the phone. "Word is they all got hit at the same time. Like, the whole team dead except for a few of 'em."

"What about Dej?"

"She good. I just spoke with her," confirmed Jeremy.

"There's a whole bunch of them niggaz lurkin' out there if they took out the whole GBM just like that," stressed one of the others, Yella Tim.

With the shake of his head, Kahlil told his crew about Tank and where they stood at that moment. When Jeremy and two more of their HCG members finally arrived on the scene, minutes later, shit got real. One look at his cousin's dead body slumped in the passenger seat was all it took to bring that demon out of Jeremy.

"Nobody know who these niggaz is other than them being Ly's people?" said Kahlil.

Jeremy, who was holding back his tears said, "All we know is them niggaz came from up there in Georgia somewhere. But Delani and 'em are up there now lookin' into thangs." At the mention of his main man, Kahlil knew that Delani would not rest until he'd saw all them dead.

"Fuck it! What family do that nigga Ly still got livin' around here?" Yella Tim was ready to put in work.

Neither one of them had a clue.

"I know who would know," said Jeremy. He gave the orders to two of his men to take care of Tank's body and make sure the car was disposed of. Then he called his Uncle Tommy to get the 411 on Lyonell's possible remaining relatives. Meanwhile, Kahlil called Shamar to check up on him and the others.

"You won't believe who I'm lookin' at right now?" said Shamar.

"Who?"

"That nigga Spanky."

Kahlil felt his heart skip a beat. Spanky was one of Ly's men.

"Where you at?" he demanded icily.

"Parked right outside your mama's house," he said.

Chapter 37

When the gunshot rang out outside the bar, everybody who knew better ducked instinctively. So many things happened at once in that instant. Several of the hooliganz bolted for the door with their guns drawn. Marlon shoved Jamir aside to shield Dejah from any possible harm. More gunshots rang out in the night, causing all the patrons to react in a panic. Jamir drew his gun and glared up at Marlon menacingly.

"I got her, Jay. Go secure the area," said Marlon.

Jamir gave him a dark look. "You got two seconds to get the fuck away from her," he replied.

Marlon hesitated.

"One," Jamir upped the gun and aimed it at Marlon's head as his finger caressed its trigger.

That's when Dejah stepped from behind Marlon and took Jamir politely by the arm. She reassured him that she was okay, that her worries were only in regards to what's going on outside.

"Ruger, Jock, Tay." Jamir regarded the three remaining hooliganz standing in his proximity. "Get him the fuck outta here. If he bucks, I want you to shoot him." He then watched as the three hooliganz snatched Marlon up and forced him towards the exit of the bar, just as Ced had been done minutes ago.

Next, Jamir took Dejah by the hand and escorted her towards the exit behind the others.

Outside, Ced was laid out on the ground with a bullet in his chest. By the looks of his still body, there was no mistaking his demise. Several feet away from him lay another body that was not one of the hooliganz. He appeared to be an older nigga, another goon, having died still clutching his weapon.

It was then that Booby hurried up to them the moment they stepped through the door.

"It was an ambush. One of the two men shot Ced and the other one ran. Mojo and Youngin gone after him right now." Dejah interpreted from the sign language communication Booby was delivering hastily.

"Thank you, Booby. Now get me away from here," she replied.

Booby nodded and ran for the car, which Dejah and Jamir climbed into together.

One after the other, the HCG members got into their cars and sped away from the scene, with Marlon taking that gangster ride and probably wondering if he would live to see tomorrow after all this.

After sliding into traffic with Dejah riding along next to him, Jamir leaned over and inquired about the phone call she had received back in the bar.

Dejah turned a gaze over at him, but only saw his shadowy outline. She was just reminded that the phone she'd been clutching all along was the starting point of the hell that was coming. It was then that a wave of emotion washed over her as she leaned over and laid her head upon his shoulder.

"You a'ight?" Jamir shifted next to her.

"That was Ida Mae from up on the block." Dejah leaned harder against him.

"What did she say?" Ida Mae was a well-known hooker, who worked the block area, picking up johns and running errands for the crew when needed.

"Donte is dead," said Dejah. "Him, Fangz, and Big Duke. Ida Mae said some bitches took them out right there up on the block."

"Some bitches?" he blurted out.

"The only bitches I know crazy enough to do that shit is already dead and gone. And me," she replied. "But you saw where I was." Right then Dejah's phone sounded off in her hand and she just let it ring several times before answering it. She sat upright in her seat and checked the caller I.D. to see who was calling. "What's up, Youngin?" she asked.

"We caught that rabbit," he said breathlessly. Youngin was referring to the second gunman that had taken off after shooting Ced earlier.

"Is Mojo okay?" He was one of her favorites.

"We good. He's one of Ly's men, that much we know already. We about to take him to the spot and see what we can get outta him right now."

"Which spot?"

"By the pit," he said.

Pepper Hill, thought Dejah. They were taking Ly's man back to the hood, where they were more comfortable. She wanted to witness the procession. She told Booby to take her to the hood.

Dejah spoke a few more words with Youngin and ended the call. The instant the call ended the phone sounded off again, and she answered it with a grudge.

Meanwhile, Jamir sent a text message to the others to inform them where they were headed.

"All of them?" Dejah said into the phone. "How the fuck? Where the fuck was you, Amp? You know what? Round everybody up and…"

Jamir laid a hand upon her arm squeezed it reassuringly. "Calm down," he said humbly.

Surprisingly, Dejah took a deep breath and exhaled, then she gave the order she so desired. After disconnecting with

Amp, who was one of Killa Don's goons, Dejah growled and slammed the phone down.

Beside him, Jamir heard the unmistakable sound of his queen sobbing into her hands. This was the first time he ever heard her cry. Knowing Dejah like he did, to make her cry, something very serious had to happen.

Somebody else was about to die.

All Jamir could do was gather her up into his arms and hold her closely.

"Whateva it is, I'm right here," said Jamir. But he had a feeling where her pain was coming from. It had something to do with Killa Don dying. It was a loss that Jamir knew his queen would take very hard, which meant more blood, more death, and Jamir was willing to do whatever it took to ease her pain.

By the time they made it to their intended destination, without further incident, Jamir jumped out the car with a whole new attitude. With his gun in hand, Jamir entered the old bando house where Youngin held the back door open for them to enter. This was one of the few old homes that not many people knew had a basement still. Down the steps Jamir went as he already knew where he was about to find his man.

"We just got here just before y'all," said Mojo the moment he saw Jamir descend the basement steps. "We haven't even started on the nigga yet."

"It doesn't even matter," said Jamir. He then walked right up to the bloody and battered goon as he laid upon the dusty floor of the basement unconscious. Jamir slapped him a few times to wake him up. When he finally came to and gazed frighteningly up at Jamir, Jamir shot him in the leg and made his demands.

By this time, Dejah had found her way down to the basement, where Booby brought forth a metal folding chair for her to sit and watch Jamir do his own thing.

Her baby.

And boy what a bloody sight it was.

For the next twenty minutes, Dejah watched, without interruption, as Jamir tortured the goon, with the help of Youngin. By the time the goon, whose real name was Simon Sullivan, was begging to die to escape the pain, she had learned all that she cared to know. The goon had spilled everything he knew. It was said pressure bust pipes, and tonight proved how true that was. When Jamir was done with Simon, aka Turbo, he gave the nod to Youngin to finish him off. Youngin was glad to do it, and he put a bullet through his forehead, scattering blood and brain matter all over the floor.

"So what do you think?" said Jamir, once he and Dejah finally made it back outside.

"About which part?" she asked.

"Any of it."

She shrugged. "He didn't tell us somethin' that I didn't already know, Jay, except for two thangs," Dejah told him quietly.

"What?"

"First off, that shit about him having a son. I need you to get on the phone wit' Dee immediately and give him the heads up," Dejah beckoned him to follow her to the car, where Booby and several other hooliganz stood guard. "The other is Ly's godmother, Heather, is over in Cairo, Georgia in a spot called The Hot Bed. If what Turbo said is true about her, then we need to send a team out there like yesterday."

"Say less," Jamir told her and retrieved his phone.

"And Jay?"

He glanced over at her.

Dejah said, "Where the fuck is Marlon?"

Moments later, she was led to the trunk of one of the cars parked out back, behind the bando. When the trunk opened, Marlon stared up at her, and to her own amazement, he climbed up out of the trunk. She allowed him to stand before her, as five of her hooliganz surrounding him.

"Give me one good reason why I shouldn't kill your ass right here, right now," said Dejah.

"One reason is all I have," Marlon answered.

She didn't even blink.

"Because you still love me," he spoke up. "And you know killin' me won't stop you from loving me. And just so that you know, I never told on no man. I'm not a rat. I'm still the same nigga, Dee. I respect you-" Marlon froze when suddenly Dejah materialized with her pistol and placed it directly against his left temple.

"None of that shit don't matter, Marlon."

"Then do as you should," he said.

"My pleasure," Dejah pulled the trigger and killed the man she still loved right where he stood. In her heart of hearts, she didn't want to do it, but to allow him to live would only complicate things further. The last thing she wanted was to go back on her word. She said and vowed to kill Marlon Jones when she got in position, and by all means, she did what she should have done years ago.

Chapter 38

Shamar was parked outside Kahlil's mama's house after hooking up with Vermani, who joined him, Rikah, and Spud on the scene. They were in the midst of politicking on some real shit, while sitting in Rikah's black Audi SUV, when Spanky pulled up in a burgundy sedan. The car parked two houses down from where Kahlil grew up at.

When it was confirmed that it was Spanky that went inside the house, it was then that Shamar decided to call Kahlil. Not only was Spanky his cousin, but Spanky was one of Lyonell's goons, one of the ones that skipped town with him years ago. Also, Spanky was the cause of Kahlil being locked up from the beginning, when he was just a juvenile. He sent Kahlil on a dummy mission that led him to losing his freedom. Then he didn't take care of his Aunt Kim, who was Kahlil's mama, as Kahlil had asked him to do while he was gone.

So when Kahlil called Shamar's phone, when he was contemplating doing the same, Shamar knew right then that the powers that be were working in their favor.

Kahlil was definitely on his way.

Trouble was coming.

"So what? We wait?" Spud was itching to get some shit popping off. It was also confirmed that Lyonell had struck the first blow, and he wanted some get back.

The whole team did.

"There's somebody else in that car, too," Rikah pointed out, her Beretta .9mm sitting upon her lap.

Both Vermani and Shamar leaned forward to look at the car. It was then they decided that they should get the ups on them before Spanky made it back outside.

"It's a war going on, so Spanky won't be visiting long," said Vermani. "May as well press play right now, and slide up on them niggaz real smooth-like."

"I'm down wit' it," said Rikah.

"Me too," Spud nodded.

Shamar remained silent for a long moment as he dwelled on the possibility of utilizing this situation to get the answers they might need to get to Lyonell.

"What we gon' do?" Rikah replied impatiently.

Shamar was considered the leader of the pack right now, and it was the leader's obligation to see that the mission gets handled accordingly. So he thought up a quick plan of attack to catch the occupants of the burgundy sedan by surprise. Rikah would be used as the key player to get them what they wanted.

"Go," Vermani said, and Rikah exited the SUV and began walking up the sidewalk.

Moments later, Spud eased out of the truck and darted into the shadows across the street to the other side. This position would bring him up along the blindside behind the car. Rikah would no doubt get the attention she wanted, while Spud moved in for the kill.

"You don't have to do this if you don't want to, Vee. I know that's your family and all, but I don't want you feelin' no type of way about it," said Shamar.

"I'm good, Shamar. I got this." Vermani and Spanky were also cousins. His and Kahlil's mothers were siblings to Spanky's father. He was their big cousin, one who never really cared to share a life with his younger relatives. The only time when he did, Kahlil ended up getting jammed, and Spanky didn't even keep it real.

So Vermani had a right to allow it to go down, because he didn't like how he treated Kahlil.

"I hope it's done quietly, though."

Inside Ms. Kim's house was Vermani's mama and daddy, both of whom were too stubborn to leave their own home. Instead they chose to be there for Kim, who was in the process of battling stomach cancer, while the streets bled of vengeance.

Down the street was the house that belonged to Mildred Andrews, the wife of Spanky's late father, who passed away three years prior. And Spanky was about to have a cruel awakening.

Just as he knew she would, Rikah worked her magic and was now leaning down in the window on the passenger side of the car. With one hand behind her back, where she had her pistol tucked in the back of her jean shorts.

Shamar then watched as Spud crept towards the car from the shadows. He opened the driver door and slid inside the car like a silent fog. That was when Rikah came up with her Beretta and aimed it at the person she had been stealing the attention of. Within seconds, both her and Spud had two of Spanky's men lying face first on the ground.

"Let's get it," Vermani opened the door and got out of the truck, along with Shamar.

Together, Shamar and Vermani moved toward the front door of the house, where Spanky was visiting. From the short distance, Vermani watched as Spud repeatedly bashed his man in the back of the head with his pistol. Only then, when he stopped, it was evident that he'd beat him unconscious.

Rikah had her man silent and still.

A minute later, three vehicles turned onto the street up ahead and came roaring forward. Shamar cussed under his breath at the thought of Kahlil having just arrived with his team, only to interrupt their plan.

Right then, Spud sprang into action and waved the cars down. He rushed in and made them kill the lights, then

Kahlil jumped out with his crew, and Spud gave him the scoop on what was going on. When Kahlil looked in the direction of the house, he nodded and spoke to the rest of his men.

Seconds later, the front door opened and Spanky stepped outside. He paused instantly when he looked out in the street to see what awaited him.

Vermani was the first to move in on Spanky, then Shamar fell in step, and together, they restrained him and dragged him towards the street.

"The fuck is you niggaz doing?" Spanky tried to buck halfway there and Shamar damn near caved his face in with two solid blows with his pistol.

"What it do, cuz?" Kahlil stepped forward, flanked by five of his loyal goons.

When Spanky finally realized what he was faced with, he hurriedly started pleading his case, until Jeremy punched him in the nose, sending it gushing blood and snot all over himself.

"You'll get your opportunity to talk later," Kahlil replied with a wicked smirk on his face. Then he snapped his fingers and ordered his men to strip Spanky naked right there in the street. Then he told them to toss him in the trunk, take his ass to the spot, and wait for him.

"What about them other two niggaz?" asked Spud.

"Take them, too," he said. "Information is key, and we gonna milk all three of them for it. One way or the other we gonna get what we want."

"Say no more," said Rocko.

"And Vee," Kahlil turned his attention on his cousin and beckoned him to step aside with him. The two cousins separated themselves from the others and Kahlil rested a hand upon Vermani's shoulder. "I thought we had an agreement, Vee?"

"I didn't ask for this shit, cuz."

229

"You wasn't supposed to be out here in the trenches at all, Vee. I know you wanna get down wit' the team but you must obey the orders given."

Vermani just shrugged.

"You did good, cuz. Real shit. But your job right now is to look after the fam and get that degree. We got this out here. A'ight?"

Reluctantly, Vermani nodded and said, "I gotcha, Kahlil. Understood. But you know I only play the cards that's dealt."

"You'll know if we really need you," said Kahlil.

Vermani didn't even respond, he just turned around and made his way back to his Aunt Kim's house. Kahlil watched him go, fighting the urge to follow him inside to check up on his mama. But he didn't need that right now, so he turned back toward his team.

Kahlil hopped in the SUV with Rikah and Shamar, and to stick close to his superior, Lil Monsta, got in the back, along with him. The rest of the crew was headed out to the spot, where they were about to unite with more of their team members who were still in the process of handling Turbo's body.

Back on the road again, Kahlil filled them in on what all he knew about the attack on the GBM clique.

"We just lost thirty-two of our niggaz tonight. Why Ly didn't target anybody in the HCG crew, I don't know. But what I do know is that that muthafucker came here wit' an army, and by any means necessary, we gotta do our part and do it right." he said.

Shamar didn't even reply to that.

"Thirty-two people at one time?" Rikah said.

When Kahlil started naming names of the ones that were left of GBM clique, the truck got quiet as they knew what a loss like that would bring.

"Lyonell targeted Killa Don and his crew because they were the original ones that were responsible for forcing his hand to begin with," said Shamar.

"We only existed after the fact."

"Correct."

"So what now? You don't think they'll try to hit us next?" asked Rikah.

"If they really wanted us, they coulda been got us, just like they did wit' the others," Shamar said. "Now we gotta use that leverage against them. We got three of their own, who can tell us what we need to know to hit them back where it hurts."

Lil Monsta sparked up the Backwoods blunt he had pre-rolled, but kept in the clutch for the perfect occasion. This was that occasion and he needed to get his head right after all he'd just learned. To hear that the GBM clique was no more was a very sobering experience.

"And that's not all," said Kahlil.

"What else is new?"

"Marlon," said Kahlil. "He's back from the dead. And Jay was the one that found him."

If only they knew…

Chapter 39

The crew had just made the drive to Summer Hill, Atlanta when Delani got the call from Jamir. He listened without much response, and shifted uneasily in his seat. Due to the low tune of Mook Boy playing in the background throughout the SUV, no one heard the deep menacing growl that escaped Delani's mouth. It was all the indication needed to know that he was in that dark place, where the only thing that mattered was murder.

Up ahead in the car before them was Lil Cam, Bizzy, and White Boy Ty. They were leading the way to where they would find Zeek, once and for all. Lil Cam said the young nigga was making a lot of noise in the city. The HCG crew was about to see just how much noise they could make together.

Vengeance melodies, a sad song.

When Delani was done with his phone call with Jamir, he disconnected the call and stared out his side window.

"What's going on?" asked Wank Wank.

Delani told them what was told to him. Skinny, who was behind the wheel, damn near veered off the road in sudden astonishment.

"We being played by this clown up there," said Skinny in that serious tone of his.

"I'm hittin' Ty up right now about this nigga." Wank Wank pulled out his cell phone to contact his brother in the car up ahead. Delani turned in his seat and put a hand on his arm to stop him.

"Not right now, Wank."

"Not right now?"

It was just confirmed that Lyonell indeed had a son, but he wasn't Zeek. Whoever this Zeek person Lil Cam had them on the hunt for was not Lyonell's biological child, and maybe didn't even know who Zeek was. Because from what Jamir provided, Lyonell had a three-year-old son by the name of Adonis, who lived over in Etheridge, on a quiet street, next to Fulton County police station. If Delani believed what Jamir said to be accurate, then Lil Cam was sending them on a mission for his own personal benefit.

Why was Lil Cam playing them for fools? Wondered Delani as he dwelled on the situation.

That's when it was decided that they would follow through with the mission. Delani was about to use this situation to get to the bottom line of Lil Cam's real reason for doing this.

Minutes later, they reached the area of Summer Hill, which Lil Cam claimed was Zeek's headquarters. It was said that Zeek was a vicious gangster, and even at the age of twenty-one, he was considered a hood legend. He lived in a nice four-bedroom house with his wifey and infant daughter. From what he'd gathered from Zeek's social media page, he owned a silver Lexus truck and a candy apple red Dodge Challenger. His crew consisted of three other niggas, Elmo, Ralo and Mecca, all of whom Zeek trusted like brothers and were getting to the money bag.

The house that Lil Cam led them to, no doubt, sported a silver Lexus truck and a red Challenger in the gravel driveway, along with a black BMW. Apparently Zeek was home with his family. And if he wasn't, he would wish that he had been.

They drove past the house and White Boy Ty hit Delani up on the phone to see how they should go about handling the situation.

Delani told him the truth.

"What?" White Boy Ty said with surprise, but Delani warned him not to blow their cover just yet.

"I got a plan," Delani voiced and then ran down the plan he knew would work, if they would just work together, without having to do Lil Cam in, as they should.

Skinny wanted to murder Lil Cam himself.

"The usual routine," said Delani, "two through the front and two through the back. White Boy Ty and Lil Cam will stand guard outside. Everybody got their vests on, and everybody strapped. Try to avoid killin' this nigga or his family because we're gonna use him once this shit is all over." He spoke with authority.

"Use him how?" asked Skinny.

"You'll see," said Delani in response.

Five minutes later, they kicked in the front and back doors of the house and went in like a team of army mercenaries. Unfortunately for Zeek, he was caught lacking in the bathroom, taking a shit and smoking on a blunt laced with Molly. When he looked up and saw two young killers in the doorway, the truth shone in his eyes that he was doomed.

"Consider this moment your lucky night, Zeek," said Bizzy, his AR-15 locked and loaded.

Zeek was too stunned to speak.

That's when Delani stepped forward inside the bathroom and crinkled his nose in disgust at the stench. He reached over and flushed the toilet, and then he stepped back against the far wall of the bathroom.

"What or who is Lil Cam to you?"

"Lil Cam?" Zeek said. When Delani described who Lil Cam was and where he came from, Zeek finally registered who he was talking about.

"Cameron. Lil Cam. I know exactly who he is. That bitch ass nigga was my stepbrotha. My old boy killed his mama not too long ago. They were both crackheads and she ran into my old boy wit' some bad dope. We been beefin' ever since that shit went down."

Both Bizzy and Delani looked at each other.

"So Lil Cam sent y'all?"

Delani nodded.

"Pussy muthafucka," snarled Zeek. "The coward couldn't come face me himself and paid you niggaz to come flip me? I'll do you one better," he said. "Whateva he paid you, I'll triple that shit. Easy."

"I got a better deal," Delani exclaimed. Then he told Zeek why they were there in Atlanta, without having to name names, and what they expected from this situation. Zeek shared their sentiments, and together, they reached a mutual agreement and shook on it.

Later, when Lil Cam looked up and watched as Zeek exited through the front door of the house, he didn't expect to see him wearing a cocky grin.

"Bizzy." Delani snapped his fingers. "Ty."

At once, Bizzy and White Boy Ty rushed Lil Cam hard and fast, before he could react. The pistol was wrenched from his hand as he was thrown to the ground. Lil Cam struggled against them, demanding to know what was going on and why.

"You know exactly what's going on, nigga," Skinny said to Lil Cam, before kicking his teeth in.

"Good thang my baby mama is over at her sista's house t'night," said Zeek. Then he pounced on Lil Cam with cruel intent and begin pounding him brutally with his fists. The HCG crew stood around watching as Zeek took a seat upon Lil Cam's chest and was beating his face to a bloody mess.

"You know Koenisha knew about this shit, too," Wank Wank moved over next to Delani and said.

"She'll get hers next."

"And that bitch that's wit' her," added Skinny.

They all agreed.

After Zeek beat Lil Cam to sleep, and broke his hand in the process, he took up the gun Bizzy gave him and filled Lil Cam's chest with hot lead.

From there, they went back to Koenisha's house and killed her and Shaunta together. By this time, the HCG crew had met Elmo, Mecca, and Ralo. They met up with them on the scene, after Zeek had called them up and gave them the scoop on what was happening. When they arrived on the scene, both Ralo and Mecca were exiting the house next door, where they left the bodies of Gunz and his crew stretched out in the house.

"So y'all after that nigga Lion, huh?" said Ralo. He was a short nigga with a bushy beard, slender built but very deadly and loyal to his crew.

After the mission on Glenwood Drive, they all relocated to another one of Zeek's spots, where he was getting his broken hand tended to by one of his side bitches, who worked as a nurse over at Wellstar Douglas Hospital.

"That's the mission," said Delani. "Yeah, why?"

"Good," said Ralo. "I've been itchin' to pop one of them niggaz melon anyway."

"Then t'night's your night, too, my nigga. Because we ain't leaving till we get our man," said White Boy Ty, hyped from the bloodshed and the promise of murder again.

"No exceptions," said Delani.

Bizzy nodded. "No exceptions at all."

Chapter 40

If there was one thing Dejah was sure of, it was the love and loyalty that Redd had for her. But after finding out that Redd had gone against her word, Dejah was definitely going to be upset with her. But to Redd, her reason for doing it was out of that warrior nature of hers, especially where Dejah's well-being was concerned. It had always been her duty, since committing to Dejah, to do her part accordingly.

And that part is what led her to the Circle Drive neighborhood. She had to put herself in Lyonell's shoes to put herself in the position she was at that moment. After learning about the massive attacks on the GBM clique that had now generated the attention of every law enforcement agency throughout two surrounding counties, she had to make her move. Redd knew Dejah and her team would be distracted by the heavy blow that was delivered against them, just like she knew Lyonell would use that very same distraction to his advantage.

Redd was already lying in wait when Lyonell finally made his way to his brother's house. Lyonell couldn't fight the urge to stop by, even if it was just for a minute, to check up on his only sibling. This Redd knew and decided to beat him to the punch.

Hidden in the shadows alongside the house next door, Redd watched as Lyonell arrived and went inside the house. To see that she now had the power to end the war made her pussy wet. To know that this act of stealth and loyalty would satisfy Dejah gave her cold heart warmth. And from the shadows, she watch Fat Boy and CJ stand guard outside the house. They had no clue of the threat that was about to swoop in on them.

Redd slipped out her blade and palmed it. Then she stepped from the shadows out into the open, like she belonged there. She played the role of a dope-head looking for some drugs. But that was only to get up on them and slit their throats. Redd killed them both right where they stood, quietly and swiftly, but also messy, due to their arteries spraying blood every which way, and even onto her. She left them both laid out on the ground dead.

When Redd was moving in on the front door of the house, the first car turned onto the street, then another and another. Suddenly, a dozen vehicles came charging toward the house. Dejah and her youngins. Redd had phoned Dejah the instant Lyonell had pulled up on the scene. Now here they were in full force, with Dejah leading the way and her whole crew behind her.

Looking from the house back to the approaching cars, Redd was anxious for some more action.

Suddenly, the front door opened and there stood Lyonell in the doorway. Due to the darkness of the night, one could see the shocked expression written on his face. Redd turned to look at him, and Lyonell stepped back inside and shut the door behind him.

Jamir was the first to jump out of one of the cars, as Redd informed him that Lyonell was inside. Jamir, along with LJ and Jeremy, barked out orders to the rest of the hooliganz. At once, at least ten of them circled the house, making it hard for Lyonell to escape. There was no way Lyonell was leaving that house alive.

At the sight of Dejah approaching her amidst her team, Redd shifted on her feet, awaiting the interaction that was about to take place. But instead of chastising Redd for going against her word, Dejah hooked an arm around her waist and kissed her passionately.

"I'm ready when you are," Kahlil responded excitedly, as he watched the two women for a moment.

Stepping away from her woman, Dejah turned towards the house and drew her pistol. "Light that muthafucker up." She ordered.

"Shoot," commanded Kahlil.

There was at least thirty hooliganz present outside the house with probably every caliber of gun. Upon command, they aimed and let loose on the house. The sound of multiple guns exploding at once was unbelievable, and the whole area lit up in harmony as fire burst from some of the cannons.

When Dejah gave the signal, all gunfire gradually ceased and an eerie silence filled the air for a second. Then came sounds from inside and outside of the house, cracking and breaking noises as it caved in on itself.

You could smell the death of gunpowder in the air as they all stood outside the house.

"Go," said Dejah.

Four hooliganz forced themselves through the front door into the house. Two more followed suit moments afterwards, going in to check and assess to the damage.

A minute later, Dejah was beckoned forward and led into the house by two of her youngins. Redd and Kahlil were right on her heels.

"He's in here," said one of the hooliganz, Juvy, still toting his Draco in his hands.

In passing, they saw the body of Aaron slumped in the hallway. It appeared as though he had been stopped in the process of running for the back door, but never made it. Blood was spread all around his body from being shot multiple times. But it was in the den area where Dejah found Lyonell, still clinging on to life after taking at least ten bullets to his person. He had been headed for the side patio sliding glass door before he realized it was a trap.

Lyonell was determined to live and was still slowly crawling towards the patio door.

"Turn that nigga over," said Dejah.

When Lyonell was forced over onto his back, they saw he had been shot in the face as well. The nigga was hard to kill, but that status had finally reached its end.

In the distance, police sirens blared in the night. But Dejah didn't care one bit, and her focus was solely on the dying gangster at her feet.

"I want you to look into my eyes before you die," said Dejah. She stood over him and squatted down near his face, up close and personal.

"No," Lyonell struggled.

"Yes, Lyonell," she said. "Game over." She pressed the gun directly upon his forehead, took a deep breath, held his gaze for a second, and squeezed the trigger. Then she rose up to her feet and turned to her youngins. "Burn this muthafucker down to the ground."

Back on the road, minutes later, with Redd sharing the backseat with her, Dejah laid her head on her lap and sighed deeply.

"What's wrong?" asked Redd, stroking her hair ever so gently and holding her close.

Dejah didn't say a word, she just cried.

It was over.

EPILOGUE

Two months later.

It was like old times. Jamir, Shamar, Heaven, Vermani were Delani were all sitting around the living room with glasses of champagne in their hands. Today was a good day for them all, a day of peace and harmony. Today was MoMo's birthday, and everybody in the hood was celebrating the death and life of her legacy. She was being remembered as, not only a dope fiend, but a mother, sister, and friend as well. There were t-shirts worn with her face and inscriptions on it, free dope for all the addicts, a big barbecue grill and a food truck on standby. Today was MoMo's Day, the celebration of the streets.

While sitting around the living room, smoking weed and drinking champagne, the crew reminisced about MoMo and told some memorable MoMo stories. Shamar was reminded, despite the conflicts he had with his mama, she gave him life and he was appreciative of that blessing.

Delani, having just not too long ago forgiven his crew for leaving him out of watching Lyonell die that fateful night, was even in tears himself. He and MoMo had had their differences, too, but he loved her as though she was his own mama.

They all loved her, especially Vermani, he was more like putty in her hands, as he'd always been her favorite of Shamar's friends. It was Vermani who met Shamar first, actually, but when Heaven came along, they became inseparable.

Like today, Shamar and Heaven leaned against each other like the truest of friends, taunting and teasing each other, just like siblings. Shamar couldn't be more grateful to have such a loyal crew as the one he was now in the company of. Even Jamir was turnt up for the cause, having now found the gist of being a young gangster. Since that one fateful night, two months ago, Jamir had not been himself. He was experiencing some dark space within, now quick to lash out or do great bodily harm for any little thing. He was a ticking time bomb that was bound to explode at any second. And Delani just loved his little brother, for they were becoming so much alike.

The Hooliganz had a big future ahead of them. Dejah promised to see to it that they did.

But all that changed when there was a knock at the front door and the twins' detective cousin, Angie Galloway, stepped inside. Upon her entry, there was a quiet but grave look on the woman's face. At the sight of her, the hooliganz knew something serious was up. Angie Galloway never just showed up, without having some type of official reason for being there.

Rising up from where he was sitting, in the leather recliner, across from the others, Delani was the first to speak up. "What's up, cuz?"

"Trouble as always," she answered.

"Trouble?" said Jamir.

She nodded gravely. "Big trouble indeed."

Both Vermani and Shamar exchanged a silent look of dismay between each other.

"No matter what happens from here, I just want y'all boys to know that I'll do my best to get down to the bottom of it. That's my word," she said. "I'll handle it."

"What're you talkin' about, Angie?" Heaven stood up next. Right then, there was a loud commotion going on outside, and all eyes swiveled towards the front door and windows.

Shamar bolted to his feet at once, then Delani rushed over to the window to peer outside.

"What's going on?" asked Heaven.

That very instant, the front door exploded open and a team of FBI field agents entered the house in tactical gear, with weapons drawn. The hooliganz were advanced upon, thrown to the floor, and cuffed, all except Heaven, who was so stunned she couldn't even move.

"I'll take care of it," Detective Angie Galloway said.

"Fuck you, bitch," Delani said. Then he hawked up cold and spat it in her face. He was shoved towards the front door and out of it first, leading the way as the others followed behind him.

The Hooliganz had finally come to an end.

Or had they not?

Heaven was the last one left, the remaining soldier, one whose loyalty to the crew was beyond measure. But how would she carry the weight of responsibility that had now befallen her?

Why her? When it was all said and done, Heaven knew it was her time to put on for her crew.

"Don't worry," she said to herself when reality finally hit that she was left all alone to fend for herself. "I know what to do," replied Heaven. Then she stepped up to the plate and went for what she knew.

Time to change the game. She had a plan.

With the whole team having fallen under one of the biggest federal indictment cases, Heaven was the only one left to pick up the pieces. Why the Feds didn't take her too, she had no clue, but what she did know was that she had the ability to do what needed to be done.

It was her turn.

Her chance to become Queen.

The last Hooligan.

Lock Down Publications and Ca$h Presents
Assisted Publishing Packages

BASIC PACKAGE	UPGRADED PACKAGE
$499	$800
Editing	Typing
Cover Design	Editing
Formatting	Cover Design
	Formatting
ADVANCE PACKAGE	**LDP SUPREME PACKAGE**
$1,200	$1,500
Typing	Typing
Editing	Editing
Cover Design	Cover Design
Formatting	Formatting
Copyright registration	Copyright registration
Proofreading	Proofreading
Upload book to Amazon	Set up Amazon account
	Upload book to Amazon
	Advertise on LDP, Amazon and Facebook Page

***Other services available upon request.
Additional charges may apply

Lock Down Publications
P.O. Box 944
Stockbridge, GA 30281-9998
Phone: 470 303-9761

Submission Guideline

Submit the first three chapters of your completed manuscript to ldpsubmissions@gmail.com. In the subject line add **Your Book's Title**. The manuscript must be in a Word Doc file and sent as an attachment. Document should be in Times New Roman, double spaced, and in size 12 font. Also, provide your synopsis and full contact information. If sending multiple submissions, they must each be in a separate email.

Have a story but no way to send it electronically? You can still submit to LDP/Ca$h Presents. Send in the first three chapters, written or typed, of your completed manuscript to:

LDP: Submissions Dept
P.O. Box 944
Stockbridge, GA 30281-9998

DO NOT send original manuscript. Must be a duplicate. Provide your synopsis and a cover letter containing your full contact information.

Thanks for considering LDP and Ca$h Presents.

NEW RELEASES

BLOODLINE OF A SAVAGE 1&2
THESE VICIOUS STREETS
RELENTLESS GOON
RELENTLESS GOON 2
BY PRINCE A. TAUHID

THE BUTTERFLY MAFIA 1-3
BY FUMIYA PAYNE

A THUG'S STREET PRINCESS 1&2
BY MEESHA

CITY OF SMOKE 2
BY MOLOTTI

STEPPERS 1,2&3
BY KING RIO

THE LANE 1&2
BY KEN-KEN SPENCE

THUG OF SPADES 1&2
LOVE IN THE TRENCHES 2
BY COREY ROBINSON

TIL DEATH 3
BY ARYANNA

THE BIRTH OF A GANGSTER 4
BY DELMONT PLAYER

PRODUCT OF THE STREETS 1&2
BY DEMOND "MONEY" ANDERSON

NO TIME FOR ERROR
BY KEESE

MONEY HUNGRY DEMONS
BY TRANAY ADAMS

Coming Soon from Lock Down Publications/Ca$h Presents

IF YOU CROSS ME ONCE 6
ANGEL V
By Anthony Fields

IMMA DIE BOUT MINE 4&5
By Aryanna

A THUGS STREET PRINCESS 3
By Meesha

PRODUCT OF THE STREETS 3
By Demond Money Anderson

CORNER BOYS
By Corey Robinson

SON OF A DOPE FIEND 4
By Renta

THE MURDER QUEENS 6&7
By Michael Gallon

CITY OF SMOKE 3
By Molotti

BETRAYAL OF A G
By Ray Vinci

CONFESSIONS OF A DOPE BOY
By Nicholas Lock

THA TAKEOVER
By Keith Chandler

Available Now

RESTRAINING ORDER 1 & 2
By **CA$H & Coffee**

LOVE KNOWS NO BOUNDARIES 1-3
By **Coffee**

RAISED AS A GOON I, II, III & IV
BRED BY THE SLUMS I, II, III
BLAST FOR ME I & II
ROTTEN TO THE CORE I II III
A BRONX TALE I, II, III
DUFFLE BAG CARTEL I II III IV V VI
HEARTLESS GOON I II III IV V
A SAVAGE DOPEBOY I II
DRUG LORDS I II III
CUTTHROAT MAFIA I II
KING OF THE TRENCHES
By **Ghost**

LAY IT DOWN I & II
LAST OF A DYING BREED I II
BLOOD STAINS OF A SHOTTA I & II III
By **Jamaica**

LOYAL TO THE GAME I II III
LIFE OF SIN I, II III
By **TJ & Jelissa**

IF LOVING HIM IS WRONG…I & II
LOVE ME EVEN WHEN IT HURTS I II III
By **Jelissa**

BLOODY COMMAS I & II
SKI MASK CARTEL I, II & III
KING OF NEW YORK I II, III IV V
RISE TO POWER I II III
COKE KINGS I II III IV V
BORN HEARTLESS I II III IV
KING OF THE TRAP I II
By **T.J. Edwards**

WHEN THE STREETS CLAP BACK I & II III
THE HEART OF A SAVAGE I II III IV
MONEY MAFIA I II
LOYAL TO THE SOIL I II III
By **Jibril Williams**

A DISTINGUISHED THUG STOLE MY HEART I II &
III
LOVE SHOULDN'T HURT I II III IV
RENEGADE BOYS 1-4
PAID IN KARMA 1-3
SAVAGE STORMS 1-3
AN UNFORESEEN LOVE 1-3
BABY, I'M WINTERTIME COLD 1-3
A THUG'S STREET PRINCESS 1&2
By **Meesha**

A GANGSTER'S CODE 1-3
A GANGSTER'S SYN 1-3
THE SAVAGE LIFE 1-3
CHAINED TO THE STREETS 1-3
BLOOD ON THE MONEY 1-3
A GANGSTA'S PAIN 1-3
BEAUTIFUL LIES AND UGLY TRUTHS
CHURCH IN THESE STREETS
By **J-Blunt**

PUSH IT TO THE LIMIT
By **Bre' Hayes**

BLOOD OF A BOSS 1-5
SHADOWS OF THE GAME
TRAP BASTARD
By **Askari**

THE STREETS BLEED MURDER 1-3
THE HEART OF A GANGSTA 1-3
By **Jerry Jackson**

CUM FOR ME 1-8
An LDP Erotica Collaboration

BRIDE OF A HUSTLA 1-3
THE FETTI GIRLS 1-3
CORRUPTED BY A GANGSTA 1-4
BLINDED BY HIS LOVE
THE PRICE YOU PAY FOR LOVE 1-3
DOPE GIRL MAGIC 1-3
By **Destiny Skai**

WHEN A GOOD GIRL GOES BAD
By **Adrienne**

A KINGPIN'S AMBITION
A KINGPIN'S AMBITION II
I MURDER FOR THE DOUGH
By **Ambitious**

THE COST OF LOYALTY 1-3
By **Kweli**

A GANGSTER'S REVENGE 1-4
THE BOSS MAN'S DAUGHTERS 1-5
A SAVAGE LOVE 1&2
BAE BELONGS TO ME 1&2
A HUSTLER'S DECEIT 1-3
WHAT BAD BITCHES DO 1-3
SOUL OF A MONSTER 1-3
KILL ZONE
A DOPE BOY'S QUEEN 1-3
TIL DEATH 1-3
IMMA DIE BOUT MINE 1-3
By **Aryanna**

TRUE SAVAGE 1-7
DOPE BOY MAGIC 1-3
MIDNIGHT CARTEL 1-3
CITY OF KINGZ 1&2
NIGHTMARE ON SILENT AVE
THE PLUG OF LIL MEXICO 1&2
CLASSIC CITY
By **Chris Green**

A DOPEBOY'S PRAYER
By **Eddie "Wolf" Lee**

THE KING CARTEL 1-3
By **Frank Gresham**

THESE NIGGAS AIN'T LOYAL 1-3
By **Nikki Tee**

GANGSTA SHYT 1-3
By **CATO**

THE ULTIMATE BETRAYAL
By **Phoenix**

BOSS'N UP 1-3
By **Royal Nicole**

I LOVE YOU TO DEATH
By **Destiny J**

I RIDE FOR MY HITTA
I STILL RIDE FOR MY HITTA
By **Misty Holt**

LOVE & CHASIN' PAPER
By **Qay Crockett**

TO DIE IN VAIN
SINS OF A HUSTLA
By **ASAD**

BROOKLYN HUSTLAZ
By **Boogsy Morina**

BROOKLYN ON LOCK 1 & 2
By **Sonovia**

GANGSTA CITY
By **Teddy Duke**

A DRUG KING AND HIS DIAMOND 1-3
A DOPEMAN'S RICHES
HER MAN, MINE'S TOO 1&2
CASH MONEY HO'S
THE WIFEY I USED TO BE 1&2
PRETTY GIRLS DO NASTY THINGS
By **Nicole Goosby**

LIPSTICK KILLAH 1-3
CRIME OF PASSION 1-3
FRIEND OR FOE 1-3
By **Mimi**

TRAPHOUSE KING 1-3
KINGPIN KILLAZ 1-3
STREET KINGS 1&2
PAID IN BLOOD 1&2
CARTEL KILLAZ 1-3
DOPE GODS 1&2
By **Hood Rich**

STEADY MOBBN' 1-3
THE STREETS STAINED MY SOUL 1-3
By **Marcellus Allen**

WHO SHOT YA 1-3
SON OF A DOPE FIEND 1-3
HEAVEN GOT A GHETTO 1&2
SKI MASK MONEY 1&2
By **Renta**

GORILLAZ IN THE BAY 1-4
TEARS OF A GANGSTA 1/&2
3X KRAZY 1&2
STRAIGHT BEAST MODE 1&2
By **DE'KARI**

TRIGGADALE 1-3
MURDA WAS THE CASE 1-3
By **Elijah R. Freeman**

THE STREETS ARE CALLING
By **Duquie Wilson**

LAND OF THE HOOLIGANZ | IRA B

SLAUGHTER GANG 1-3
RUTHLESS HEART 1-3
By **Willie Slaughter**

GOD BLESS THE TRAPPERS 1-3
THESE SCANDALOUS STREETS 1-3
FEAR MY GANGSTA 1-5
THESE STREETS DON'T LOVE NOBODY 1-2
BURY ME A G 1-5
A GANGSTA'S EMPIRE 1-4
THE DOPEMAN'S BODYGAURD 1&2
THE REALEST KILLAZ 1-3
THE LAST OF THE OGS 1-3
By **Tranay Adams**

MARRIED TO A BOSS 1-3
By **Destiny Skai & Chris Green**

KINGZ OF THE GAME 1-7
CRIME BOSS 1-3
By **Playa Ray**

FUK SHYT
By **Blakk Diamond**

DON'T F#CK WITH MY HEART 1&2
By **Linnea**

ADDICTED TO THE DRAMA 1-3
IN THE ARM OF HIS BOSS
By **Jamila**

LOYALTY AIN'T PROMISED 1&2
By **Keith Williams**

YAYO 1-4
A SHOOTER'S AMBITION 1&2
BRED IN THE GAME
By **S. Allen**

TRAP GOD 1-3
RICH $AVAGE 1-3
MONEY IN THE GRAVE 1-3
CARTEL MONEY
By **Martell Troublesome Bolden**

FOREVER GANGSTA 1&2
GLOCKS ON SATIN SHEETS 1&2
By **Adrian Dulan**

TOE TAGZ 1-4
LEVELS TO THIS SHYT 1&2
IT'S JUST ME AND YOU
By **Ah'Million**

KINGPIN DREAMS 1-3
RAN OFF ON DA PLUG
By **Paper Boi Rari**

CONFESSIONS OF A GANGSTA 1-4
CONFESSIONS OF A JACKBOY 1-3
CONFESSIONS OF A HITMAN
By **Nicholas Lock**

I'M NOTHING WITHOUT HIS LOVE
SINS OF A THUG
TO THE THUG I LOVED BEFORE
A GANGSTA SAVED XMAS
IN A HUSTLER I TRUST
By **Monet Dragun**

QUIET MONEY 1-3
THUG LIFE 1-3
EXTENDED CLIP 1&2
A GANGSTA'S PARADISE
By **Trai'Quan**

CAUGHT UP IN THE LIFE 1-3
THE STREETS NEVER LET GO 1-3
By **Robert Baptiste**

NEW TO THE GAME 1-3
MONEY, MURDER & MEMORIES 1-3
By **Malik D. Rice**

CREAM 2-3
THE STREETS WILL TALK
By **Yolanda Moore**

LIFE OF A SAVAGE 1-4
A GANGSTA'S QUR'AN 1-4
MURDA SEASON 1-3
GANGLAND CARTEL 1-3
CHI'RAQ GANGSTAS 1-4
KILLERS ON ELM STREET 1-3
JACK BOYZ N DA BRONX 1-3
A DOPEBOY'S DREAM 1-3
JACK BOYS VS DOPE BOYS 1-3
COKE GIRLZ
COKE BOYS
SOSA GANG 1&2
BRONX SAVAGES
BODYMORE KINGPINS
BLOOD OF A GOON
By **Romell Tukes**

THE STREETS MADE ME 1-3
By **Larry D. Wright**

CONCRETE KILLA 1-3
VICIOUS LOYALTY 1-3
By **Kingpen**

THE ULTIMATE SACRIFICE 1-6
KHADIFI
IF YOU CROSS ME ONCE 1-3
ANGEL 1-4
IN THE BLINK OF AN EYE
By **Anthony Fields**

THE LIFE OF A HOOD STAR
By **Ca$h & Rashia Wilson**

THE STREETS WILL NEVER CLOSE 1-3
By **K'ajji**

NIGHTMARES OF A HUSTLA 1-3
By **King Dream**

HARD AND RUTHLESS 1&2
MOB TOWN 251
THE BILLIONAIRE BENTLEYS 1-3
REAL G'S MOVE IN SILENCE
By **Von Diesel**

GHOST MOB
By **Stilloan Robinson**

MOB TIES 1-6
SOUL OF A HUSTLER, HEART OF A KILLER 1-3
GORILLAZ IN THE TRENCHES
By **SayNoMore**

BODYMORE MURDERLAND 1-3
THE BIRTH OF A GANGSTER 1-4
By **Delmont Player**

FOR THE LOVE OF A BOSS 1&2
By **C. D. Blue**

KILLA KOUNTY 1-5
By **Khufu**

MOBBED UP 1-4
THE BRICK MAN 1-5
THE COCAINE PRINCESS 1-10
STEPPERS 1-3
SUPER GREMLIN 1-4
By **King Rio**

MONEY GAME 1&2
By **Smoove Dolla**

A GANGSTA'S KARMA 1-4
By **FLAME**

KING OF THE TRENCHES 1-3
By **GHOST & TRANAY ADAMS**

QUEEN OF THE ZOO 1&2
By **Black Migo**

GRIMEY WAYS 1-3
By **Ray Vinci**

XMAS WITH AN ATL SHOOTER
By **Ca$h & Destiny Skai**

LAND OF THE HOOLIGANZ | IRA B

KING KILLA 1&2
By **Vincent "Vitto" Holloway**

BETRAYAL OF A THUG 1&2
By **Fre$h**

THE MURDER QUEENS 1-5
By **Michael Gallon**

FOR THE LOVE OF BLOOD 1-4
By **Jamel Mitchell**

HOOD CONSIGLIERE 1&2
NO TIME FOR ERROR
By **Keese**

PROTÉGÉ OF A LEGEND 1&2
LOVE IN THE TRENCHES 1&2
By **Corey Robinson**

BORN IN THE GRAVE 1-3
CRIME PAYS
By **Self Made Tay**

MOAN IN MY MOUTH
By **XTASY**

TORN BETWEEN A GANGSTER AND A GENTLEMAN
By **J-BLUNT & Miss Kim**

LOYALTY IS EVERYTHING 1-3
CITY OF SMOKE 1&2
By **Molotti**

HERE TODAY GONE TOMORROW 1&2
By **Fly Rock**

WOMEN LIE MEN LIE 1-4
FIFTY SHADES OF SNOW 1-3
STACK BEFORE YOU SPLURGE
GIRLS FALL LIKE DOMINOES
NAÏVE TO THE STREETS
By **ROY MILLIGAN**

PILLOW PRINCESS
By **S. Hawkins**

THE BUTTERFLY MAFIA 1-3
SALUTE MY SAVAGERY 1&2
By **Fumiya Payne**

THE LANE 1&2
By Ken-Ken Spence

THE PUSSY TRAP 1-5
By **Nene Capri**

DIRTY DNA
By **Blaque**

SANCTIFIED AND HORNY
by **XTASY**

BOOKS BY LDP'S CEO, CA$H

TRUST IN NO MAN
TRUST IN NO MAN 2
TRUST IN NO MAN 3
BONDED BY BLOOD
SHORTY GOT A THUG
THUGS CRY
THUGS CRY 2
THUGS CRY 3
TRUST NO BITCH
TRUST NO BITCH 2
TRUST NO BITCH 3
TIL MY CASKET DROPS
RESTRAINING ORDER
RESTRAINING ORDER 2
IN LOVE WITH A CONVICT
LIFE OF A HOOD STAR
XMAS WITH AN ATL SHOOTER

www.ingramcontent.com/pod-product-compliance
Lightning Source LLC
Chambersburg PA
CBHW051629260626
47170CB00004B/1106